MW00529537

These things matter most.
How well did you love?
How fully did you live?
How deeply did you let go?"
~Jack Kornfield~

the *Life*
We Dream Of

By

Jennifer Leigh Pezzano

Copyright © 2022 by Jennifer Leigh Pezzano All rights reserved.

No part of this publication may be reproduced, distributed, or transmitted in any form or by any means, including photocopying, recording, or other electronic or mechanical methods, without the prior written permission of the publisher, except in the case of brief quotations embodied in critical reviews and certain other noncommercial uses permitted by copyright law. Any references to historical events, real people, or real places are used fictitiously. Names, characters, and places are products of the author's imagination.

Front cover image by Virtually Possible Designs.

Book formatting by Jillian Michaels.

First printing edition 2022.

www.jenniferleighpezzano.com

This book goes out to all of you
May you find healing within the darkness
Courage beneath the fear
And beauty in all your imperfections
May everyday bring you closer to the life you dream of.

How long have I been sitting here, watching shadows play on the walls?

Life tosses you around, and sometimes all there is left to cling to are the fragments of reality.

The stability of the upholstered chair beneath me.

The faint smell of the marine wind as it drifted through the window.

The honking of traffic and the rushing of people below.

The gentle murmur of the city, its constant pulse a heartbeat you can never slow down. Unlike mine. My heartbeat will eventually fade to a climactic finish long before my body is ready.

Mortality is a smirking companion, impervious to the ego's desperate plea.

I gripped my phone. The urge to reach out and spill my sordid fate to another was a frantic bird pounding against the splintered bars of its cage. But who would I call? There was no one to console me. I was alone in a world of my own making.

With a broken sigh, I threw my phone across the living room; it bounced once, hit the wall, and landed on the polished grain of the hardwood floor. My anger was not even strong enough to break something. And I wanted to break something. I wanted to scream, to cry, to claw through the walls I had erected and release the entrails of myself.

But something had shut down inside of me so long ago, and

all I was able to muster was a fury, blanketing the emptiness that engulfed me.

Chapter One

"What is it that suffocates you?"

I sat on the plush beige couch opposite my therapist. A chunk of dark hair scattered with strands of grey had fallen into his face, and I resisted the urge to brush it back and slip off his wedding ring. Many a fantasy had started that way. I knew it was a pathetic cliché. So many nights he had become fodder for my lonely imagination and wandering fingers. But I couldn't help myself. There was something so comforting about a cliché. It was safe. An impression that couldn't touch me. A blessed distraction from the dark reality now lay burrowed beneath my skin.

"My life is suffocating me."

A tangled inhale grappled within my throat, the hiss of anxiety twisting inside as I recalled my doctor's words last week. The words that had constricted my world, causing each day to press tighter around me until all that was left was an outline. The ink of who I was, already fading.

He shifted in his seat, quiet blue eyes resting on me. "And what is it about your life right now that you find so suffocating, Julia?"

He did this a lot, used my name as a way of establishing some sort of intimacy between us. It had been almost six months since I'd first come to him, hoping to still the discontent lurking like shadows that kept me up at night. But I had never really let him in. I'd never taken my guard down. Perhaps I didn't know how? This vestige of strength I portrayed was only a cloak keeping me veiled, and he was just another prop in my life. A habit. Something to fill the empty space between work and home. Someone to remind me I still existed. I hadn't even told him about my diagnosis yet.

"All of it. My job, my apartment, my..." The words caught on my tongue, like slivers of uncertainty as I sought relief in the view out the window. Autumn had crept in overnight, stealing away the last of summer's bright optimism, and the maple outside the office trembled with a hesitant blush of color against the bone white of the Seattle sky. The impermanence was a bleak reminder of the truth holding court in my gut.

"Julia? What else feels suffocating?"

"My solitude." The unexpected prick of tears stung my eyes, and I pushed them back like shameful secrets. I had never cried in front of him and didn't want to start now.

From the corner of my eye, I noticed him jot something on his notepad. "You have never mentioned this before. You have always spoken about your independence and how your life was an extension of your ambition. You have said on numerous occasions that you are happy with your solitude."

I bit my lip, staring out into the city. How many lies had I told him? How many of my words had been coated in confident fabrications, as if I could convince myself of these things simply by saying them out loud?

He tilted his head toward me, trying to pull my attention away from the window. "Julia?"

Vulnerability pressed against me, whispering threats of exposure, and I dug my nails into the palm of my hand, the welcoming sting like an anchor. "What?" My voice came out clipped as I swung my gaze back to him.

"Why do you think you're now addressing this? Because I

must admit, I feel we have been dancing around this topic for quite some time."

"Oh, have we? I didn't know I was so transparent."

He leaned forward, clasping his hands together and resting his elbows on his knees. "Julia. Everyone craves companionship in their lives. It's not a sign of weakness."

"I know that." I brushed his words aside with a quick wave of my hand, my impatience coiling within, ready to strike.

"Do you ever think that perhaps you have used your career as a distraction to buffer yourself from getting close to the people around you?"

I shot him a scathing look, the talons of my anger extending. "My career is not a *distraction*."

"I'm not saying it is. But you have been coming to me for some time now, and we still have yet to go very deep."

"Oh, have I been *boring* you?" I tossed my words at him, bitterness coating my tongue. "Because if I am, I can gladly stop our sessions."

He leaned back in his chair with a sigh. "Do you want to stop therapy, Julia? I feel like we're finally touching on some important topics here."

My silence filled the room as I struggled to hold back a retort. The truth was too big. If I opened my mouth, it would swallow me whole.

"How about this? How about I ask you why it is you come to me every week?"

My eyes fell back to the window. The morning sun had finally managed to peek through the fine layer of clouds, bathing the room in a tepid glow and teasing my skin with warmth. "I don't really know anymore."

"Well, when we first started, you were having trouble sleeping." His eyes rested on mine, full of his endless questions. "But if I am correct, you stated recently that this is no longer an issue. So, what is it that compels you to continue our sessions?"

5

I shrugged, biting the edge of my lip. "Someone to talk to, I guess."

"Well, beyond the day-to-day sharing you do here, what is it that you hope to achieve by coming to me every week?"

A puff of air escaped my lips. I was suddenly tired of words. Tired of the clinical back-and-forth. What use was there in talking? It never changed anything. "Since you're the professional, why don't you tell me?"

"This isn't about my opinion, Julia. This is about you, and what it is *you* want to get out of our sessions."

I crossed my legs, my foot rapidly tapping the floor. "Well, you seemed to have some opinions of your own just a second ago."

"I'm only trying to address this feeling of isolation that you spoke of." He closed his notepad and set it on the table beside him. "You talk about feeling suffocated. What exactly has caused this sudden shift for you?"

"My future."

He looked at me quizzically for a moment. "And what is it about your future that is causing these feelings for you?"

I glanced to the clock on the wall, a wave of relief washing over me as I grabbed my purse. "Time's up."

With a nod, he regarded me with a look that held all the unspoken words between us. All the half-truths I doled out like a reluctant child.

"I suppose it is."

I stood and breezed past him, my heels clicking a staccato heartbeat against the polished tile. "See you next week."

Shutting the door behind me, I pulled my phone out of my purse and dialed my office as I walked toward the elevator. My assistant answered on the first ring, her chipper voice grating in my ear.

"Sylvia, I need you to cancel all my meetings for today."

"Sure thing. Will you be coming into the office this afternoon?"

"No."

A cool wind hit me as I hung up the phone and exited the four-story brownstone of my therapist's office. I needed to stifle these feelings inside me, hissing and scratching like a cornered animal.

I stopped at the first bar I saw. Darkened windows obscured the view inside, while a faded neon sign flickered above. Slipping inside, my eyes adjusted to the dim light as I walked over to the bar and sat on the cracked leather stool, which seemed to sigh beneath me.

This was a fitting backdrop for my current mood. Only a few people populated the room, all of them curled around the comfort of their chosen vice like a lover, their eyes heavy with detachment. That was what I longed for. Detachment from my life, which had now begun to feel so bleak and meaningless that it sucked the air out of me.

Signaling to the bartender, I ordered a gin on the rocks. My fingers traced the worn grooves on the wood of the counter, imagining what my daughter would think of me now. She often came to me in these moments of self-reflection, like a timid ghost of my own disapproval.

My drink slid into view, and I reached for it, resting the cold glass against my lips. I watched as the clear liquid swirled around the ice before tipping it back and allowing the warm, welcoming burn to slide down my throat.

"You don't look like you belong in a place like this."

I swiveled my head in the direction of the tired pickup line and took in dark eyes and a scruffy five o'clock shadow. A small smile tugged at my lips as I regarded his moderately attractive features and put-together attire. Crisp dress shirt, expensive shoes. He would do.

"Well, please enlighten me as to what place you think I should be right now."

He cocked his head at me, his eyes playful. "Somewhere with more light. Your beauty is wasted in here."

"Is that so?" I downed the rest of my drink and retrieved a ten-dollar bill from my purse, placing it on the counter. "Does *your* place have better light?"

* * *

Ushering me into his apartment, he backed me against the bedroom door, his lips on mine, urgent and tasting of beer. I pulled back and turned my head from him as I reached for his pants, unbuckling the belt.

"No kissing, huh?" His voice was gravelly in my ear.

I slid my hand lower and cupped his erection through the fabric of his pleated pants, causing a disjointed groan to spill from his mouth.

"I didn't come here to be kissed." I pushed him down onto the bed, his eyes wide and full of a simplified lust as he watched me undress. All men were the same, so pliant and predictable.

Straddling him, I pinned his arms to the sheets, reveling in the feeling of reducing him to nothing but his own primal need, stripping him of his identity and revealing the animal underneath. We were all nothing but animals in the end, viciously clawing at phantoms we had created from the depths of our own fear. Seeking solace in the burrow of a warm body.

These were the moments when I was fully in charge, reduced to sweat, skin, and a pleasure that for one brief moment, stole away all the darkness inside.

* * *

Dust danced within the beams of weak sunlight that streamed in from the window of the bedroom. Sitting up, I went to grab my pants and shirt from the floor.

"Hey, now. Where are you going?"

His hand fell to my arm, but I brushed it off. "I gotta go."

"Can I see you again?"

I turned to him, the name he had given me in the taxi ride over suddenly eluding me. "No, I don't think so."

Slipping on my shoes, I grabbed my purse and headed out the door, not bothering with a goodbye. What was the point of empty words? I had nothing to give.

My eyes scanned the flow of traffic hissing by as I waited for the Uber I had called to take me back to my apartment, longing for a hot bath and the crispness of clean sheets.

As I slid into the car and directed the driver to Capitol Hill, my mind drifted back to my therapist's response when I told him in sordid detail about all my one-night stands. Perhaps I was trying to get a rise out of him, to maybe see him shift uncomfortably in his expensive leather chair.

"After you sleep with these men and leave, how does that make you feel?"

"I feel powerful, like I'm in control."

"And how long does this feeling last for you?"

"Not long enough."

And this time was no different. When I entered my apartment, the rush had faded, and I was greeted by the kind of silence that made me agitated and restless.

I was alone once more with all the thoughts I did not want to sit with.

Chapter Two

id-afternoon sun angled through the windows of my living room. Prisms of warmth danced across my skin, washing the walls in a curtain of light.

As my bow slid over the strings of the cello, the deep resonance filled my body. A vibration of wood dancing with sound, the mournful notes stretching across my skin. Back and forth, my arms strained from the force of movement as the bow drew out a language that cradled me, banishing the noise within my mind, and settling into the spaces beside me like a silent audience.

Lost in the fluid rhythm of the strings, time stepped back from me. My limbs merged with the sleek maple, my heartbeat twining through the grooves of the neck. Embracing the body of the cello, I allowed the music to become my lover, the companion I fell against. And in these brief moments of reprieve, it was enough.

A dissonant noise sliced through the notes, breaking the trance, and the bow stilled in my hand. My eyes skirted to a number flashing across the screen of my phone, and my breath caught in my throat, icy tendrils gripping at my neck. Gravity yanked me from my moment of weightlessness and pulled me back into the depths of reality. Leaning over, I turned off my phone, the blue glow fading to black.

Resting my head on the curved wood of the cello, I closed my eyes, willing the world to stop spinning so fast. I was not ready to face what stood waiting on the other side.

I stared blankly at my computer screen, the words blurring together into meaningless patterns. The usual flow and focus I found myself in while editing was nowhere to be found. My mind was stuck between gears, the dull weight of inertia a crippling force.

A soft knock sounded on my office door, and my boss, Steven, poked his head in. "You got a minute, Jules?"

Shooting him a wan smile, I motioned for him to come in. The scent of Old Spice trailed after him as he placed a file on my desk and took a seat across from me. "I got you those articles to take a look at for next month's publication."

"Thank you." I opened the file, absently glancing through the pages.

"How's the editing going on the Williams piece?"

I sighed and rested my back against the chair. "Slowly."

"You want me to take a look at it for you?"

"No, I can handle it."

"I know you can handle it, Jules." He leaned forward, a half-smile edging the corner of his mouth. "Maybe I just miss those days when you used to come to me for help."

The intercom on my desk phone sprang to life, and my

assistant's voice cut through the space between us. "Julia, Doctor Henderson is on line two. Do you want me to take another message?"

I stiffened, gripping the edges of my desk as Steven stood with a nod. "I'll let you take that."

The door closed softly behind him, leaving me alone with my hesitancy, and I reached out, pressing the reply button. "No, it's okay, Sylvia. I got it."

Picking up the phone, I felt the familiar fatigue pulling at my limbs, the same lethargy which had been plaguing me for weeks. My pulse accelerated as I stared at the blinking light. I couldn't avoid this any longer.

"Julia, this is Dr. Henderson." The soft cadence of her voice filtered through the receiver. "You haven't returned any of my calls."

I fiddled with a pen on my desk, my eyes glancing at the various editorial awards lining my walls. The framed achievements that kept me company and defined so much of who I was. None of it felt real anymore, and none of it could save me. "I know, I'm sorry. I've just been really busy with work these past few days."

"We discussed this at your last appointment. There is only a very small window where this treatment is going to help. And we need to start immediately."

A burn gathered in my mouth, corrosive and biting as I choked on the measured words. "Yes. I understand."

"Can you come in this afternoon?"

A wave of panic rippled through me, and I looked down at my hands. Nail polish once so meticulously applied, was now chipped and worn, a small detail now glaringly insignificant. So many things in my life were beginning to take on that tone. Flimsy routines were crumbling away, leaving only the outline of substance behind.

"What time?"

"Two."

I took a deep breath, summoning the willpower I needed right now, even though all I wanted to do was run. To hide behind the consoling veil of denial that beckoned me. "Okay, I'll be there."

Before she said anything more, I hung up and pushed myself off the chair, pacing back and forth across the room in a flurry, as if movement could still the torrent of anxiety bleeding through the cracks of my façade. It was the same anxiety that yanked me from sleep during darkened hours, following me like an incessant companion, loud and always impossible to outpace.

"*How old were you when you first started having anxiety attacks, Julia?*"

"*I was eight.*"

"*Was there an event that may have preceded the onset of your anxiety?*"

"*I don't want to talk about it.*"

"*Why not?*"

"*It's pointless.*"

"*Why do you feel it is pointless?*"

"*Because it won't change the fact that my childhood was ugly, and people have only hurt me.*"

"*Is that something you truly believe?*"

"*I have yet to be proven otherwise.*"

Looking out at the skyline from my window, I took a deep breath and tried to still the racing of my heart. Fog settled low and heavy, like an ominous shroud obscuring the city below. This view always seemed to anchor me, as if I were above the world and it couldn't touch me. All my life, I had tried to be untouchable. But in the end, it was my own body that betrayed me.

* * *

I sat awkwardly on the edge of the cushioned seat of the waiting room, my fingernails digging into the palms of my hands as I awaited the arrival of Dr. Henderson. I gazed out the window to the Space Needle, which towered above the city center like a sentinel piercing through the marine layer. In the background, soft classical music drifted through the speakers, and a vase of flowers sat on the table beside me, its cloying scent infusing the room, making me feel like a ghost at my own funeral.

The rancorous taste of bile rose in my throat as I realized I probably wouldn't even *have* a funeral. Who would show up besides Steven? My co-workers? A handful of people who barely knew me beyond the surface. Had my entire life been reduced to nothing but an obituary? Dry words on a page highlighting my accomplishments like death's resume.

"Julia."

A voice jarred me from the heaviness of my thoughts, and I looked up to see Dr. Henderson standing in the hallway. "Please, come with me," she said, sweeping her hand toward her open office door.

With shaky legs, my body involuntarily stood and followed behind her like a marionette bound to the strings of a performance I was forced to play out.

She sat across from me at her desk, gaze solemn. "Thank you for coming in today. I want to go over the procedure with you, and then we can schedule a time to start proton therapy sessions." She paused for a moment, glancing at my file on the computer screen. "I feel this is the best course of action, considering the location of the tumor and the difficulty in removing it. This targeted radiation will hopefully slow the growth and give you some more time, all the while eliminating the side effects of traditional chemotherapy."

Her words receded, growing muffled as I recalled the last time I had sat across from her. The glowing screen in front of us holding my test results like a bomb waiting to be uncovered. How my body slowly detached as she opened her mouth, spilling shrapnel across the room, the walls rippling as if some unseen force had abruptly halted the rules of physics. Solid matter turning to liquid. Life folding in on itself.

Numb. That's what I had been. That's what I had always been. Impassively navigating through my life like a habit I could not define. A deep dreamless sleep I stumbled through. And I suddenly wanted to wake up.

I tried to respond, but all that came out of me was a long exhale. My eyes skimmed her shelves and landed on a photo of her and a child. A tiny piece of her life tucked between her files and reference books, a tangible artifact of her existence. While mine trembled beside me, undefined and already fading.

"Now, please keep in mind that there is a limit on how many people can accompany you to your sessions."

I pulled myself back to her composed gaze and shook my head. "That won't be an issue. It will just be me."

She nodded and bent down to open a bottom drawer, sliding a brochure across the desk. "I know this is a lot for you to take in right now, and it is really important to have people in your life who can provide support." Her finger tapped the folded paper in front of me. "This is a great support group. I think it would really benefit you."

My hand brushed across the glossy brochure depicting two men with wide smiles, their arms draped across each other's shoulders. They looked happy, and I wondered if these people in the picture even had cancer? Or was it only a stock photo that came up when you typed in the keywords, *friendship, closeness, family?* Words I didn't have in my life.

Dr. Henderson leaned across the desk. "Statistics show that

having a support group in place greatly increases the outcome in patients."

I furrowed my brow, choking back the tears that once again threatened my composure, and quickly slipped the pamphlet into my purse. "When do we start?"

Bathed in the harsh glare of the clinic's overhead bathroom light, my reflection stared back at me. Dark features and crimson lipstick against a starched white hospital gown. The days since the appointment with my doctor had been spent in a state of restless detachment, skirting the boundaries of a life that no longer felt like mine. I had become only a tenant housed in a body that would soon evict me.

Taking a shaky breath, I reached up to smooth back my long strands of hair, securing them tightly in place with a clip. Even now, with the unrelenting grip of my illness keeping vigil, my vanity sighed in relief. I wasn't going to lose my hair. I clung to this fact with a desperate sense of pride. It was all I had left.

The technician led me into a white room where a large oval machine stood in the center, the interior emitting a cool, blue glow. Positioning myself on the table, I lay back, my eyes fixed on the bright emptiness of the ceiling as she applied the cast around my chest that had been fitted for me the day before, and pushed a button, sliding the table forward.

"Now, I need you to lie as still as possible," the woman spoke in a soft tone, gently adjusting my body beneath the cast.

She looked young, with unblemished skin and blond hair tied up in a bouncy ponytail that swayed with her movements. "The procedure will take roughly fifteen to twenty minutes. Are you ready?"

I nodded as she disappeared from my view, leaving behind the sound of a closing door. The room dimmed and the blue light intensified above me as a steady hum filled the air. Closing my eyes, I tried to wash out my thoughts, not wanting to focus on the tiny beams of radiation that were now piercing through the delicate fibers of my chest.

A war raged within me, and I had no weapons. Only a battered shield that could buy me more time. But what was the use of time? What was I fighting for? Beyond my career, my life was a barren landscape. A desperate plea to a vacant room. All I had was the persistent whisper of survival. A tiny bud pressing through the weight of the earth, searching for a sliver of light.

The minutes passed by in slow, agonizing breaths as my body itched to move and a dull pain settled in my lower back. My heart pounded out a steady rhythm of blood against veins and bone, and I felt like screaming.

* * *

"Now, you're going to have some fatigue for the next few hours, so I suggest you take it easy and rest," the technician said as she walked me over to the reception counter, where a woman slid an appointment card to me. "We will see you for your second session the day after tomorrow."

I nodded blankly, pushing through the double doors and out into the hazy sunlit parking lot, my shiny red sports car standing out like a flame among all the grey and black sedans. Across the street lay a cemetery, rows of gravestones lining the manicured green like a cruel, ironic joke, and I skirted my eyes away, unable to look at the foreboding reminder of my own impermanence.

The rush of cars drowned out the noise of my mind, which tumbled around like loose stones with no direction. I could already feel the ache in my body creeping over me. I had grown accustomed to fatigue these days, but this was a weakness that tugged at me, demanding attention, and I wondered if I should have called an Uber to take me home.

Navigating my car through the streets and into the current of the Bay Freeway, I flipped through the radio stations, trying to distract myself from this new reality that had taken me hostage. Claiming me.

Forty-two years, and all I had to show for it was an executive office and a penthouse apartment on Capitol Hill. A cage full of lonely artifacts.

"What is your definition of success, Julia?"

"I don't know. I guess, wealth, accomplishment. The freedom to carve out my own life without having to answer to anybody else."

"And what about happiness? Does that factor into what success looks like for you?"

"Happiness is such a vague and subjective term. It never sticks around. You can't control when life's going to knock you down. But you can *control your attachment to the outcome."*

"And what does that mean for you, exactly?"

"It means that if you aren't looking for something, you'll never be disappointed when it doesn't come."

I somehow made it home and into my apartment, where I shed my clothes, legs trembling as I collapsed on the bed. Gripping my pillow, I willed my mind to release itself to sleep. Though every muscle in my body was stripped and weary, my thoughts commanded attention, clinging like a harsh, sticky residue I was unable to wash away. It was moments like these I wished I had a pet, something warm and breathing to curl into. How had I managed to push everything I could lose in my life so far away that I couldn't even remember what it felt like to hold something?

And I suddenly wanted to hold something.

I wanted to feel another heartbeat against my skin. The gentle rhythm of existence reminding me I was still here, that my own heart was still beating.

Chapter Three

The brick building loomed above me as I clutched the cancer support group flyer in my hand. I paced beside the entrance; the click of my heels hesitant against the sidewalk as I debated opening the door to the Queen Anne Community Center.

Anxiety twisted inside, leaving my mouth dry, limbs shaking. The last thing I wanted to do was to sit in a room full of strangers. Their eyes on me like whispers, intense and prying. But the idea of another day spent staring at my mortality amid the silence of my apartment filled me with a crushing dread.

A dread I no longer had the strength to face alone.

Warmth hit me as I entered, the air tinged with a faint smell that reminded me of school cafeterias, remnants of diluted bleach and lemon floor cleaner. Long buried memories flooded me with a visceral force only the power of scent could evoke. *Lunch trays and the dissonance of chatter. The chill of the metal seat on my bare thighs, my hair obscured around my face, hiding the bruises. The sting of loneliness. For friends were dangerous, they asked too many questions.*

I shook off my thoughts, pushing them back into the locked compartments of my mind as my gaze fell to an open door, the soft buzz of voices filtering out into the hallway.

Gathering my courage, I took a deep breath and stepped through the doorway. I cringed inwardly as heads turned in my direction, feeling like an interloper as I took in the faces before me. Some looked gaunt and fearful, others wore the lines of a deeply etched sorrow. But they all shared the same expression in their eyes, the look of resigned futility. Age held no sway in this room. Youth was only an afterthought. We had all been whittled down to the same fleeting timeline.

"Sorry I'm late."

My voice came out clipped and loud, seeming to slam up against the abrupt silence within the room as I weaved between the circle of chairs and found an empty seat.

"Welcome to our group." An older woman with dark-rimmed glasses sat across from me with a clipboard in hand. "Would you like to introduce yourself?"

I set my purse underneath my chair. "Um, my name is Julia Marino."

The woman nodded and wrote something down on her clipboard. "Thank you so much for joining us today, Julia. My name is Susan." Leaning forward, she rested her elbows on her knees, regarding me with rehearsed, sympathetic eyes. "Since you're a new face here, is there anything you'd like to share before we start with our group exercise?"

I looked around the room. The gentle sound of rain as it began to patter on the roof above us buffeted the oppressive silence. "No, thank you."

Susan sat back, the gentle press of her gaze resting on me. "That's okay. You can share with us whenever you *feel* ready. We all have our own process."

Murmurs of agreement rose around me, followed by collective nods and smiles. I felt like something enclosed in glass and on display. Their empathy was stifling, and I fought back the urge to get up and leave.

"So, who would like to open up group today?"

Susan swept her hand across the room and a frail, older man cleared his throat, shuffling his feet as he leaned forward. "I would like to share something." He dug his fingers into his thighs, his eyes shimmering with unshed tears. "My daughter moved in yesterday. She insisted she was staying to help me with chemo. And I should be thankful. I should be grateful that she would do this for me. And I am..." He trailed off, his gaze bouncing across the room as he gritted his teeth and pounded his fist against his leg. "But I'm also angry. I'm angry because I can't take care of myself anymore. That *my* cancer has to affect *her* life."

The force of his emotion hit me like a blast to my gut. *Perhaps I was lucky?* I didn't have to worry about my cancer becoming someone else's problem. Perhaps there was a veiled fortune behind my solitude. Nobody's life would change after I was gone.

"Thank you so much for sharing, Paul." A heavy silence fell across the room, heads bowing low as if lost in their own private prayers, until Susan spoke again. "We are now going to divide ourselves into groups of two. Please find a quiet corner, and I will pass out the answers we came up with in our last session."

The room suddenly came alive with movement and chatter as the man sitting next to me turned and spoke close to my ear. "Care to be my partner?"

I looked at him for the first time. Dark hair and warm chocolate eyes met mine. He wore a wide, easy smile that spoke of confidence, though his appearance did not convey that. His hair was in a state of erratic dishevelment, and the cheap fabric of his clothing lay loose and wrinkled over his tall, lean frame.

I shrugged. "Sure, why not."

"Great." He stood and grabbed his chair, motioning for me to join him. "Let's snag that spot over by the window."

I picked up my folding chair and reluctantly followed. "So, what exactly are we doing?"

"It's something called *Exercising Our Fears,*" he said as he settled himself by the window. "The group wrote down all their fears last week, and we divided them into jars. Today we're going to pick from them at random, see if they apply to us, and then deconstruct them."

"And why are we doing that?" I asked, smoothing the wrinkles on my shirt as I sat across from him.

He cocked his head, a faint look of amusement drifting across his face. "Well, I guess it's so we can better understand that we're not alone in our fears, and that maybe we share the same ones."

I nodded, throwing him a thin smile as Susan breezed by carrying a tray of mason jars with folded scraps of paper inside. Bending down, she set one on the floor between us.

"Thanks, Susan," he said before leaning toward me and extending his hand. "I'm Quinn, by the way." His hand enfolded mine, his grip strong and warm against my skin.

"Julia."

He smiled. "Yes, I gathered that."

"Right." I absentmindedly began to fiddle with my necklace, running the diamond charm back and forth over the chain as I angled my gaze out the window, watching the rivulets of water slowly trickle down the glass.

"Do you want me to go first, Julia?"

I nodded, but kept my eyes fixed on the window as he rooted through the pieces of paper in the jar.

"*Being alone.*" There was a long pause before he continued. "I guess that's a fear of mine."

My shoulders tensed. Once again, my isolation stared down at me with judging eyes demanding answers. "Why are we taught to be so scared of being alone?" I turned to him,

THE LIFE WE DREAM OF

attempting to brush aside the feelings that hissed inside me. The sorrow I had no name for.

He ran his fingers through his hair with a sigh. "Well, what's the point of life if you're not able to share it with someone else?"

I glanced around the room, taking in faces stretched against the mask of their own private stories. How many of them truly revealed their life to others? How many of them only lived side by side like friendly neighbors that shared a wall but locked their doors at night?

"We're all alone in one way or another."

"Okay, there's some truth to that." Quinn settled back in his chair, looking out the window for a moment before turning his gaze to me. "There is a difference between being alone and being lonely. For me, I think the fear lies in a sense of emptiness. It's the relationships in our lives and the way we love others that define us in a lot of ways. Without those, who are we really?"

I raised my eyebrows at him. The familiar taste of my own regret rested on my tongue, bitter and impossible to wash away. "I don't see why we need to seek others to define who we are."

"We don't have to, but it sure does help give us perspective, don't you think?" He looked down at the piece of paper in his hand, his fingers folding back the edges. "I mean, without the mirror of other people, we become disillusioned and cut off from the world around us."

I bit my lip, the sting slicing through the heaviness of my thoughts. I had grown so accustomed to building windows that did not open. "I'm not scared of being alone. I've been alone all my life."

"But are you lonely?"

Quinn's words challenged me, and his eyes met mine with an intensity I felt uncomfortable with. It was as if he were trying to reach inside and extract something private and delicate, and it pricked at my defenses.

"My turn." I reached for the jar and placed it on my lap, pulling out a piece of paper. "Suffering." I set the jar down with a long sigh, this exercise feeling suddenly trite and meaningless. *Who wasn't afraid of suffering?* "This is pointless."

"What's pointless?" Quinn leaned forward and regarded me with a look of mild curiosity.

"All of this." I flung my arm out in the direction of the people huddled in pairs, talking softly. "Everything."

"So, you're angry?"

"Of course, I'm angry. I'm angry that I'm sick and there's *nothing* I can do to fix it." I was growing loud, and a bloom of heat rose to my face as a few people turned in my direction. I swiveled my head back to the window, seeking solace in the steady thrum of rain blanketing my vision in a wash of grey.

"I'm angry, too."

I looked at Quinn, his eyes meeting mine in a silent nod of solidarity, his gaze momentarily stilling the storm inside. My voice came out tattered, like a weary traveler seeking shelter in the remains of a battered house. "Well, I guess we have something in common then."

* * *

I waited until the stream of people filed out the door before I got up, my limbs cramped and aching from the uncomfortable metal seat.

Susan stood by the window, adjusting the blinds. "Thanks for coming, Julia. I hope to see you next week."

"We'll see." With a tight smile, I bent down and grabbed my purse. Slinging it over my shoulder, I briskly walked out of the room, leaving the echo of my footsteps behind me.

Pushing open the doors, I stepped into the chill of the

afternoon. It had stopped raining, and the sky hung heavy and indifferent as a gust of wind startled the tree above me, scattering wet leaves onto the pavement.

"It was nice talking with you, Julia."

I whipped around and saw Quinn standing underneath an awning beside a motorcycle.

"Is that yours?" I gestured toward the bike, the gleam of silver and chrome like a flash of brightness against the grey.

"It is." A slow, teasing smile stretched across his face. "You feel like going for a ride?"

"No, thanks," I quipped, pulling out my phone. "I prefer an Uber."

"Ever ridden on one of these?" Quinn grinned as he slipped his helmet on and adjusted the straps. "They're pretty fun."

"No, and I have no desire to." I looked over at him as he positioned himself onto the motorcycle, his thighs straddling the seat, and that familiar itch began to crawl through me. "But we could go back to your place."

A flicker of surprise darted across his face as he stared at me. "And what would we do at my place?"

I slid my phone back into my purse and walked up to him. "Well, we could fuck."

A nervous chuckle spilled out of him. "Oh, *you're* funny."

"I wasn't joking." I met his stare head-on as if I could expose him, that feeling of power rising in my gut and taking hold. I wanted to reclaim myself, to wash away the thoughts that burned within me. To obliterate the clawing fear that battered against the cage of my chest.

Quinn leaned forward and casually folded his arms across the handlebars. "And what makes you think I don't have a wife and children waiting for me at home?"

I nodded at his hand with a flirtatious smirk. "I don't see a ring. Plus, when has that ever stopped a man?"

"Well, I don't know what kind of men you've been hanging

around with." A faint smile played on his lips. "But I *could* have a girlfriend, you know."

"Something tells me you don't."

"And what makes you think that?"

"Because you were just flirting with me."

"I was?" Quinn cocked his eyebrow, regarding me with a playful look.

"Yes. I know when a man is flirting with me. Besides, you wouldn't be inviting a woman to ride on your bike if you had a girlfriend."

"You're very observant." He shot me a crooked smile as his gaze slid over me. "And as enticing as your offer is, I'm going to have to respectfully decline."

I stepped back from him, unaccustomed to being rebuffed, the dynamic of power shifting, leaving me deflated. "Well, that's your loss. You're not really my type, anyway."

"And just out of curiosity, what *is* your type?" Quinn's eyes appeared to twinkle with amusement.

Still feeling stung, I gestured at him dismissively. "Well, someone who knows how to dress, for one thing."

With a laugh, he started up his motorcycle. The noise abruptly cut through his words, forcing him to shout above the rumble of the engine. "I hope to see you next week, Julia."

Heaving a long sigh, I wrapped my arms around myself, attempting to suppress all the emptiness shrieking inside like a hollow wind. I watched as Quinn threw me a wave and guided his bike across the sidewalk before accelerating down the street, leaving me standing there with a strange mixture of annoyance and intrigue.

Chapter Four

"So, you like it rough, do you?"

He slammed into me, eliciting a sharp wave of pain to mingle with my pleasure as I clutched the sides of the table. His fingers dug into my skin as he gripped my hips from behind, his grunts filling the dark, unfamiliar room.

"Do you ever take any of these men back to your place?"

"No. They could be creeps, and then they would know where I live."

"So, you know that these men could be creeps, but yet you still have sex with them?"

"Yes."

"Do you ever find this blatant disregard for your own well-being concerning?"

"I know how to take care of myself."

"God, you're so fucking hot," he growled, thrusting into me even deeper, his pace harsh and animalistic.

Sliding my hand down to cup my sex, my fingers rubbed the folds as he filled me and pressed me over the table, my nipples brushing against the fabric of my bra. The pressure inside curled and twisted, and my orgasm rushed forward, enveloping me in a silent release.

I never shared my pleasure with these men. It was not for them. It was my own private secret.

Tilting my head back, I stared into the mirror above the table, watching this stranger in a suit contort his face into something vile and livid as he tensed up and exploded into me with all the fervor of a man draining his own wounds.

With a groan, he slid out and zipped up his pants while I bent down to pull up my own, shooting him a forced smile as I slipped past him and into the bathroom.

Turning the light on, I leaned against the door, closing my eyes for a moment. *"Do you feel better now?"* A sharp voice hissed inside me as I looked into the mirror, but only vacant, dark eyes stared back. I no longer had answers. Whatever satisfaction I once gleaned from my sexual exploits had now begun to falter to a dull, throbbing ache. I couldn't avoid the truth any longer.

I was dying.

Primary Cardiac Sarcoma.

Those three words cut me open like a knife, and there was no way to stanch the flow of blood. No matter how hard I tried, I couldn't run from this anymore.

So fitting, really, that I would have cancer of the heart.

"Hey, gorgeous, you all right in there?"

His voice jarred me from my thoughts, and I turned on the tap, my hands shaking as I splashed cold water over my face, washing off the lipstick that clung to my mouth like a dark blemish. "Yep, I'll be out in a sec."

Opening the door, I brushed past him and grabbed my purse from the bed.

"Well, thanks for the late-afternoon pick up," he said with a grin. "If you feel like doing this again sometime, I left my business card in your purse."

I shot him a tight smile and made my way to the front door, closing it behind me. I wouldn't be calling him. I never called them.

Stepping outside, I propelled myself down the street, my footsteps carrying out a frantic rhythm of heeled shoes against worn concrete. Darkness pushed through the city as the glow of streetlights sliced my skin into shadows. The murmur of cars slid past like the rush of an exhale as I walked, the wind washing away the debris that clung to me. The scent of a man I did not know. The anxiety that coiled within.

I didn't walk with a destination in mind. I wasn't trying to get home. I was only trying to outpace my own thoughts, turning corners, and allowing them to lead me down the stream of sidewalks, the steady rhythm of the city mocking the beat of my failing heart.

Passing through the business section, the persistent hum slowed to a crawl, and I found myself in the residential area, streets that trickled into neighborhoods. A discovery of houses tucked away and untouched by daylight.

Each home held a history engraved within its walls, windows tinted with the warmth of light, flickering images of bodies obscured by curtains, the breath of humanity enclosed between wood and glass. The story of people living.

The quiet I found here was comforting, and it eased the agitated pulse of my heart. The gentle acceptance of the night clung to me like a shield, buffering me from the splintered pieces of myself, and the rush of my own discontent softened.

For one brief moment, I could imagine what it would feel like to have lived a life full of something more than the space I occupied.

The machine hummed above me. I had grown used to these sessions. Closing my eyes, I tried to visualize the radiation piercing through the tender layers of my heart and halting the growth inside.

Brittle time. It was all I had left, and I clung to it with a desperation I'd never felt before, praying it wouldn't crumble in my grasping hands. This vulnerability was like delicate skin stretched over bone and tissue, and I feared that if I moved too quickly, it would tear, leaving nothing to hold me together.

The overhead light turned on, signaling the end of the therapy, and I sat up, my limbs shaking and heavy. Grabbing my clothes, I quickly changed and exited the building, skirting past the receptionist with a nod. My phone buzzed incessantly within my purse as I walked through the parking lot, reminding me of all the deadlines at work I was evading, all the unavoidable questions I didn't have the strength to answer.

All of it seemed so pointless now. The clients and staff meetings, the advertising sales, and editorial budgets. The work that defined me. The six-figure income I didn't need anymore. *What if I just resigned?* Handed over my position to Lillian, the young and eager copy editor who had her whole life in front of her. Why was I clinging to a career that only brought meaning to a life still full of possibility?

I had no more possibilities left. All I had were clawing questions ripping at the fabric of myself and a fear that stood beside me like a shadow. The inevitable weight of it all was crippling. What was I to do with these last fragile pieces of myself?

I sat staring at the email. I must have read it a hundred times over the past two years. The words I had memorized by heart. The reply I never had the courage to send.

The door to my office opened, and Sylvia poked her head in. "Sorry to bother you, but you told me to remind you about an appointment scheduled for this afternoon?"

"Oh, shit." I leaned back, running my fingers through my hair.

Sylvia walked in and softly closed the door behind her. Resting against it, she regarded me with a look of concern. "Are you okay?"

"I'm fine."

She fiddled with the bracelet on her wrist, glancing around the room nervously. "I mean, you've just seemed really distracted lately, and I'm not the only person who's noticed. Steven has mentioned it a few times. We're all a little concerned."

"I told you, I'm *fine*." My words came out harsher than intended as I stood and grabbed my purse.

"I don't mean to pry. It's just that you haven't been yourself these past few weeks."

Feeling cornered, I briskly strode to the door and held it open for her. "I appreciate the concern, Sylvia, but it's really none of your business."

A mottled blush spread across her cheeks as she stared up

at me, her eyes wide and full of a gentle openness I suddenly found myself envying. Life had not crippled her yet.

"You're right, it's not. I'm sorry."

I nodded curtly to her as she slid past me and back to her desk. "And I won't be returning this afternoon, so please send over my drafts to Lillian and have her finalize the edits for this week."

"Of course."

I could feel her eyes following me as I walked toward the elevator and pushed the green button, the sting of remorse tugging at me. "Sylvia."

"Yes." She turned to me, the edges of her mouth quivering as if unsure of their direction.

I gave her a tired smile. "I didn't mean to snap at you just now. Don't worry about me, okay?" Stepping onto the elevator, the doors shut behind me with a whoosh, enclosing me in a tempered silence; my vulnerability a tight band stretched across my skin.

"Why do you feel you always have to keep people at arm's length, Julia?"

"Because it's easier that way."

"And what do you think will happen if you let someone in?"

"I'd lose my power."

"And why is power so important to you?"

"Because it's all I have."

* * *

Stepping into the room of the support group, my eyes scanned the faces of people who stood in small, cloistered circles, clutching white paper cups and chatting quietly. I had surprised myself by returning. This longing for solidarity and a desire to push past my comfort level was unfamiliar. I felt like a small child in a room full of adults who spoke in a language I couldn't decipher but desperately wanted to understand.

I spotted Quinn in a corner talking to another man. My eyes quickly skirted away, hoping he hadn't noticed me watching him as a vague rush of warmth washed across my skin. My proposition from the week before lingered awkwardly within me, the memory tasting crass and ugly as my hands fumbled for a cup at the refreshment table, pouring myself some coffee from the dispenser.

"You're back."

I turned around and found Quinn's deep brown eyes on me.

"Yeah." My voice wavered as I swept my arm across the room. "I figured I'd give this thing one more shot."

He nodded at the cup in my hand. "You're not going to drink that, are you?"

I looked down at the watery brown liquid and grimaced. "I was hoping this would be coffee."

He chuckled. "I think it's only supposed to be the *idea* of coffee."

A smile slipped out as I set the cup on the table. "Hey, I wanted to apologize for last week."

"Really?" His eyes danced with a playfulness. "I would have taken you for more of the bold, unapologetic type."

"I usually am." I looked away, my finger absentmindedly tracing the smudges on the wooden folding table. "I'm just trying to make things less awkward."

Quinn raised his hands up in the air. "No awkwardness here. In fact, I was quite flattered. I don't get propositioned by women very often," he said with a lighthearted grin. "You know, with me being unable to dress myself and all."

A small laugh escaped me. "Okay, now you just make me sound shallow."

"Are you shallow?"

His response caught me off guard, the look in his eyes

intense and probing. *There it was again.* That challenge. But this time, it felt refreshing. There was something about him that made me want to loosen my armor.

People began to move around us, taking their seats within the circle. Quinn gave me a nod and motioned toward a chair. "Shall we? It looks like we're about to start."

I sat down beside him as the energy in the room shifted from the buoyancy of casual banter to the heaviness of a reality we all shared. A somber silence settled among us as Susan took a seat and adjusted her glasses.

"Thank you everyone for coming today. Who would like to open the circle?"

From the corner of my eye, I saw Quinn's hand go up.

His brow furrowed as he leaned forward in his chair, clasping his hands tightly together. "Well, I still haven't told my son about my cancer."

His voice came out strained as he spoke, and a pang of sorrow hit me as understanding nods moved like a wave across the room. I wondered how many had children of their own? How many put on a brave face to soften the truth that clung to them, like a stain they could not erase? I took in these faces awash in the tide of their own private sorrow, and I saw a courage there, embedded in the act of loving something beyond yourself. The sharp sting of regret rose within as I realized it was a sacrifice I had never been willing to make.

Voices rose and fell around me as the hour slowly passed, cocooned in a space fashioned from collective misfortune. Tangled sunlight pierced through the clouds like a fleeting reprieve and streamed through the windows as I sat there and listened to these people share their stories of love, loss, grief, and fear, while my own story sat locked tightly within the cage of my chest, daring me to release it.

People began to trickle out the door as the meeting ended,

and I joined them, stepping outside to find Quinn beside his bike, tucking a long-lens camera into the folds of a saddle bag.

Crossing my arms, I leaned against the wall beside him. "Do you always ride that thing?"

He looked at me. "I try to. Best way to get around in my opinion. You sure you don't want to go for a ride? I'm actually headed to Mount Baker Ridge to do a shoot. We're not going to get many more nice days like this."

The truth saturated the edges of his words, coating them in a meaning that went far beyond the weather, daring me to push past the walls of my isolation, to shed the stagnant layers I had woven so carefully around myself. Stepping up to him, I touched the seat of his bike, running my hands across the soft leather. "It is a nice day out, isn't it?"

Quinn bent his head down next to mine, wisps of hair falling into his eyes as he shot me a crooked smile. "So, what do you say? Want to go on a little adventure?"

Chapter Five

"I can't believe I'm doing this." I eyed the motorcycle like it was a wild animal. Quinn grinned and handed me an extra helmet he pulled from a saddlebag. "Don't worry, I'll drive slow. I promise." He slid onto the seat and patted the space behind him.

Clipping the helmet on, I was grateful to be wearing my black ankle pants as I cautiously swung my leg over and settled in. Hooking my stiletto heels onto the footrests, I stiffly gripped the sides of the seat.

"You're going to have to hold on to me, you know," Quinn chuckled as he started up the motor.

The engine vibrated between my thighs as I tucked my purse between us and encircled my arms around his waist, surprised at the definition hidden beneath his shirt. I curled my fingers against taut muscle and scooted closer. His warmth radiated through me, and I detected a faint aroma of spice hovering along his neck.

Quinn turned back to me, raising his voice over the rumble of the motor. "So, all you need to do is keep your feet on the foot pegs, try to relax, and lean in the same direction as me."

"Okay. Got it." I clutched him tighter as we lurched forward and out onto the street. The wind rushed at me as we weaved through traffic in a fluid dance of movement and sound. My heart picked up speed, and the tingle of exhilaration bubbled within, finding the thrill mildly intoxicating.

The stretch of road grew denser with the lush greenery of trees as we wound our way up to the viewpoint. The sharp, invigorating scent of pine filled the air, and a chill clung to the shadows.

As we reached the top, Quinn slowed the bike to a gentle putter and cut the engine, the sudden silence permeating me like an out-breath.

"Be careful," he said as I dismounted. "The exhaust pipe can get pretty hot."

I slid off the bike and took in the view stretching past the city skyline to the shimmering blue of the Puget Sound.

"You've been up here before, right?" Quinn asked as he pulled out his camera, draping the strap over his shoulder.

"Yes, but it's been a long time." I took a deep breath and crossed the parking lot, the breeze flirting with my skin and tugging at my hair. Shadows flickered across the ground as I walked over to the lookout and clasped my hands around the steel bars of the railing. "I forgot how beautiful it is."

I stared down into the yawning space below, and a fleeting question tore through me, pressing the air from my lungs.

How easy would it be to jump?

"This is one of my favorite spots." Quinn stood beside me and fiddled with the lens on his camera before holding it up and taking a shot of the view. "And the light is so perfect right now, with the way it's hitting the water."

I glanced at him with a small smile, attempting to push away my morose thoughts. "So, I take it you're a professional photographer?"

"Yes. Mostly freelance. I have done a few spreads in various magazines."

"Really?" I drew back the loose strands of hair the wind had blown askew. "Well, I'm surprised we haven't crossed paths before."

"Oh yeah, why's that?" Quinn leaned precariously over the railing with his camera to get another angle, letting off a short series of shuttered clicks.

"I'm the executive editor for a magazine here in town."

"Huh, would've guessed lawyer, honestly."

"And why would you guess that?"

Quinn shrugged, lowering his camera. "You have a commanding presence." He smiled at me. "You'd be very effective in a courtroom."

"You think so?" I gazed off into the distance of the water, watching as the sun danced along the surface. "I used to love my job. It's been my whole life. But lately it all seems so trivial."

"Cancer will do that to you."

I turned to see him looking at me. Caught within the light reflected in his eyes, there was a depth that I found unnerving. As if he could reach within and see all the cracks carefully concealed. I broke away from his steady gaze.

"Do you mind me asking what your diagnosis is?"

Quinn's question tugged at the locked doors and shuttered windows inside me. With a sigh, I retreated to the bench beside us and kicked off my heels, folding my knees against my chest. The words hovered in my throat, bitter and sharp. I had never spoken them out loud before. I had never claimed them as my own.

My breath spilled out, trembling and hesitant as I untethered my truth into the space between us, hoping it could somehow lessen the weight that pressed on me. "I have stage four heart cancer."

Quinn sat next to me, his arm brushing mine and creating a warmth I found myself suddenly wanting to lean into. A tender sadness swam in his eyes as he looked at me. "How much time do you have?"

I bit my lip, fighting the tears that threatened to surface. My doctor had given me a rough number, a dark truth I was too terrified to look at. And a part of me still clung to the illusion of denial like a shaky lifeline. But here I was, sitting beside a stranger, and all I wanted to do was unburden myself. The reality was too much to carry alone.

"Six months, give or take." My words came out strangled as a lump rose in my throat, the reality of it all hitting me like a slap of cold air. Six months was not enough time. Suddenly, the world felt so achingly beautiful, and all I longed for was the chance to see it through new eyes. To live beyond the cage I had encapsulated myself in.

I tore my gaze from the horizon. "What about you?"

His eyes rested on me, full of an understanding that was unspoken and genuine as he sat back against the bench. "Stage two pancreatic cancer. It runs in the family. I lost my dad to it seven years ago. I finished my final round of radiation therapy a week ago, which did manage to slow the growth a little, but not stop it." His jaw tightened as he looked up at the sky, his voice growing low. "I've got a year or two, if I'm lucky."

I swallowed the growing lump in my throat, resisting the urge to reach out and entwine my fingers through his, as if the very act of touch could save us from the tumbling speed of time. "And you have a kid?"

Quinn nodded. "I do. He's ten and lives with his mom. I get him on the weekends." He shook his head, emotion gathering in his eyes like storm clouds. "And I just can't tell him." Leaning forward, Quinn vigorously ran his hand through his hair. "How do I tell my kid that his father is dying?"

I had no words of comfort for him, but I could feel his anguish. It was visceral, and large enough to encompass my own. We sat in a hushed silence for a moment, lost within our own entangled thoughts like two weary soldiers comparing battle wounds.

"How do you do it?" My question broke the stillness between us.

Quinn looked over at me, his brow furrowing. "What do you mean?"

I clenched my hands together, pale fragile skin against the black cloth of my pants. "How do you find the meaning anymore? Knowing that all your plans have been taken away."

"I just get up every day and try to make the most out of what I have left." Quinn's voice grew deep, the outline of his sorrow cutting through the words. "And hopefully give my kid something to remember me by."

A deep sigh tumbled out, my voice coming out in a knotted whisper. "That's all we can do, I guess. Hope that our lives leave some mark on the world."

I stared out at the white peaks of the Olympic Mountains towering in the distance, their presence solid and unmoving. Such a stark contrast against the chaotic fragility of our own lives. Would my daughter even care if she knew I was dying? I was nothing to her. Only a name on a birth certificate and a scattering of genetics. The vast emptiness of my life hit me. What mark would *I* leave on this world? Would anyone even mourn me when I was gone?

Quinn fiddled with his camera and squinted into the sky as if searching for something. "I'm going to get a few more shots in before I lose the light."

* * *

We stood beside Quinn's bike as the last of the sun's rays filtered through the trees, bathing our skin in fractured shadows. "Thanks for bringing me up here."

"Thanks for coming." A slow smile bloomed across his face. "I had a feeling you could use a little change of scenery." He pulled out a card from his back pocket and handed it to me, his eyes heavy with sincerity. "My number's on there. If you ever feel like talking, please don't hesitate to call me, okay?"

I fiddled with the black embossed card, his number and address printed below a silver outline of a camera. "So, do you give out cards to all the women you meet?"

"Nope." He shot me a wink as he clipped his helmet on. "Only the ones brave enough to ride on the back of my motorcycle."

"You think I'm brave, huh?" I let out a soft chuckle and pocketed his card inside the folds of my purse.

"I think you're *very* brave."

I looked up to find his penetrating gaze cutting through me, and a heaviness twisted inside, causing my words to come out constricted. "I don't feel brave."

Quinn leaned on the bike as a gust of wind blew over us, causing the branches above to moan and creak, bowing low against the last remnants of blue sky. "I think cancer makes you brave. I think every day that we continue to fight is an act of bravery."

My vision wavered with tears for a moment. "I'm still trying to figure out what I'm fighting for."

"You'll find it. We *all* have something to fight for."

A silence settled between us for a moment as we stood staring at each other. Like a leaf tumbling in the air, I had nothing to hold on to. But there was something in the way he looked at me, and it made me feel like I wasn't going to fall.

I shivered as the chill crept through my sweater, and the familiar grip of fatigue took hold of me. "Do you mind dropping me off at my place? I live over on east twenty-fourth avenue."

Quinn stood from the bike with a soft smile, letting out a low whistle. "Capitol Hill, huh?"

I rolled my eyes. "I'm not *that* rich. But yes, I do have a nice apartment there."

Stepping closer, Quinn shrugged off his leather jacket and handed it to me. "For the ride down."

"I'm fine." I brushed off his offer with a wave of my hand.

He raised an eyebrow. "Sun's going down. The ride back is going to be a little cold."

"I said I'm fine."

"Just wear the damn jacket, Julia." Quinn's eyes sparkled with a playfulness as he thrust the jacket at me.

I reluctantly took it, draping the warmth around me as I slid onto the seat behind him. Enclosed in the remnant of his scent and pressed so close to him, a rush of heat rose to the surface, and I tried to push away the sudden image of him taking me up against a tree. The feel of the rough bark on my skin. That delicious mixture of pleasure and pain I had used for so long to distract myself from my own emotions.

But I knew it would no longer stifle the ache inside, and my body was too tired. I couldn't run from this anymore. Something much larger was demanding attention, and for the first time, I felt compelled to sit beside it and gaze into the swirling darkness, to ask the question which had been gnawing at me for weeks now.

What was I going to do with the time I had left?

Chapter Six

"*I*t's good to see you, Julia. You missed our session last week."

I sat against the over-plumped cushions of my therapist's couch. "Yeah, something came up."

"Care to talk about it?"

"No, not really." My foot tapped on the floor as I looked out the window at another rainy day, the heavy grey blanket of the sky matching the bleak palette of my mood. Each day was just another unraveled cord bringing me closer to the inevitable, and my dreams had become nothing more than dark shadows taunting me.

"You seem a bit agitated."

"I *am* agitated."

He cleared his throat and leaned forward, regarding me with a look of concern. "Do you want to talk about why you're feeling this way?"

"I'm running out of time." I bit my lip hard, the sting piercing through the layers of my resolve.

"Would you care to elaborate on what you mean?"

I was growing so tired of this dance between us, all this empty correspondence I had willingly created. My silence was not going to change the outcome. I knew it was time to tell him.

Whipping my head in his direction, anger rose inside like a hot flame buffering the desolate wind of my own anxiety.

"I mean, I have cancer. I'm fucking *dying*." The words flew from my mouth like ugly shards of glass I could not retract, slicing the air between us.

His face furrowed with a mixture of surprise and sadness as he stared at me from his chair. "How long have you known?"

I glanced at the picture hanging above his head. A framed painting of a garden path leading to the water, sunlight shimmering on the surface like diamonds, its soothing, quaint beauty suddenly cruel and mocking. "About a month."

"Why did you wait until now to share this with me?"

I shrugged, acidity coating me like armor as I leaned back against the couch, defeat pressing down on me with its rigid grip. "I don't know. So you can clear your calendar, I guess."

He set his notepad on the table beside him and drew his hands together. "Anger can be a common reaction to this kind of news. And this dismissiveness, it's a way of protecting yourself." He looked at me with soft eyes. "You are cycling through the stages of grief right now, and they don't necessarily come in a fixed order. It's different for everyone."

A sudden breeze danced with the tree outside, shaking loose the last of the leaves which clung to the branches. The harsh grip of winter was on its way, and I wondered if I would even see another spring. Would I ever be able to watch the breathtaking colors of life unfold again? My throat tightened, and my vision trembled like the rain against the window.

He leaned forward and placed a box of tissues beside me. "It's okay to let this out. You need to be able to work through all these emotions inside you."

Shaking my head, I tried to push past the tears, but they broke through, leaving thin trails of warmth on my cheeks, my vulnerability no longer a secret.

I looked over at him, my voice wavering as I choked on all the thoughts I was too afraid to speak out loud. "When does the acceptance come?"

"It comes when you are ready for it."

Doctor Henderson sat across from me as I clenched my hands together. The look on her face revealed the answer long before it left her mouth.

"It isn't working, is it?" My words came out in a rasp against my tongue.

She looked up from the computer screen, her face pinched and grave. "I'm afraid not. Your scans indicate no slowing of tumor growth. We knew we only had a forty percent chance of the proton therapy yielding results." Turning away from the screen, she reached into a drawer, gathering a stack of pamphlets. She slid them across the desk to me, her gaze solemn. "What we need to discuss at this point are your options regarding palliative care."

Her words fell on me like a blast of frigid air as I stared at the papers, the brutal slap of finality sucking the breath out of me. Brochures, that's all she had left. Hollow information on glossy folded pieces of paper.

Panic crashed into me as I shook my head. My hands clenched into fists in my lap, nails biting into the flesh and drawing out that comforting ache.

"No. There *has* to be something else we can try. An experimental therapy? Holistic herbs?" My words came out harsh and knotted while my mind scrambled around in panicked disbelief, refusing to accept this bleak and unforgiving reality laid out before me.

How much time did I have left? How many breaths? How many sunsets? How many hushed mornings when the hum of the city had not yet woken, and the air was rich with the echo of the ocean like a soft, comforting sigh? The claws of desperation pressed the air from my lungs. I wanted more of those moments I had so foolishly taken for granted.

She leaned back in her chair. "There are a few experimental trials available, but unfortunately, your cancer is too far advanced for you to be a viable candidate. I'm sorry. I wish we had more options."

"So, this is it then?" A cold sweat crept along my skin, and nausea rose in my gut as the walls closed in on me. My life, reduced to pamphlets and doled out words of condolences. *I have to get out of this room.*

"Please take a look at these." She slid the papers closer to me. "There are a lot of valuable resources and information for you. To help make things more comfortable." The blue of her eyes pierced into me, full of a sympathy that felt clinical and rehearsed. "Have you been going to the support group I recommended?"

I nodded, my limbs laden as I pulled on a loose thread in the hem of my shirt, watching it slowly unravel between my trembling fingers.

* * *

I don't remember how I got home. My body had taken over, performing a series of meaningless gestures that resulted in me curled up in bed, watching light play over the walls while I clutched my covers like a life raft.

What was the point of it all? There was nothing left. My life had been whittled down to a handful of months, and all the control I so fervently clung to had slipped from my grasp. The crushing truth hit me with a cruel and unrelenting force, stealing my breath.

I was alone.

Gasping, I clutched at my chest as if I could rip away at the truth and expose a different answer beneath. The violent pace of my heart screamed within like a frenzied captive banging against the walls of its cage, hoping for a rescue it knew would never come.

I stumbled from the bed, but the weight on my chest did not release. It gripped itself tighter, and my lungs struggled for air.

I can't breathe. Was this it? Was I dying? Had my battered heart finally given up?

My vision blurred, and the room spun as the wild animal of panic thrashed inside. Like a last desperate plea, I fumbled for my phone on the nightstand, my hands weak and shaky as I dialed nine-one-one.

The voice on the other end was tinny and detached. Questions filtering through a tunnel. I was only a number. A list of symptoms. A body that needed tending to. Nothing more.

I lay on the floor, gasping for breath with the phone cradled to my ear while the dispatcher insisted I stay on the line. Everything now filtered down to the frantic pull of my lungs and the warning cry of my heart as I waited for the sound of sirens.

* * *

Against the stark whiteness of the hospital bed, the sheets were cold and abrasive on my skin. Wires crisscrossed me like a road map, tethering my body to the steady blinking monitor beside me.

The last hour had been a haze of images and sensations. Disconnected from my body, I watched it all unfold like a dream. Paramedics with their gloved hands quickly lifting me off the floor and onto a stretcher. The sound of sirens as we sped through the city. Then the hiss of the emergency room doors sliding behind me, encapsulating me in a room devoid of color.

My limbs lay like broken weights beside me as the rush of my heart pounded within. Still beating, fast and frantic, as if it no longer wanted to reside within the walls of my body.

The door opened, and a doctor walked in. "Julia Marino," he said, glancing down at his tablet.

"Yes." My words came out like sandpaper, course against my tongue.

"I just got off the phone with your oncologist, and our tests show no indication of a heart attack." He pulled up a chair beside my bed and sat down. "My guess is that what you had was a panic attack."

I turned to him. "I've had panic attacks before. *This* was different."

"Well, panic can present itself in a myriad of symptoms. Given the added stress of your recent diagnosis, this is often a common occurrence among cancer patients." He began to tap away on the screen of my chart. "What I'm going to do is prescribe you a mild sedative."

"No." A lurid memory flashed into my mind. White pills cupped in the cold and unyielding palm of my mother's hand. Her eyes staring up at me, wide and vacant. All the life inside stolen away. "I don't want drugs. I don't want to be doped up."

"What I'm prescribing for you is a *very* low dose. You will not be doped up. This medication will only help relax you a little, so that heart rate of yours can come down." He leaned back and rested the tablet on his lap, regarding me as if I were a child.

I flinched and turned my head from him, focusing on the pulsing lights on the monitor, a rapid staccato of colors on a screen. "Fine." I knew I wouldn't take them. My words were only a pale agreement to mollify his concerns.

"Okay, I'll go get your prescription and discharge papers ready for you, then." He stood from the chair. "Is there someone you can call to come pick you up?"

"Not really. No." My eyes drifted to the window as I remembered the card Quinn had given me last week, still nestled in the pocket of my purse like a faint beacon of comfort.

A nurse breezed in and silently removed the wires attached to my chest, her fingers quick and efficient as she turned off the machine. And then she was gone, the door clicking softly behind her, leaving me alone with my tattered thoughts.

I rose from the bed and sucked in a sharp breath as a strong wave of dizziness overcame me once more. Gripping the railing of the bed, anxiety clawed at me. I no longer trusted my body and what it was capable of. Like a child terrified of the monsters lurking in the dark, the idea of going back to my apartment filled me with an overwhelming dread.

My hands shook as I waited for the instability to subside. Fumbling with the ties of the hospital gown, I retrieved my clothes from the chair next to me and rooted through the contents of my purse until I found Quinn's card; and before I lost the nerve, dialed his number.

He answered on the second ring. At the sound of his voice, pleading words I could barely decipher tumbled out, abrupt, frantic, and punctuated by a stifled sob. "I'm at the hospital right now. I had a panic attack."

"What hospital are you at?"

"I'm at Swedish Medical Center. They just discharged me." I

rasped, pacing the room in a restless blur as I gripped the phone tightly against my ear.

"Okay. I want you to go find a seat in the waiting room, and I'll be there soon."

"No, it's fine. You don't have to do this."

"Julia. Don't go anywhere. I'll be there in twenty minutes."

Chapter Seven

hy had I called Quinn?

I knew he couldn't save me. All I knew was that there was something about him that made me feel safe, and I couldn't remember the last time I'd felt safe with anyone.

I sat stiffly against the chair in the waiting room, a place perpetually infused with quiet trepidation. People sat hunched over, staring into the chasms of their phone as if the blue glow could distract them from whatever it was they were anticipating. News about a loved one. An unplanned visit. An unexpected diagnosis. Layers of unspoken questions hung in the air like an invisible stain, while the world went on around us, impervious and unrelenting as we sat here, waiting for an answer.

A warm hand touched my shoulder, jolting me from my swirling thoughts. I looked up into Quinn's deep brown eyes, his calm gaze instantly slowing the racing of my heart.

Taking a deep breath, I stood, my legs shaking as I clutched my purse to my chest and allowed him to silently lead me out of the hospital.

The double doors closed behind us with a shudder, and a blast of cold air hit me. Angry rain pummeled from the sky, bathing the sides of the awning we stood under in a steady cascade of water. Quinn turned to me, his face a heavy mask of concern. "What happened?"

"I don't know." My words came out in a whisper as I leaned against the brick wall, dropping my purse to the ground. "I thought I was having a heart attack. I thought I was dying. I don't think..." I covered my face with my hands, trying to hide the flood of tears that rose to the surface. "I don't think I can do this alone."

"You're not alone." Quinn took my hands in his, gently pulling them away from my face. "I'm right here."

"You know what I mean." I yanked away from him, clutching my arms to my chest. "I *am* alone." My voice spilled out in a snarled cry as I stared out into the ashen sky of an afternoon quickly fading. "I've always been alone. And I'm going to *die* alone!"

My legs crumpled beneath me, and I slid down the wall. Entangled in the debris of the day, I allowed the unrelenting weight to overtake me as my words became a strangled whisper. "The proton therapy isn't working."

Quinn crouched in front of me, his eyes wide and full of sorrow as he reached out and grasped my shoulders, his touch like an anchor, calming the storm inside. "Okay, I want you to take some deep breaths with me."

Swiping the tears from my cheeks, I released a trembling exhale followed by a shaky in-breath.

"*Good*. Now another one."

His gaze remained fixed on me, warm and soothing as our breath merged like waves washing against the shore, until the churning pace of my heart settled back with a trembled sigh.

"Do you feel a little better?"

I nodded and pushed myself off the ground, trying to regain what shred of composure I had left.

Quinn drew up his collar and squinted at the rain. "I'm going to go pull my car around for you. I'll be right back."

"Where's your bike?"

He pulled some keys from his pocket. "Back at my house."

My hand fell to his arm. "Why did you come?"

"Because you called. Because nobody should be alone and scared in a hospital. And because I wanted to." He glanced back at me with a faint smile before dashing out into the downpour.

* * *

We parked in front of my building. The patter of the rain against the car roof was like the low beat of a drum pulsing through the silence, hollowing out a tender and delicate space inside me.

Quinn cut the engine and turned toward me. "Do you want me to come up with you?"

I twined my fingers together, biting the edge of my lip. The habitual urge to push myself away rose for a moment, only to dwindle to a vague murmur inside. Something much stronger demanded attention. I suddenly wanted to be seen.

"Would you mind?"

"No. Not at all." He stepped out of the car and briskly walked around to my side, the rain drenching his hair and spilling patterns across his jacket as he opened the door for me. Pulling myself from the seat, another rush of lightheadedness hit, and his hand rested on my back, steadying me. "Are you okay?"

"I'm not sure. I've been dizzy ever since I got back from my doctor's appointment today."

Quinn nodded and slid his hand around my waist, pulling me closer to him, his warmth permeating my skin like a sedative. "Your nerves are shot. Let's get you inside so you can lie down."

I leaned into his shoulder, sinking into the solidity of him as he ushered me into the lobby and toward the elevators. Here I was, broken and frayed against his pillar, a small body clinging to a mast.

We reached the top floor lobby, and the doors opened to an expanse of glass with the view of the city stretching out before us. Drawing myself away from him, I fished inside my purse for my keys and unlocked my door while Quinn stood there taking in the view.

"Nice place you got here."

"Thanks," I replied, throwing my purse on the kitchen counter with a heavy sigh. "It does feel too big for me at times, though."

He stepped inside, his eyes scanning the floor-to-ceiling windows, polished oak floors and sleek, high-end, minimalist décor, everything in tones of grey and white. He was a breath of life amid the sterility. The first man I had ever allowed into my apartment. And the realization of this felt deeply significant.

"How about I make us some tea or something?" he said, turning to me. "Or some food, if you're hungry?"

"You really don't have to stay, Quinn. I'm sure you have better things to do right now." I sunk down onto the couch, resting my elbows on my knees as I ran my fingers through my hair. "And what about your kid?"

Quinn shook his head. "My son is with his mom for the next two days." He crossed the room and crouched beside me, placing his hand on my arm. "I would like to stay. But only if you want me to."

His touch was a beacon, coaxing me back to myself. My hand found his, curling my fingers around his palm, and a spark of heat traveled through me when he squeezed back. Pulling away, I leaned against the couch, watching him as if he were a mirage, an outline of something good that would fade if I got too close. "I would like that. Thank you."

"Okay, why don't you go lay down, and I'll rustle us up some food." Quinn stood and threw me a smile as he crossed the room and went into the kitchen.

I made my way into the bedroom and collapsed onto the sheets, wrapping my blanket around me while the sounds of Quinn in the kitchen filtered through the doorway. My body felt torn and dislodged from the events of the day, mind swimming as fatigue gripped my limbs, but Quinn's presence was a comforting support I wanted to reach for, and gratitude washed over me. Closing my eyes, I allowed the gentle sway of exhaustion to claim me for a moment.

The sound of Quinn walking into the room startled me, and I jerked my eyes open as he set a cup of tea and a bowl of soup on my nightstand. "You didn't have much in your kitchen to work with. But I *did* manage to find some cans of soup."

"Thanks for making this," I said, sitting up and propping my back against the pillows. "I guess I haven't eaten anything today."

I stared down at my bare fingers. The rings I used to wear no longer fit, and I had taken them off weeks ago. I wasn't sure if it was the cancer, my lack of appetite, or a combination of both, but I no longer liked what I saw in the mirror. My reflection was a stark reminder of a body slowly disappearing, and it terrified me.

Quinn settled in a chair beside me, his hair curled from the rain and falling into his eyes. Stretching out his long legs, he took a sip of the tea in his hand. "How are you feeling?"

I shook my head and reached for the bowl of soup, dipping my spoon into the murky broth. "That's a loaded question, you know."

He shot me a faint smile and glanced out the darkening window. "It always is, isn't it?"

His eyes traveled around the room, falling to my cello, which stood propped up on a stand in the corner, the encased bow leaning beside it like an unbroken companion. "You play the cello?"

I nestled the soup in my lap and shifted beneath the covers, sweeping my hand through the air. "I don't know if I would call it that. I used to play when I was in high school. But then I stopped."

My fingers clenched, digging into my palm as I recalled the sound of splintering wood hitting plaster. My father's eyes glazed with drink as he violently hurled the instrument against the wall, obliterating the last bit of beauty I had tried so desperately to cling to.

"I found that cello at a flea market about ten years ago. Thought I would see if I still remembered how to play." A tired smile tugged at my lips as my hand skittered across the sheets, tracing invisible patterns on the fabric. "It helps relax me."

"I would love to hear you play sometime." Interest rose in Quinn's eyes as he looked over at me.

"I don't play in front of people."

"Why not?"

I stared at the cello, so many years of unspoken emotion embedded in the strings, my heartbeat hidden between the groves of the wood like secrets no one could touch. "It's private."

"I get it." Quinn nodded and leaned back in his chair. "I think it's important to have things that we do only for ourselves."

A sharp chime pierced the air between us, and Quinn slid his hand into his pocket to retrieve his phone. Motioning that he would be back in a minute, he pressed the phone to his ear and left the room.

As I forced spoonfuls of the bland tasting soup into my mouth, I listened to the deep drone of his voice from the living room, soft and full of affection.

"I love you, too, bud."

My heart clenched, and that loneliness I spent years convincing myself was never there, rose once more and settled beside me. I suddenly ached for a little piece of love to call my own, an island I could swim to when the waters grew too deep.

Quinn appeared in the doorway, leaning against the frame while he slipped his phone back into his pocket. "That was my son. He wanted to tell me about the score he got on his math test today." His voice was thick with a wistful pride as he spoke.

"What's his name?"

"Jasper." He crossed the room and sank back onto the chair next to me with a sigh. "He's such a good kid. Best damn thing that's ever happened to me."

Setting the half-empty bowl on the nightstand, I grabbed my cup of tea, the warmth seeping through my hands as steam softly rose into my face. I wondered how much I had missed out on. How much meaning would I have found in being a mother? I knew in the end, my career had only been a paltry substitution for a life lived.

"And he still doesn't know about your cancer?"

"No, and neither does his mom. She and I don't have the best relationship." Quinn shook his head, his eyes flashing with sorrow. "Every time I'm with Jasper, I tell myself, this will be the day I sit him down and tell him. But then he looks at me with this big smile..." His voice cracked and sudden tears welled up in the corners of his eyes. "And I just can't do it." He leaned forward, and with the heel of his palm, wiped at a stray tear which had snuck down his cheek. "He's such a happy kid. I can't bear to be the one to take that away from him."

Quinn's unabashed emotion cut into me, and I reached over, placing my hand on his. I wanted to rest against his tenderness as the edges of my protective shell shifted and stretched, longing for release, longing to show him what was underneath.

"I'm sorry. I can't imagine how hard that must be."

Quinn's fingers rested over mine, his thumb sweeping a slow circle across my skin. "I take it you don't have kids?"

I shook my head as I released his hand, my teeth pressing hard into my lip. "I'm not a mother, no. But I did have a child once."

"Really?" A mixture of sadness and confusion flashed across his face.

"Yes. I was nineteen, and I gave her up for adoption." A sharp tug of pain pierced into me. For so long, I had tucked away this skeleton of mine, a secret full of shame, regret, and all the years spent wondering who she was and who she had become, my heart aching for a child I never knew.

"You had a girl?"

I nodded, choking on the words. "Yes. She's twenty-three now, I think."

"And the father?" His question was a scar tearing at the threads beneath my skin, and I skirted my eyes past him, seeking solace in the rainy canvas of nightfall that lay beyond the window.

A memory I had not unearthed in years burrowed up. Standing in the dark outside of his house, clutching the growing swell of my belly while the cold sting of the rain soaked my clothes. My eyes pleading with him as he watched me through the living room window. The anguish that burned inside as he drew the curtains shut and turned off the porch light, the sudden darkness shutting me out like a jarring and brutal slap.

"I'm sorry, I don't mean to pry. You don't have to tell me what happened." The soft tone of Quinn's voice yanked me back from my thoughts.

"No, it's okay. It's an unoriginal story. Cliché, really. I was young and stupid, and I fell in love with my college professor. A much older man who was married with kids. He told me he loved me, that he was going to leave his wife for me, and like a fool, I believed him." My words came out bitter and flippant, as if I could bury once more, that broken, needy girl. Cover her with the weight of the earth. But she had always been there, clawing at the surface. And I could still remember the way his hand felt slowly traveling up the length of my thigh for the first time as I sat beside him in an empty classroom going over a paper. The furtive glances that undressed me. The clandestine trysts in my one-room studio that smelled of Chinese takeout and desperation. The way he said my name, as if it was the most beautiful sound in the world.

"And then what happened?

My eyes had drifted to my hands which clenched the cup of tea, and I looked up at Quinn. "I got pregnant. He panicked, and wanted me to have an abortion, but I refused." I took a deep breath, biting on the edge of my lip. "I guess... I hoped... that he would come around. That we would run away together and start a new life. But of course, that never happened. Instead, he transferred to another college, uprooted his family, and moved out of town. I never heard from him again."

"Wow. What a piece of shit." Quinn's jaw tensed as he shook his head, strands of hair falling into dark eyes that held sympathy.

"Yeah. He was." I took in a shuddering breath, feeling the weight of my past shift as I extracted the snarled threads and laid them bare between us. "I was working on my journalism degree. I had plans for myself. But at the time, I was struggling and barely able to make rent. How was I going to take care of a kid? I had no family to support me. I was an only child. My mom died when I was ten, and my father was an abusive drunk. I left home as soon as I got a job, and I never looked back."

I set the cup of tea on the nightstand, and folded my knees up against my chest, clasping my arms around myself while Quinn watched me with a sadness that flickered across his features. His gaze was so open, I felt like I could fall into him, that he would catch me if I asked him to. "I wanted this kid to have a better life than I had."

Reaching over, his hand rested on my knee for a moment, warm and grounding. "Have you ever tried to contact her?"

I sucked in a sharp breath. "She actually reached out to me. She sent me an email about two years ago, said she had tracked me through some old birth records. Apparently, I had kept them open. Though I have no memory of doing that." My hand fluttered to my chest, fiddling with the chain of my necklace. "I guess it was another thing I just... locked away."

"So, you've talked to her?"

"No." The bitter sting of remorse tugged at me as I slid my hand across the sheets, smoothing the wrinkled creases. "I've never been able to find the courage to respond."

"What do you have to lose?" He leaned back and rested his head against the plush fabric of the chair, his gaze intense and probing. "Don't you think it's time you met your daughter?"

So many years of regret pressed into me, and I feared I would never have the strength to face it. "I don't know if I can." My hands clenched the covers, pulling them tightly around my body. "What would I even say to her?" I shook my head, biting back the sting of emotions that threatened to suffocate me. "I've waited too long. It's too late now."

"I don't believe that." Quinn's eyes were soft, but tore into mine like a challenge, a demand I couldn't look away from, as if daring me to face myself. "It's never too late."

* * *

The evening enclosed us as we talked, sharing pieces of our lives, stories that knitted together a vague outline of who we were and who we were trying to become before time had stepped in demanding urgency. Every moment was valuable, and we sat steeped in this knowledge, our voices hushed and full of a delicate fervency as we exchanged words for a solidarity that felt intimate and authentic.

Quinn shared slivers of childhood memories, images of open fields, skinned knees and trees he would climb, hours spent watching the branches dance with the sky. I sat and listened, my own childhood locked away tight, too dark, and ugly to share. There were no happy memories there, only tangled thorns that drew blood. And so I borrowed his, trading the remnants of my shrouded trauma for his warm blue sky.

My anxiety had softened to a dull hum, coiling back, and releasing me from its pallid grip. I stretched and looked over at the clock beside my bed. "It's getting late. I'm sure you're wanting to go home and get some sleep."

The dim light threw shadows across his face, accentuating the strong curve of his jaw and a faint peppering of stubble. With his deep brown eyes and tousled hair, he had a rugged but playful handsomeness about him I found alluring. His soothing presence took up space among the empty corners of the apartment and quieted the restlessness inside me, and I didn't want him to leave.

"Honestly, I could stay up all night talking with you." He leaned forward with a smile. "But I think it's *you* who needs to get some sleep."

I nodded and burrowed into my blankets, allowing the pulse of exhaustion to slip in beside me. "You're right, but I don't want you to leave just yet."

My confession exposed something fragile, and I reached my hand out to him, owning this vulnerability as I threaded my fingers through his, so large and warm against my own.

Quinn gave me a gentle squeeze. "Then I'll stay."

"Just until I fall asleep, okay?"

His voice was a whisper in the darkness, filling me with solace. "Okay, Julia."

Chapter Eight

*M*orning light streamed in through the windows and crept across my sheets. I turned over in bed and found Quinn still in the chair next to me, his face soft and uncovered with sleep. Sitting up, I watched the steady rhythm of his breath, like a comforting sigh filling the empty spaces inside.

The intimacy of waking to a man beside me, in a room that had only ever enclosed my own thoughts, sent a warm rush to the surface of my skin. Without thinking, I reached out and ran my fingers through his hair, the dark strands thick and silky between my fingers.

Quinn's eyes fluttered open with a look of diffused longing as his hand clasped around mine. My heart tumbled in my chest as I fell into the depths of his gaze. Suspended in something unspoken and heavy, I pulled away, breaking the moment between us.

"I can't believe you slept in that chair all night."

"I wasn't planning to." He stretched and shot me a grin. "But this chair is surprisingly comfortable."

I looked out the window. The thick cover of clouds had broken overnight, and sunlight peered through, illuminating the water beyond the city in a shimmering brush of gold. "We could go get some coffee or something to eat if you want. There's this really great café around the corner."

"I would love to," he glanced at his phone that lay on the nightstand, "but I actually have to go pick up Jasper from his mom's this morning." He stood and grabbed his coat, which he had draped over the chair. "Can I take a raincheck on that?"

"Of course." I waved my offer away with a flick of my hand. "I've already taken up too much of your time."

He regarded me with a look that seemed to reach through the layers I was once more scrambling to erect. "You haven't taken up anything, Julia. I really enjoyed talking with you last night."

"Me too." My eyes dropped to the floor as I tried to push away the uncomfortable sensation that overcame me. I wanted more of these moments with him, and this reality left me brittle and exposed, my yearning a frightened animal cowering in the corner.

"Julia, what is it about intimacy that scares you so much?"

"Who said I'm afraid of intimacy?"

"It's clear by your avoidance of it."

"Intimacy is overrated."

"And why do you feel that way?"

"It's messy."

"What is it about intimacy that you find so messy?"

"You strip too much of yourself away."

"What do you think will happen if you strip yourself away?"

"People will see inside."

"And what is it you don't want them to see?"

"All the ugliness."

I stood abruptly from the bed, slipping the familiar edges of my walls back into place like a habitual shield, hoping to hide away the sting of my emotions. "I'll see you at the next meeting, okay? I'm going to go take a shower. Feel free to let yourself out."

Quinn stared at me for a minute as if waiting for me to say something else, and I wanted to say something. But all my words were locked up tight, choking the air from my lungs.

With a nod, he made his way out of the room, the sound of the door closing behind him filling the apartment once more with a familiar crushing silence.

I stood in the office hallway, hovering outside the door to the boardroom. My hands clenched nervously together. The voice inside that had been persistently growing louder for days now had quieted. I knew this was what I had to do. It was time to pass the torch. For me to say goodbye to a life I no longer had room for.

A hush fell across the table as I entered, twelve pairs of eyes watching me with a mixture of uncertainty and apprehension. I took a seat, adjusted my tailored suit jacket, and summoned the resolve I knew I would need for this.

"I apologize for the last-minute meeting, but I need to discuss some important changes which will be occurring." I folded my hands against the table and took a deep breath. "As of today, I will be stepping down from my position as executive editor."

Murmured voices rose and looks of confusion washed across the room.

"I am also recommending that Lillian take my position. She has been working under me for three years now, and I feel confident she has the ability and skill needed to take my place and help move this magazine to the next level."

Steven leaned forward from his seat beside me. His face was creased and wrinkled from years of laughter and warm, open smiles, but there was no smile this time. "Julia, you're not leaving us, are you?"

A lump rose in my throat. Steven had always been like a father figure to me, gently guiding me when I had been an eager but under-confident intern. The closest thing to a friend I had. I swallowed back the emotion that threatened the surface. "Yes, due to personal reasons, I will be resigning. This decision will be effective immediately."

I had to rip the bandage off. I wouldn't be able to sit with all the long, drawn-out goodbyes. The veiled questions and pensive looks. If I didn't leave now, my resolve would suffocate me.

"Thank you all for being such an amazing team. It's been an incredible honor working with each and every one of you."

And just like that, over a decade of my life had come to a close. The finality hit with a blunt force as I looked around the room at the faces I had worked tirelessly beside for so many years. Taking a deep breath, I stood and gave everyone a tight smile before striding out of the room, leaving a stunned silence behind.

My hands shook as I closed the door to my office and surveyed my meticulously organized desk; a pen holder, my computer, a tiny bonsai tree Steven had given me as a Christmas gift the year before. So much of myself was embedded within the shiny oak panels, its drawers holding memories and accomplishments like talismans of a life I no longer recognized.

"*What would you do without your job?*"

"*What do you mean?*"

"*Well, you speak about how your work defines you. How would you identify yourself if that work were suddenly taken away? Who do you think you are beneath the external persona you present to the world?"*

"I have no idea."

"Don't you think that would be something important to explore?"

Where had all the time gone? I had spent so much of my life consumed by my career, chasing down success while the years snuck by until I couldn't even recognize them anymore.

With a sigh, I pulled out a box from the closet and sifted through the various artifacts I had accumulated throughout the years. Photos and gag gifts from staff parties, framed magazine editions, various awards; my entire career now neatly tucked away.

A knock on the door startled me, and I looked up to find Steven walking into the room, his eyes somber. "Julia. Care to tell me what's going on?"

Steven had always been able to see beneath the rough exterior I presented to the people around me, and our relationship had been forged from an unspoken understanding, one I had always been deeply grateful for. But I couldn't tell him. I wanted him to remember me as a woman somewhere out there in the world. A woman living.

I resumed my careful packing, trying to quell the tears I could feel rising inside. "Life has decided to make other plans for me." Leaning across the desk, I picked up the bonsai and handed it to him. "Take this."

"You don't want it anymore?" He looked at me, his brow furrowing.

"You'll be able to take better care of it than I can." I turned from him and placed my laptop into the box. "Plus, you'll have something to remember me by."

"I don't think I need a *tree* to remember you. This place is not going to be the same without you, Julia. You've made quite an impact on this company. That is something that will never be forgotten." His hand fell to my shoulder, and I whipped around, a tear escaping down my cheek. "Are you sure you don't want to tell me what's going on?"

"Please, don't make this any harder than it already is," I choked out. "You know how much I hate goodbyes."

"This doesn't have to be goodbye." He looked at me with a sad smile, his eyes reflecting a softness I suddenly wanted to fall into.

"But it is." My lip quivered, and the words rushed out of their own volition, tangled and longing for someone else to hold them for a moment. "I have cancer, Steven. I'm dying."

Silence gripped the space between us, his face crumpling in disbelief. And then his arms were around me, pulling me into a hug. I tensed up for a moment and then let go, allowing the tears to spill out and stain his jacket.

There was nothing to say. He didn't try to mollify the moment with platitudes. He just held me, his hands strong against the shell of my body as I released my walls and breathed goodbye to a story that was no longer mine.

The rain poured down, washing out the city in a heavy blanket of grey. I stepped from my car and sprinted through the parking lot, flinging open the doors to the community center. Stopping in the doorway to shake the rain off my coat, I couldn't help the smile that crept across my face as Quinn

THE LIFE WE DREAM OF

locked eyes with me from across the crowded room. A wordless hello infused with a warmth that caused my pulse to accelerate.

People had already begun to take their seats as I joined the group, and I quickly nabbed the empty chair beside Quinn.

"How are you doing?" He dipped his head close to mine, his voice soft and low, like a caress against my ear.

"I'm okay." I let out a long exhale and fumbled with the straps of my purse, flustered by the depths of his gaze.

"Thank you, everyone, for joining us today. Who would like to open our circle?" Susan's voice cut through the room, and my hand impulsively raised in the air.

"Julia." Her calm eyes met mine with a look of surprise, and I bit my lip, wondering what had compelled me to volunteer.

"Um." My eyes darted across the room, trying to find something solid and impassive to cling to as everyone waited for me to speak. "I found out my proton therapy isn't working." My voice came out shaky, my mouth dry. There were no more deals to be made with the truth. I had nothing left to bargain with. "I have maybe six months." The sting of tears clouded my vision as I drew in a trembling breath.

Quinn reached out and gripped my hand firmly in his, and I squeezed back in gratitude, his touch a soothing anchor stilling the hurricane inside. "Three days ago, I quit my job. For so long, my work has been my entire life. I poured all of myself into my career. And now, I have no idea who I am without it."

I looked at the woman across from me, her face pale and hollow, disease ravaging the light in her eyes, and I was overcome with a sudden desire to wrap my arms around her fragile edges, to weep with her. We were all castaways here in this room, adrift in a sea of shattered dreams, clinging to the remnants.

I wiped at a tear that crept down my cheek. "I'm trying to figure out what it is I want with this time I have left. And even though I don't have those answers yet, I *do* know what it is I no longer want."

* * *

Rain battered the roof as Quinn and I sat together in my car after group, the windows obscured by the heat of our breath.

"It was brave of you to share today. I know it wasn't easy."

I let out a long sigh. Baring myself to a roomful of strangers had left an unexpected lightness behind, as if the layers were slowly chipping away, leaving behind cracks where the air could get through. I only hoped the space inside held room for something new to grow.

I ran my finger along my seat, fidgeting with the embroidered seam on the leather upholstery. "I've been wanting to apologize for the other day at my apartment. I didn't mean to brush you off like that." I looked up to find him watching me like an open invitation. "I've always struggled with feeling vulnerable."

"I know."

I shot him a wan smile. "Is it that obvious?"

He leaned in close, the warmth of his eyes enveloping me. "Only to someone who wants to see what's on the other side of that vulnerability."

His candid words caused a flutter to bloom inside, and I took a shaky breath, caught within the pull of his gaze. "I don't even think *I* know what's on the other side."

"*You* are."

The sting of tears crept through, blurring my vision. His answer was so simple, yet profound. It was as if beneath all the scars lay an unbroken version of myself, just waiting to be found. And I only hoped he was right. I wanted so desperately to find that woman.

Quinn settled back against the seat. "If you could go anywhere right now, Julia, where would it be?"

"I don't know." I turned toward the window, watching the rivulets of water snake down the glass. "Somewhere warm and tropical would be nice. I'd love to get away from all this rain."

A slow smile tugged at the corners of his mouth as he sat up. "I think we can do something about that."

I glanced at him. "What are you talking about?"

He leaned over and plucked the car keys from my hand. "Why don't you let me drive, and I'll show you."

Chapter Nine

Quinn pulled the car into the parking lot, and I leaned forward, squinting up at the looming Space Needle. "Why are we at the Seattle Center?"

"You'll see," he said with a playful wink.

I sighed and crossed my arms, fatigue pulling at me. "I don't know if I feel up to being around crowds of people right now."

"It's midweek. It won't be that crowded." He cut the engine and looked over at me. "And where we're going will be nice and quiet. I promise."

Reluctantly, I slid from the seat and followed him through the parking lot. The cold sting of rain slapped against my face as the wind tugged at my clothes, and all I wanted was to curl in bed among covers that muffled sound. To wait for sleep to strip everything down, a gentle hand leading me far away from the foreboding grip of time.

Climbing a set of stairs, Quinn led us through an empty playground and toward the elegant white arches of a large building.

"Are we going to the Pacific Science Center?" I asked, turning to him.

"Have you been here before?"

I shook my head. "No, I haven't, actually."

"Well, good. It'll be a surprise then. You'll like it."

We walked into a room awash with light and high ceilings. Only a few people milled about, their voices a low hum echoing across the walls. Quinn stepped to the front desk and pulled out his wallet.

"No, I got this," I said, fishing through my purse.

With a playful grin, he slid a ticket across the counter to me. "Too late. It's on me."

He led me down a series of hallways, past various science displays, and through a set of double doors. Warm, humid air hit me as we walked into a large room enclosed in panels of glass and tropical plants. As my eyes took in the space, I noticed movement, tiny creatures fluttering among the foliage, their delicate wings alight with color.

"It's a butterfly garden. The closest thing to a tropical oasis you'll find here in Seattle." Quinn's words came out in a whisper as if he didn't want to startle them. "I used to bring Jasper here all the time when he was little."

I breathed in the rich scent of earth and flowers, an intoxicating blend of hibiscus and jasmine. The warmth of the room curled around me, contrasting the chill from outside. Removing my jacket, I leaned against a rock ledge and looked up, watching the butterflies glide through the air in their graceful dance of flight. "This place is really peaceful."

"It is, isn't it?" He thrust his hands in his pockets and joined my gaze upward. "Kinda wish I'd brought my camera with me."

I looked over at him. "How long have you been a photographer?"

"All my life, pretty much. I was a very introverted kid, and the lens was a way for me to interact with the world." He rested his back against the wall beside me. "Photography gave me the confidence I needed to come out of my shell."

With a sigh, I glanced down at my hands. "Aside from playing the cello, I loved to draw when I was young. I really wanted to be an artist." A sadness tugged at me as I recalled that little girl tucked away in her room. Hours spent building fantasy worlds with crayon and ink, lost in a visual realm born of color, imagination, and endless possibility.

"So, what happened?"

"Life happened, I guess. I lost my spark." A gentle tickle brushed across my skin, and I took in a breath as the wings of a butterfly landed softly on my hand, its own mortality fleeting, but so beautiful. A reminder of life. We were all ephemeral. Could I grasp ahold of what I had left and find a way to make it beautiful?

"I don't think your spark is lost, Julia. It's not too late to start over."

"But *isn't* it?"

I met the depths of his gaze. How differently would I have lived my life if I'd only known what little I had to bargain with? So many precious moments I had wasted. All those years spent running from myself, from the brutal memories of my father and the paralyzing loss of my mother, all the while trying to outpace the yearning for a daughter I never had the chance to know.

Sorrow pressed against the tight spaces inside of me and my words came out in a choked whisper, a desperate plea for absolution. "I don't like the person I have become."

Quinn leaned forward and swept back a loose strand of hair which had fallen into my face, his eyes full of tenderness. "I see so much strength inside you. You're a fighter and a survivor, Julia. And I think *that* is remarkable."

Caught under the weight of his stare, a desire took hold of me, molded not out of control, but a longing to let go. His fingers rested against my cheek like a kiss, and my breath hitched in my throat.

The sound of the door opening broke us from our moment, and I pulled away as a mother and two kids stepped into the room, their soft chatter rising and falling between the thick foliage surrounding us.

My hands fidgeted with the strap of my purse like nervous birds uncertain of their flight. "Are you scared?"

Quinn looked at me. "Of course I'm scared."

"You just seem so calm all the time."

"I've had more time to process everything, that's all." He lifted his hand out for a butterfly, watching as it flickered down to his open palm. "But I still wake up in a cold sweat some nights."

I leaned my head on his shoulder, his scent enveloping me as I sank into this soft connection with him that felt so honest and effortless, tethering me to a possibility of something more. Something bigger than myself.

A gentle silence took hold of us as we rested against each other, watching the vibrant colors of wings swirl around the room in a breathtaking dance of impermanence.

Afternoon light slanted through my living room window as my fingers hovered over the keyboard. The words I needed lodged within the cage of my chest. What do I say to someone I have never met, but who came from my blood and marrow? Who grew inside my belly like a hopeful seed? A miracle. Someone who had reached out to me in open vulnerability, while I never found the courage to respond.

Fragile but lucid images I could never erase flooded

through me. The feel of her tiny hand as it wrapped around my finger, the soft downy fuzz of her jet-black hair. The way my lips pressed against her forehead in a kiss I knew would be my only one.

"Go live a bold life full of love," I had whispered before the nurse took her from my arms, my words a gift I hoped would bless her with the kind of happiness I never had as a child. A childhood void of rage, rough hands, and a mother's blank stare, the light within her snuffed out so long ago. I wanted my daughter's life to be filled with warmth and laughter, with a love that cradled her.

Shame and guilt gnawed at the edges of my thoughts. Had my fear of confronting my past, a past that defined so much of who I was, caused me to miss my one chance with her?

With a deep, shaky breath, I began to type.

Amelia,

I'm sorry it has taken me so long to get back to you...

"Thank you for coming with me." I sat stiffly in the car beside Quinn, my hands fiddling with my hair. "I was afraid I would lose my nerve if I did this alone."

But it was more than that. Something unexpected had happened. The fierce independence I always identified with had begun to feel more like a tightly locked door. Between Quinn coming to the hospital and our time in the butterfly garden, he had woven himself into my life somehow, becoming a thread of solace, a steady light within my darkened corridors.

Quinn nodded and leaned back in his seat. "I'm really glad you called me." He motioned out the window. "Which house is it?"

I looked down at the piece of crinkled paper in my lap I had nervously clutched the whole drive here. "Sixteen forty-two Freemont Avenue." I surveyed the rows of houses lining the street and pointed to a blue one with faded prayer flags snapping against the wind. "I think it's that one."

I had not expected Amelia to get back to me so quickly, and I was even more surprised when she offered to meet at her house. "*I would very much like to see you in person,*" she had written, opening a door to me that I didn't feel I even had the right to walk through.

I never imagined she would be living here in Seattle. This whole time we shared the same breath of the city, and I wondered if we had ever crossed paths before. Did we brush past each other on the street? Stand in the same line at a grocery store?

Was life only a random series of insignificant events tethering us together?

I bit my lip and stared out at the blue house as if the contents within could destroy me. "I still don't know if I can do this."

Quinn's hand rested lightly over mine. "You *can* do this. And I'll be waiting right here for you the whole time, okay?"

"You don't have to, you know," I said, turning to him. "You can just drop me off, and I can call an Uber."

He shook his head, a small smile creeping across his face. "Nope, I'm here to make sure you don't run off, remember?" He cocked his thumb towards a small stack of photography magazines sitting in the back of his seat. "Plus, this is a great time for me to catch up on some light reading."

I sighed, my hand resting hesitantly on the door handle. "What if she hates me?"

"I don't think she would have invited you over to her place if she hated you." He squeezed my hand before letting go and leaning across me to open the door on my side. His hair brushed against my cheek, his face so close to mine I could make out the darkly threaded filaments of color in his eyes. My heart pounded in my chest, and I wasn't sure if it was from my nervousness or his sudden proximity.

"This is life giving you a chance to finally meet your daughter. This is what you wanted. A second chance."

"You're right." A rush of resolve took hold, and I drew in a deep breath, pushed myself from the seat, and closed the car door behind me.

My legs felt heavy as every step brought me closer to her house. I stumbled on a crack in the sidewalk, my heel twisting painfully as I righted myself and looked to her window where gauzy curtains obscured the inside.

What would she look like? Would she have my eyes? The shape of her father's chiseled nose?

These questions tumbled inside like frantic children, bathed in the persistent force of curiosity and trepidation, and beneath all that lay the sickening weight of my own remorse.

A sharp wave of apprehension took hold of me, sucking the breath from my lungs as I raised my shaking hand to the worn grooves of the white painted door and knocked.

Chapter Ten

My pulse accelerated as the door creaked open. A streak of white lunged at me, and I was met with a large labradoodle, its paws landing on my chest and nearly knocking me over.

"Oh, my God. I'm so sorry!" Hands reached out to yank the dog down, and I took a step back. "He's really sweet, just gets a little too excited sometimes."

Words caught in my mouth as I took in familiar dark features and the same brown eyes as mine, which appeared to glow an amber color when the light hit them. It was like staring into the mirror of a younger version of myself, although she wore her hair in a short pixie cut, wispy bangs framing the gentle curve of her eyebrows. The sudden prick of tears obscured my vision, blurring the edges of her like a mirage.

"Are you okay? He didn't scratch you, did he?"

I shook my head blankly, frozen in place as she stood there in the open doorway looking at me with a composed mixture of intrigue and concern. "Would you like to come in?"

I hesitated for a moment before following her into the house. Stepping inside, I was hit with an aroma of curry and amber incense. Potted plants crowded her living room, their long leaves trailing across walls and tumbling over bookshelves. Sequined pillows leaned against a threadbare corduroy couch, and the walls were decorated in large oil paintings, their canvases splashed with a vivid cacophony of color and patterns.

A wet nose nudged my hand, and I looked down into the brown, eager eyes of the dog.

"That's Ziggy," she said, closing the door behind her. "If he jumps up on you again, just tell him *no*."

An awkward silence fell between us as we stood in the cramped living room, looking at each other, and I realized I hadn't spoken yet. I cleared my throat, words coming out dry and brittle. "Amelia, thank you so much for being open to meeting me like this."

"Thank you for coming." Her smile was genuine, filled with a warmth that softened me, stilling my nerves. "I just put on some water for tea. Would you like some?"

"Yes, tea would be nice. Thank you."

I followed her down a narrow hallway and into the kitchen.

"I have chamomile, mint, or green tea?" Amelia said as she grabbed two ceramic mugs from the cupboard.

"Chamomile would be nice." My gaze drifted across the room to where a few smaller paintings adorned the walls, full of life and an unrestrained vibrance. "Did you paint all these?" I asked, motioning around the kitchen.

"I did."

"So, you're an artist?"

She nodded. "Yes, I guess I would call myself that."

"They're beautiful." An unexpected feeling of pride rose inside me. She had a gift, born from the same spark that used to burn within me. But hers had caught fire and blazed across the walls.

"Thank you." She looked at me with a small smile. "People are always telling me I should get them into an art gallery or something. But I don't know..." she trailed off, running her fingers through the strands of her hair. "I guess they're like close friends to me. I don't want to let any of them go."

"Well, I think they should be shared with the world in some way. They're really beautiful."

"Thanks. We'll see." She shrugged and took the kettle off the stove, steam curling around her as she poured the water into two cups. "Maybe one day."

There was a fluid grace to her as I watched her move about the kitchen. There were no hard edges, no sharp eyes filtering out the world around her. She seemed happy.

I took a seat at a small table beside the window, the wicker chair creaking beneath me as my hands nervously fiddled in my lap. I stared at the faded finish, stains embedded into the wood from years of cups and plates sliding against it. "Did you have a good childhood?" The unexpected question rushed from my lips, causing Amelia to whip her head in my direction, regarding me with a look of surprise.

She carried the mugs of tea over to the table and took a seat opposite me. "Okay, I guess we're going to dive right in, huh? Um, I guess I did, yeah." Her eyes grew wistful as she spoke. "My mom and dad are really great. They have always supported and encouraged me. Even when I decided to drop out of college and go backpacking around South America." She let out a soft chuckle, a smile pulling at the edges of her lips as she slowly twirled her cup of tea over the worn grooves of the table. "They always tell me that the most important thing in life is to find yourself, no matter what road that leads you down."

A long sigh spilled from me, and I glanced out the kitchen window where bare branches quivered against the late autumn sky. I had spent my whole life running from myself. Who would I be right now if I had only stopped for a moment and looked into the depths?

"Sounds like you have some pretty smart parents." I turned

back to her. "Did you know that I was only nineteen when I had you?"

"I know." She ducked her head down for a moment, her fingers playing with the handle of her cup. "And I never faulted you for doing what you did, by the way. I'm sure you had your reasons."

"I did." Gripping the cup, I gazed into the amber liquid, watching as the steam rose and curled between us. There was so much I wanted to explain to her. Years of silent conversations molded from my own regret, but all the words lodged themselves in my throat. "I could never have given you the kind of life you had growing up."

Amelia leaned back in her chair. "This is all so surreal. I can't believe I'm sitting here having tea with my birth mom." She shook her head. "I've thought about you a lot throughout my life, you know."

"Amelia." I had a sudden urge to take her hand. Reaching across the table, I tentatively brushed my fingers over hers. Her skin was so soft and unblemished against my own. Her fingers long and slender like mine. She didn't pull away from my touch, and a bittersweet longing welled up inside. All these years suddenly filtered down to this moment. "I think about you *every* day."

She looked at me, a sudden trace of anger and sadness hovering in her eyes. "Then why did it take you two years to get back to me?"

Her words slammed into my own shame, and I withdrew my hand, caught between the urge to defend myself and the desire to surrender to my faults. "I was scared. I've done a lot of avoiding in my life."

Her gaze pierced into mine, wide and full of questions. "Why? What happened to you?"

I shook my head, refusing to let the ugly shards of my story pierce through the gentle layers of her own.

"Well, what about my birth father, then? Who is he?"

I hesitated, biting the edge of my lip as I stared into my cup of tea. My silence appeared to frustrate her, and she leaned back in her chair with a sigh, folding her arms across her chest. "I was really hoping we could *talk*."

"I know, I'm sorry." I grappled for an explanation, running my fingers through my hair. "I'm still trying to take all this in right now. I think this may be harder for me than it is for you. I have a lot of remorse, while you just have curiosity."

"You don't know what I have." Her words came out clipped, and a sudden intensity flared in her eyes as she stared at me. *I knew that look.*

"Do you know how much it hurt me that you never responded when I e-mailed you? I spent my whole life wondering who you were and why you gave me up. And you couldn't even be bothered to write me back."

Her fire was crisp, the bold potency of youth burning like an unextinguished ember, and I admired her for not shirking her emotions.

"I'm so sorry, Amelia. The last thing I ever meant to do was hurt you."

She shrugged, brushing off my apology as she stared out the window. "Can you at least tell me what compelled you to contact me now?"

The swell of panic crashed against me. I wasn't about to tell her I was dying. That I may never have reached out to her at all if life hadn't brutally yanked me to the curb, forcing me to stare down at the cold and empty fortress I had built around my life.

"I guess I'm realizing that life is too short, that I have a lot of things I need to face in order for me to heal." I spread my hands out flat on the table. "And it all starts with you." A tear formed in the corner of my eye, running a slow trail down my cheek, and I quickly moved to brush it away. "I wanted you so bad. But I was too young and broken, and I knew I'd never make a good mother." I looked up into her eyes, so wild and full of all the years ahead of her. "Your father, he was married with kids of his own. I was only meant to be a prop in his life, not a part of it."

She crumpled her brow, appearing to be lost in thought for a moment. "Does he know about me?"

"Yes, he does, but he left town shortly after he found out I was pregnant. I guess he was afraid that I was going to expose our affair."

"Did you love him?"

I took a shaky breath. "I thought I loved him. But I didn't know what love was supposed to look like. I never really had it growing up."

A realization suddenly hit me with a clarity I had never grasped before. All these years of sleeping with men and then leaving was not because I wanted to feel powerful and untouchable, it was because I was angry. Angry at my father, and angry at the only man I had ever allowed myself to feel something for, and beneath all that anger was a pain so deep it cut into the very fiber of my being. There was a little girl still inside me, with her face full of tears and her skin bruised and raw, pleading for me to love her.

Emotion choked me. I had never given that girl inside the love she deserved, and I had no one to blame for that but myself.

Amelia softened and uncrossed her arms, running her fingers through her cropped hair. "I'm so sorry to hear that. I can't imagine having a life without love in it."

I looked into the eyes of my daughter, finding pieces of myself embedded in the deep richness of her gaze, pieces I had never been given the opportunity to nurture, but she had. "I'm glad you can't. Because a life without love isn't much of a life at all, really."

A silence swept over us for a minute, each caught in the private sphere of our own thoughts.

"Do I have any siblings?" Amelia's voice came out tentative.

I took a long sip of tea, feeling the warmth travel down to my belly. "I suppose you have a half brother and sister out there somewhere, but you were the only child I ever had."

"Really?" She leaned across the table as the questions spilled from her like rapid gunfire. "What about other family? aunts or uncles? Grandparents?"

I sighed, the weight of my isolation gripping me like a vise. The branches of our family tree were withered and bare, and I could not summon the strength to open the wounds of my own snarled past. "It's just me. There's no one else."

"Do you have a husband... boyfriend?"

I shook my head, a small smile slipping out. "I guess I haven't found the right person yet."

She furrowed her brow, a look of sadness creeping across her face. "You know, when I was young, I used to imagine you as a traveling artist, with a life full of dance and music, surrounded by people." Her hands waved dramatically in the air as she painted color over my grey, like an optimistic flower pushing through cement.

A tired smile cracked around the edges. "That sounds like a magical life."

"It does, doesn't it?" She rested her elbows on the table and cradled her chin in her hands, her eyes growing wistful. "I don't think it's ever too late to live the life we dream of."

And there it was. Hope. Her powerful words stretched across the table and enfolded me.

* * *

We stood together by the door, navigating our goodbye.

"I would really like to see you again," Amelia said, her voice sincere and hopeful.

"Me, too. I would like that very much." I fiddled with the

straps of my purse, feeling the heavy cloud of fatigue pressing down on me, but not wanting to break this delicate moment between us.

"Can I give you a hug?"

I looked at her in surprise. "Yes, of course." Then her arms were around me, all strong curves and soft flesh against my angular frame. She smelled of roses and soap, and I clutched her tightly, a tender ache rising inside as I fought back tears. "Thank you, Amelia," I whispered as we drew apart.

I walked down her driveway in a daze, my emotions stretched and unsteady. Quinn saw me coming and got out of the car, the wind pulling at his hair as he walked toward me. "How'd it go?"

Without thinking, I tumbled into the solid comfort of him and buried my face in his jacket, allowing the rush of tears I had been holding back to release. A mixture of joy and sorrow tangled together.

Chapter Eleven

*D*im afternoon light cast shadows across the room as I stepped into my therapist's office.

"Nice to see you, Julia." He stood from his desk and grabbed his notepad, seating himself in his leather chair and motioning to the couch in front of him. "Please, take a seat."

This scene had been played out countless times, like actors on a stage rehearsing the same lines over and over, and it suddenly felt so hollow. A reminder of a life I no longer wanted.

He regarded me with a softness as I sat down. It was a new face he wore these days, the *cancer look*, full of empathy and concern as he danced around the edges of my comfort level.

"How are you feeling today?"

"I met my daughter." The words flew from my mouth like eager wings of hope as I sank into the pillows of the couch.

"Wow, this is *big* news." As he spoke, his eyes lit up for a moment. "If I recall correctly, you only mentioned her once during our earlier sessions. Would you like to share with me what it was that prompted you to reach out to her after all this time?"

"Well, cancer is a great motivator, isn't it?"

A sad smile slipped over his features as he nodded. "I suppose you're right."

"And I'm tired of running from everything." I looked at him

for a moment, really looked at him beyond the façade of therapist and fantasy, and I saw a man who was trying to live his own life with integrity. I realized that was all that really mattered in the end. It wasn't what you accomplished that was important, it was how honestly you existed.

Taking a deep breath, I allowed this tenuous feeling of renewal to take root. "I want you to know that this is going to be my last session with you."

He looked at me with raised eyebrows. "And why is that, Julia?"

"Because I need to start over, and that means I have to let go of some things first."

Worry etched along the lines of his face. "I understand you feel this need to release certain aspects within your life right now. That is very important in this process you are going through. But it is also very important that you have someone to talk to as well."

My phone buzzed in my purse beside me, and I looked down to see Quinn's name flash across the screen. A small smile burst through, like delicate sunlight filling me with warmth. "I have someone."

"That's really good to hear." He leaned forward and folded his hands together, regarding me with eyes that spoke of sincerity. "Though I *am* sorry to hear that you want to end our sessions together. I feel like we were beginning to address some important issues. I also think you should be really proud of yourself for wanting to make bold changes in your life. When we are able to create something good out of our circumstances, that is when we truly grow."

A softness wound its way into me. Maybe it was because I knew this would be our last moment together. Or maybe I no longer needed to cling to that version of myself, but all the months of anger and hesitation I had painted upon the walls of this room suddenly diffused, leaving a clarity and lightness behind.

"You *are* a good therapist, you know that?"

He smiled, and something shifted between us as we let go of our roles and became two people sitting across from each other. "I must admit, you have been one of my *more* challenging clients." A chuckle spilled from him. The first laugh he had ever shared with me. "But it has always been a challenge I looked forward to." He grew serious again. "It's not important *how* much time we have. What is important is what we *do* with that time. And I believe you are on the path to finding that, Julia."

A tear slid down my cheek, bathed in the glow of something that felt a lot like promise. "I hope so."

* * *

"Feel like going for a ride?"

Quinn's words grew muffled over the sounds of traffic. I pressed the phone closer to my ear as I stepped out of my therapist's office for the last time and into a day that held the possibility of blue sky. "Where are you taking me?"

"It's a surprise."

I let out a little laugh and rolled my eyes. "What is it with you and surprises?"

"Have I disappointed you yet?"

His voice took on a slight raspy tone as he spoke, and an unexpected rush of heat spread through my limbs, causing me to fumble with my words. "No... Not yet."

"Okay good, I'll be outside your place in an hour then, and bring a warm coat."

An unfamiliar sense of giddiness overcame me as I hung up the phone, a lightness fluttering within my chest. I leaned against the brick wall of the office to wait for my Uber and stared into the sky, watching the clouds break and shift into feathery silhouettes above me. I took a deep breath, awash in this fragile sensation growing within. There was no hissing voice inside, no ominous knocking on the door of time. For a brief moment, I felt present in a body that was not slowly dying, but still very much alive.

A car pulling up to the curb startled me from my reverie, and I slid into the back, directing the driver to my apartment. I took in the frantic pace of the city as it hurried by the window. Each person encapsulated within their own fleeting narrative like leaves tumbling forward in the wind.

*　*　*

Quinn's bike sputtered to a stop beside the sidewalk. A wide smile stretched across his face as he handed me a helmet.

"You're late," I said with an exaggerated lift of my eyebrow.

"I got stuck in traffic." He gestured his hand in the air. "Besides, time is only an illusionary constraint created by an establishment whose sole purpose is to regulate behavior."

"Wow. Where did you come up with that long-winded theory?" I asked as I scooted in behind him.

He chuckled and glanced back at me while I clipped my helmet in place. "I read too many philosophy books in my twenties. I think I was trying to impress the ladies."

"Did it work?"

He shook his head. "I don't think so. Did it work on you?"

"Nope."

"Damn. Well, I guess I'll try flowers next time," he said with a playful grin as he started up the motor.

A weightlessness rushed over me as we accelerated through the city, trading tall buildings for densely packed houses and rolling hills. The deep blue of Lake Washington winked at us through the pine trees as we careened through the narrow streets, the wind pounding like a drum against our bodies.

As we passed a sign for Howell Park, Quinn slowed down, parking beneath a large pine tree nestled beside a winding path. "Wait, isn't this the nudist beach?" I asked, unhooking my arms from around him and sliding off the seat.

He laughed. "Relax. I promise you there are no nude bathers this time of year."

"I hope not," I mumbled under my breath.

He stood there with an amused look on his face. "You've never been to a nude beach before?"

I shook my head as I smoothed away the tangles in my hair. "I doubt you find that surprising, though."

With a grin, he leaned over and grabbed his camera and a brown paper bag from the side compartment of his bike. "I've been to a few throughout the years. It's actually quite liberating."

"Really?" I looked at him curiously. "Well, you're just full of all kinds of surprises, aren't you?"

"I am." He grinned and adjusted the lens on his camera, motioning toward the path. "But the reason I brought you here is because this also happens to be one of the best, most secluded spots on the lake."

"And what's in there?" I pointed to the bag in his hand.

Quinn gave me a slow smile. "You'll see."

Following him down the sandy footpath, I was grateful for the sturdy sneakers I thought to put on. I was beginning to care less about my clothes, the designer labels and high-heeled shoes that defined me, the sharp angles and muted tones. I suddenly longed for color and soft fabric against my skin.

The path opened to the water, an expanse of silver and blue gently lapping along the shore. Dappled sunlight flirted with the clouds, casting a golden shimmer across the lake, and in the distance, the shadowed outline of city buildings sketched across the sky.

Quinn crouched on the sand, his camera pointing toward the water as he looked back at me. "There's food in the bag if you're hungry."

I pulled out a charcuterie platter and some grapes, along with a blanket nestled beneath a small bottle of cabernet and two plastic cups. "This looks like a picnic. Are we celebrating something?" I asked, holding up the bottle of wine and raising my eyebrow at him. "And should you even be drinking?"

"Relax, I'm only going to have a glass." He stood with a smile and walked over to me, taking the bottle from my hand and settling himself down in the sand. "And yes." Pulling out a Swiss army knife from his back pocket, Quinn unscrewed the cork from the bottle. "You just met your daughter for the first time. I think that's something to celebrate." He poured some wine into a cup and handed it to me. "This is the beginning of a whole new chapter for you."

I nodded and took a sip, the rich, spicy notes lingering on my tongue. "And I just fired my therapist today."

There was a pause as he looked at me. "Why'd you do that?"

"I don't know," I said, sitting down beside him. "I walked into his office this afternoon and just realized I didn't want to be there anymore."

"That's fair, I suppose." He glanced out toward the water; his brow furrowed in thought. "I think it's important that we give ourselves permission to weed out the clutter."

"You know, it feels really freeing in a way." I took another sip of wine and ran my hands through the sand, feeling the grains slip between my fingers like silk. "Letting go of all the obligations. The habitual patterns of daily life, the work that demanded so much of me. None of it really matters anymore. None of it *ever* really mattered."

"I can drink to that." He raised his cup, lightly tapping it against the edge of mine, his gaze locking onto me. "Here's to rewriting your story. To being free."

We sat in silence for a moment, allowing the chill of the breeze to ruffle our hair and the birds to claim the space around us, their melodic notes drifting through the trees, as if unaware of their audience.

Quinn popped a grape into his mouth. "So, what do you want to do with all this freedom of yours?"

I drew my knees up to my chest and gazed out at the sky. "I don't know. Maybe I could travel somewhere exotic? I've always wanted to visit Tibet."

"Tibet, huh? Why is that?"

"I'm not quite sure. There's just something that has always drawn me to that place." My fingers traced a spiral in the sand. "It has always felt like something was waiting there for me."

"Maybe something is." His eyes rested on mine for a moment before glancing out at the water. "I was talking to my sister the other day. She thinks I need to make a bucket list."

"So, your family knows?"

He nodded. "My two sisters do. They live out in Michigan. Our Mom on the other hand..." He trailed off, his eyes growing sad. "She started showing signs of memory loss last year, and it's been a pretty rapid decline ever since." He picked up a smooth stone and cocked his arm back, chucking it into the water. "I guess it's a blessing, in a way. She won't have to deal with the pain of losing a child."

"I'm sorry to hear that." I watched him as he continued to throw stones into the water as if he were trying to release emotions too heavy to hold, a deep sorrow he was afraid to sit with. My hand landed softly on his knee, my thumb running a line down the denim of his jeans. "And what about your sisters? How are they handling all of this?"

Quinn shrugged. "They're tough, those two. All spit and vinegar." He smiled faintly as he tossed another rock into the lake, the ripples flowing out into a bloom of patterns that caught the light. "They're actually coming to visit in about a month." He looked over at me. "I think you guys would really hit it off."

"Why is that? You think I'm full of spit and vinegar?"

He leaned in close to me with a teasing smile. "No, I think you're a pussycat, Julia. One that's just been pet the wrong way."

A laugh bubbled up, causing me to choke on my wine and sending a spray of red across his shirt. "Oh, God, I'm so sorry." I grimaced and quickly opened the package of meat and cheese, grabbing some napkins that were wrapped inside.

"Was it something I said?" he asked, his eyes full of playfulness.

I shook my head and dabbed at the stains on his shirt, feeling the energy between us shift into a concentrated tension that longed to release itself. Looking into his eyes, I reached out to brush away a lock of hair the wind had blown across his cheek. "You know, when I'm with you, I *forget* sometimes."

He nodded, a tender sadness hovering in his gaze. "Me, too."

Emotion welled up, and I bit back the tremble in my lip. "It's not fair, you know."

He stood and took my hand, threading his fingers through mine and pulling me up from the sand. "You know what I like to do when I'm out here and there's nobody else around?"

"What?"

Quinn walked to the edge of the shoreline. Spreading his arms out wide, he let out a long, loud cry, shattering the quiet. He turned back to me with a playful smile. "Try it. It feels really good."

I let out a puff of air and shook my head at him. "I'm not going to stand there and scream like a lunatic."

He walked back to me and grabbed my hands, pulling me

toward the water. "Why not, Julia? Haven't you ever screamed like a lunatic before?"

"No, I haven't." I crossed my arms and regarded him with a look of measured reluctance. "What if somebody hears us?"

"Nobody's here." He swept his arm out toward the long stretch of empty beach. "Humor me for a second."

"Fine." I rolled my eyes and filled my lungs with air, letting out a stiff, sharp cry.

Quinn chuckled. "Okay, that was cute. But I think you got more in you than that." He placed his hands on my shoulders, his eyes piercing into mine. "All that anger inside. All that pain. All the fear. Just let it go for a minute."

I stared out into the water, its endless undulating dance beckoning to me, drawing out a yearning for release. A plea for relief from all that had been barricaded inside. Taking a breath from deep within my belly, I let out a scream up into the sky, harsh and angry as Quinn joined in, his voice merging with mine in a long, drawn-out battle cry.

Something broke within me as I continued this onslaught of sound and fury. A rush of grief and anger, loneliness, and disappointment spilled out, raw and unrestrained, emptying all of myself into the depths of the lake until there was nothing left but a stillness inside.

I turned to Quinn, wide eyed and spent as laughter bubbled to the surface. "Okay, you were right. That felt *really* good."

A grin stretched across his face. "Told you it would."

I didn't know if it was from the wine or our primal scream session, but a euphoria overcame me as I leaned into him. He smelled of wind and musk, and an ache coiled its way through my core as he slid his arm around my back and looked down at me with a sudden heat in his eyes.

A drop of rain landed on my shoulder, and Quinn jerked his head up into the darkening grey of the sky. "Oh, shoot. We should probably get out of here." He dashed to his camera and threw it into the paper bag as I followed behind, quickly gathering the food and the now empty bottle of wine. "I checked the weather this morning, and it said we would have at least a few hours of clear skies."

"That's Seattle for you," I said with a smirk as drops of rain began to descend upon us with an increasingly rapid force.

"I'm sorry, the ride back is going to suck, Julia," he said as we hurried down the path and over to his bike.

Quinn revved the engine as I quickly climbed on behind him and clipped on the helmet he handed me. Wrapping my arms tightly around his chest, we sped down the road, a blur of vivid green rushing past as the rain slapped against my face. I closed my eyes and tilted my head back, relishing the cold sting on my skin, my body alive and awake, every sensation heightened.

A smile hovered on my lips, invigoration coursing through me like a bright spark of fire burning away the residue, leaving behind a spaciousness that unfurled, as if my soul could finally breathe again.

Chapter Twelve

We tumbled into my apartment, leaving a trail of rain behind us. Quinn set his camera on the counter and shrugged off his leather jacket, hanging it on a hook beside the door.

"I think I'm *really* starting to like that bike of yours," I said breathlessly as I slid off my coat.

He lifted his eyebrow. "Oh, yeah? Think there's been a biker chick in you this whole time?"

"Maybe there has been," I said with a laugh as I walked into the kitchen. "Hey, would you like to stay for dinner?" I opened the fridge and pulled out some vegetables. "I actually have some food this time. I was thinking of whipping up a stir fry."

"You're soaking wet. Why don't you go change first, and I'll get the food started?"

"You're wet too, you know," I said, playfully pointing a carrot at him.

"Yeah, but I dry faster."

"And why's that?"

He stepped close to me, running his hand through my strands of damp hair. "I don't have all this luscious hair to contend with, for one thing."

His touch sent a rush of desire crashing against me, and my breath caught in my throat as he took the carrot from my hand

and nodded toward my bedroom. "Go dry off, and I'll start chopping these up for us, okay?"

With a smile, I brushed past him and made my way through the bedroom and into the bathroom, where I peeled off my wet clothes and went to grab a towel. My reflection struck me as I glanced in the mirror and took in a body I no longer recognized.

At some point, I had stopped looking as my weight began to whittle away. But here I stood, exposed. Detained under the bright light. And I couldn't look away this time.

I reached up to my breasts, cupping soft flesh now grown loose in my hands. All my curves had evaporated, leaving only angled bone behind. I ran my hand down past my belly, the gentle slope of my femininity now a flat plane.

I thought of Quinn in the other room, of his hands tracing the contours of what was left of me. *What would he see?* I sucked in a sharp breath, trying to push away the rising panic and replace it with that soft, warm elation I had felt with him only moments ago. Reaching up, I grabbed my robe from the hook on the door and loosely draped it over me.

Walking back into the kitchen, I found Quinn standing at the counter slicing carrots. I wanted his hands on my skin. To obliterate all the fear clawing inside. I needed to feel his body against mine, to remind me I was still alive in my own, that I could still be beautiful.

Coming up behind him, I drew my fingers lightly across his back, my voice a trembling whisper. "Touch me, Quinn."

He turned around, his eyes wide as they trailed down my open robe. "*Julia.*" His voice was choked as he stared at me, his gaze full of a sharp longing that sent my pulse racing.

Stepping closer, I gently took the knife from him, placing it in the sink. "I need you to touch me. I want you to make me feel beautiful."

He placed his hand on my cheek, tentatively at first, almost as if he didn't believe I was real. "You *are* beautiful, Julia. *So* beautiful." His fingers swept down my neck and across my collarbone, his breath growing ragged as his gaze fell to what was left of my breasts. I sucked in a breath as his hand delicately traced across my skin, waiting for his eyes to shift away. But they didn't. The gentleness of his touch and the burn of his eyes elicited a rush of warmth that caused my core to tighten and ache.

My words rushed out, desperate and pleading as I pressed myself into him, feeling the swell of his arousal grow against my leg. "Then make me *feel* beautiful, Quinn. *Please*. I need you to make me feel beautiful."

With a groan, he suddenly gripped my hips and lifted me onto the counter, the cutting board full of carrots clattering to the floor. Cradling my face in his hands, he stared at me for a moment, his gaze flickering with desire and a tenderness that robbed me of breath.

Then his mouth found mine, his lips soft and still tasting faintly of wine as he drew me into a kiss that was deep and unhurried but full of a hungry fire that made me lightheaded. Opening to him, a rush of sensation swirled within, foreign and uncharted, as I curled my fingers into the thickness of his hair and wrapped my legs tightly around him, not wanting to let go. Not wanting him to stop. Wanting more.

Slipping my robe down past my shoulders, he pulled me tighter to him, his mouth falling feverish and hot along my neck as I gripped his back. With a turbulent urgency, I tugged at his shirt, yanking it over his head. The feel of his skin was an electric shock as I ran my hands across the tattoo on his chest, fingers tracing the black ink of a phoenix.

He shuddered against my touch, his breath labored in my ear as I fumbled impatiently with his belt buckle and grasped the heat of him in my hand.

"Julia. Wait."

"I don't want to wait," I said with a tangled moan as I lifted my hips and guided him inside me.

His expression shifted and grew ravenous, seeming to lose whatever self-control he had as he stared wildly into my eyes and gripped my waist, a deep groan spilling from him as he filled me up with his desire.

Pleasure tore at me as we moved together, our bodies slow but fervent, his touch tender and soft, cradling me as if I were something treasured, something unblemished. Closing my eyes, I threw my head back, stifling the cry that for the first time longed to take flight from my mouth, wild and untamed.

"I want you to look at me," he whispered like a plea into my ear as he plunged deeper. "I want to see you."

But my eyes remained tightly shut, unable to meet the intensity of his gaze.

"Julia. *Please* look at me."

His voice grew imploring as his lips sought out mine, but I turned my head away from him, suddenly overcome with a feeling too large for me to handle. It was visceral and consuming, and I was suddenly drowning in it. I couldn't breathe.

"I can't," I gasped. "It's *too* much."

Quinn stilled. Placing his hands on the counter, he rested his head into my neck for a moment, his breath heavy on my skin, before slowly pulling out, leaving an emptiness behind like the cold sting of a slap.

"What the fuck, Quinn?" Shame and confusion slammed into me as I watched him buckle his pants and pick up his shirt from off the floor.

He leaned in close to me, his eyes blazing with fire as he took my face in his hands, his thumb tracing my cheek, brushing against my lips. "I want you, Julia. But I want *all* of you. Not just your body." He shook his head, anguish clouding his eyes with tears. "I want to see what is inside that beautiful mind of yours. But you have to be willing to show me."

I pulled away from him and yanked my robe closed. My body throbbed from the feel of him inside, leaving me exposed and raw. Humiliation and rejection burned within, and that familiar anger rose up, potent and comforting like a shield. "You need to leave."

"Julia, please."

"Just go."

He stood there staring at me, his face etched in turmoil.

"Fucking go!" I threw my words at him, vicious and snarling as the sting of tears blurred my vision.

He raised his hands in the air and backed away from me. "Okay, I'm going."

I slid off the counter and crumpled to the floor as he grabbed his coat and closed the door behind him.

What just happened?

The pain inside pounded at me, a snarled mess I could no longer push aside. Curling into myself, a broken sob spilled from me, loud and unhinged as all the years of grief rushed out, pooling onto the kitchen floor.

Stretched open and bare, I wailed against my own habitual self-preservation. It had always been nothing more than a trap. A cage that held no door.

* * *

Morning cast pale light across the bed, my eyes bleary from lack of sleep and a night full of tears long overdue. A night spent sifting through the debris, trying to find myself among the rubble. I had no happy memories to grab onto, no tenderness that kept me company in the dark. My whole life had been a series of misfortunes I was constantly trying to run from the memory of. *How much of my life had I avoided?*

I stared at my phone, summoning the courage to call Quinn as the familiar grip of regret tore into me. How could I explain to him my snarled history with men? The furious promise I had made to myself at nineteen, the one that assured I would never let someone get close to me again.

That girl was still there, angry and lashing out at the world.

Images from the night before rose to the surface. Quinn's hands on my skin, lips against mine. His breath in my ear like a warm caress, summoning me closer to him. I couldn't remember the last time I had let a man kiss me like he did, allowing myself to kiss back with a visceral passion that made my limbs weak, exposing a longing I had buried so deep. Everything in me cried out for him, but I was caught within my own fear, terrified to assess the damage. He had opened something inside, challenged me, asked something of me, and I did what I'd always done. I ran from it.

My hands shook as I dialed his number, but the anticipation was short-lived as my call went directly to his voicemail. I threw the phone across the room and burrowed deep into my blankets, hoping the weight would smother all the noise inside.

I don't know how long I lay there in bed, trapped between my restless thoughts and a paralyzing fatigue. Eventually, the day faded into the murky colors of dusk, and I stumbled into the kitchen, willing myself to eat something. My eyes fell to the cutting board on the floor, the carrots scattered across the tile like withered casualties from the night before. Bending down, I began to pick up the pieces, throwing them into the sink when my breath stilled, and I saw the dark shape of Quinn's camera sitting on the far counter.

Opening the leather case, I pulled out the camera and turned it on. A photo sprang to life on the small screen. Pebbles speckled with sunlight, water wrapping around them like an embrace. The branches of a tree bent over the reflection of the lake. The intricate design caught within a stone. I realized Quinn was not a landscape photographer. He saw the brilliance hidden within the small things that lay unnoticed.

I continued to swipe through his shoot from the day before when I came across a picture of myself. He must have snapped it when I wasn't looking. I was in partial profile, gazing out into the open water, the wind lifting my hair into the sky. He had captured something within my gaze, a yearning mixed with fortitude. The prick of tears clouded my vision.

He had always seen the beauty there.

A light drizzle coated my hair, and the wind blew in from the Sound, bringing with it the briny smell of the ocean. With Quinn's camera clutched in my hand, I opened the door to the community center, my heart beating rapidly as I eagerly scanned the room, but I didn't see him anywhere. His absence hit me like a burst of cold air against my skin as people began to shift around and take their seats, a few murmuring greetings to me as they passed.

I sat stiffly on the edge of my seat, my hands clasped tightly to the straps of Quinn's camera case. *Maybe he's just late?* I stared at the door, willing him to walk in with his disheveled hair and soft brown eyes. To see that smile of his, the one that always made my heart thrum. All the things I wanted to say to him hovered on my lips like fragile offerings.

The minutes ticked by unbearably slow as people began to

speak, their words muffled and far away. *Where was he?* Unease began to claw at me, worry twisting knots in my gut. The room suddenly felt too large without him.

I shifted uncomfortably in my seat and tried to stifle the images that rose in my mind like an ugly nightmare. *A motorcycle crash. His cancer.* Something could have happened to him, and I would never know.

I barely got through the rest of group, suspended in a state of silent panic. My heart pounded wildly in my ears as I burst through the doors, frantically digging through my purse for my phone. With shaking hands, I dialed his number once more, praying for the encouraging sound of a ringtone, but once again I was met with the harsh click of his voicemail.

Chapter Thirteen

I pulled my car out of the parking garage, my hands sweaty as they gripped the steering wheel. Idling the engine, I glanced down at Quinn's business card in my lap, reading the address printed in small black letters on the back.

Merging onto the northbound freeway, I followed the directions I had typed into my phone, looking for the exit to Sand Point.

Churning thoughts engulfed me as I drove through the streets searching for his apartment building. I didn't know what I was doing; all I had was an address and a faint hope he would be there when I knocked on the door. He had to be there. The alternative filled me with such a crushing panic it sucked the air out of me.

Parking outside of an old brick building, I stepped out of the car on shaky legs and gazed at the fire escapes that loomed above me, the metal rusty and worn from years of wind and rain. The entrance door hinges screeched in protest as it slammed shut behind me, enclosing me in a room that smelled faintly of mildew, the walls lined with mail slots. Unable to locate an elevator, I proceeded to make the slow climb up the narrow flight of stairs.

Breathing heavily by the time I reached the second floor, I leaned against the wall and closed my eyes for a moment, trying to slow my heart, which battled wildly in my chest, a cruel and mocking reminder of my own tragic narrative.

Struggling to pull myself together, I walked down the long hallway. Sounds drifted through doors as I passed. The laughter of a child, the blaring of a television, the melodic notes of a song. Each person encapsulated in their own private story while life teemed from behind walls.

I stopped in front of Quinn's apartment and took a deep breath, trying to calm my nerves. My hands trembled as I raised them and tentatively knocked on the door, trying to push away the fearful thoughts. Willing him to answer.

Footsteps sounded, and the door flung open. A boy stood there looking at me with the same thick hair and deep brown eyes as Quinn.

"Who is it, Jasper?"

A wave of relief flooded me as Quinn appeared behind him, surprise flickering across his face. "Julia?"

I thrust his camera out awkwardly, my voice wavering. "I'm so sorry to bother you, but you left this at my apartment, and I figured you'd want it back."

"Thank you." He took it from my hand, his fingers lingering against mine for a moment, before glancing back at Jasper. "Give me a minute, okay, bud?"

Closing the door behind him, Quinn stood beside me in the hall, his eyes somber. "Is this the only reason you came?"

"No." I bit my lip, trying to find the words which were suddenly lodged uselessly within my throat. "You weren't at group today, and I've been trying to call you, but your phone was turned off."

He ran his hands through his hair with a sigh. "I'm sorry. I had a doctor's appointment this afternoon, and I always turn off my phone when I'm with Jasper." He looked at me with a mixture of confusion and sadness.

"I was worried..." I trailed off for a moment, awash in an

emotion I struggled to find a name for, my vulnerability flailing around like a helpless animal. "I thought something had happened."

"I'm okay." Stepping closer to me, his face softened. "I didn't mean to worry you. I *was* going to call you tonight."

I glanced at his open door, feeling like an intruder in a world that held no space for me. "I should probably go. I'm sorry for barging over like this. I don't want to interrupt your time with Jasper."

Quinn grabbed my hand as I abruptly turned to leave. "You're not interrupting anything. Why don't you stay? Come in and have some dinner with us. We're making spaghetti." A small smile slid across his face, tempering the edges of my trepidation. "I'd really like for you to meet Jasper."

I stared at him, his invitation a gift I felt I did not deserve to open. "Are you sure that's a good idea?"

"I've already mentioned you a few times, and he's said that he wants to meet you." He squeezed my hand and nudged open the door, motioning me inside with a nod of his head. "Plus, we could use an extra hand with the salad."

With his fingers wound through mine, I hesitantly followed him inside. Oregano and basil simmered in a sauce on the stove, the warmth enveloping me. I looked around the open floor plan of his apartment, taking in the cluttered shelves bursting with books and photography magazines, photos stacked precariously on end tables, Legos scattered across a coffee table. His place was messy and chaotic, full of a life being lived. Such a stark contrast to the tidy silence of my own apartment, the structured muteness of my life.

In the hallway leading to the bedrooms stood Jasper, watching me with curious eyes.

Quinn released my hand. "Jasper, this is my friend Julia I've told you about. She's going to stay for dinner. Is that okay with you, bud?"

A wide smile stretched across his face. "Great." He plunked himself onto a barstool next to the kitchen counter and began to spin himself in circles. "Do you want to see my rock collection?"

"He does have a pretty impressive collection," Quinn said with a wink as he shook a box of pasta into a boiling pot of water on the stove.

"Sure, I would love to."

Jasper jumped off the stool, and I followed him down the hallway, giving Quinn a backwards glance as I did. His eyes met mine, filled with questions that caused my pulse to quicken. Stripped bare by his gaze, I attempted a smile, all the unspoken words heavy between us.

I found Jasper in his bedroom, standing beside a tall shelf lined with various sizes of geodes, quartz, and agate. "Wow. These are really neat," I said, turning to him.

"This is my favorite." He plucked a large grey rock from the shelf and handed it to me. I turned it over in my palm to reveal the intricate pieces of quartz shimmering like diamonds within the center, its stunning beauty hidden beneath the dull exterior.

"We found this one when we went to Colorado last year. Me and my dad go rock hunting all the time."

"That sounds like a lot of fun." I placed the geode back on the shelf as Jasper moved to his bed and sat down, bouncing on the mattress.

"Yeah, my dad's the coolest." His eyes lit up as he spoke, full of the burning spark of youthful admiration. "Do you know he rides a motorcycle?"

"I do." I smiled as I sat beside him. "He has actually taken me riding a few times."

Jasper hopped up and grabbed a dog-eared map from his bookshelf, a cascade of books tumbling to the floor in the process. He opened to a picture of the States, black ink dotting the pages. "My dad promised me that soon we're going on a road trip on his bike. Look, I marked all the places we're going to stop at." His finger traced along the large circles drawn hastily across the map, his face brimming with excitement.

My heart lurched in my throat, and sorrow trickled through, stinging my eyes as I listened to Jasper talk with exuberance about his dad and all the things they were going to do together.

He still doesn't know.

This joyful child had no idea what bitter truth was lurking in the shadows of his father's smile. Pain sunk deep into the marrow of my own memories. What would I have done with my mom if I had only known how much time I had left with her?

"Doesn't that sound cool?"

Jasper's words broke through my thoughts, and I forced a wide smile across my face. "That does sound cool. You're really lucky you have such a wonderful dad."

I stood in the kitchen beside Quinn, chopping tomatoes for the salad, the energy between us dancing around the tension. Around all the things I still needed to say to him.

"So, how did the doctor's appointment go?" I asked, lowering my voice so Jasper wouldn't hear.

His eyes flickered to mine as he went to pull the sauce off the stove. "Same as usual. No good news." He sighed and glanced down the hallway to Jasper's room. "At least the tumor's not growing as rapidly as they feared it would."

"So, you might have more time?"

He looked at me, his eyes clouded with a deep melancholy. "Maybe."

"I've started looking into holistic alternatives," I whispered as I placed the slices of tomatoes in neat rows within the lettuce. "I figure I have to try something."

Quinn stepped close to me, his voice brushing against my ear. "You should, Julia. Hope is a powerful thing. Sometimes, it's all we have."

A tired smile crept across my face, and I fought the urge to lean into him. We stared at each other for a moment, locked within a silent, mutual surrender to a truth that was so much bigger than our ability to fight it.

Reaching to grab some plates from the cupboard, he turned to me with a wide smile, as if trying to distill the somber energy between us, his hand motioning to the food on the counter. "I think it's time we got this show on the road."

With a nod, I handed him the salad.

"Dinner's ready, bud," he called out above the sound of cartoons coming from his bedroom. Quinn shot me a weary smile. "I wish his mom hadn't gotten him that device. I hate that damn thing. It's a gateway drug."

"A gateway drug to what?" I asked, popping a tomato in my mouth.

Quinn placed the bowl of spaghetti on the table. "To collective compliance."

I let out a soft chuckle. "I guess you could also say that about public school."

He leaned in close, his hair lightly grazing my temple, sending an involuntary rush of warmth to spill across my skin. "Oh, don't get me started on public school."

Jasper bounded into the kitchen and dropped into a chair at the table. "Can we have ice cream for dessert, Dad?"

With a smile, Quinn ruffled Jasper's hair. "Only if you finish all your salad."

* * *

I stood at the sink, stacking the clean dishes onto the drying rack as Quinn and Jasper finished up the Lego building they were erecting together in the living room. The cadence of Jasper's chatter blended with the low tone of Quinn, creating a soothing background that softened the edges around me, and the sudden thought of going home to the emptiness of my apartment filled me with dread. I didn't want to slip back into the tight skin of my life. It was a life becoming harder to fit into.

"Thanks again for doing the dishes." Quinn appeared behind me, his hand resting on my arm.

I turned to him, smoothing away a few loose strands of hair that had fallen into my face. "No problem. It's the least I could do."

He motioned toward Jasper, who bounded past us and down the hall. "I'm going to get the kiddo into bed."

I fiddled with the dish towel, unable to make eye contact, my longing a restless bird hovering in the space between us. "I was hoping we could talk, Quinn."

"Me too." He bent close to me, his words falling like a soft shiver across my neck. "I'll be right back, okay?"

A breath of relief spilled from me. "Okay."

Finishing the dishes, I went into the living room and sat on the couch, glancing at a stack of photos sitting on a side table. Most of them were of Jasper, his gentle eyes gazing back at me full of wonder. The tender love Quinn had for his son was evident in every shot, and my heart swelled as I flipped through them. How I longed to be viewed through his lens. I no longer wanted to hide myself away, and I only hoped I could find the right words to show him that.

The sound of Jasper's door shutting and Quinn's footsteps down the hall startled me from my thoughts as I sat, nervously fiddling with my hands.

"Jasper sure likes you." He leaned against the wall as he

spoke. "He said you have very pretty eyes, and you smell like flowers."

A small laugh escaped me. "That's sweet." I rose from the couch and walked over to where he stood. "He's a really great kid, and he absolutely adores you."

He nodded, a sadness resting in his eyes. "I know."

The space between us quivered with intensity, and I wanted to reach out to him, to collapse into his arms, feel his heartbeat joining with mine. So solid and comforting against my own scattered rhythm. "I'm sorry about what happened the other night." My words tumbled out, breathless and bare.

"Don't be sorry, Julia."

"But I am." I shook my head as tears pricked my eyes. "All my life I've pushed people away, so terrified of what they would find if they saw inside. And it's been easy because no one has ever really tried to go too deep. Until you." I took a shaky breath as all the pain broke through the surface. The rejection, the loss, the avoidance. Like the cancer inside, it was eating away at me. Hot tears ran down my cheeks, and I brushed them away, meeting the searing focus of his gaze. "I don't know what you see in me, but whatever it is, it makes me want to find it in myself."

"You know what it is I see in you." He leaned close and wiped at a tear with the pad of his thumb. "I see a woman whose armor is only as strong as her unwillingness to let go. And behind this wall that you have built around yourself, there is a fire that fascinates me." His fingers trailed up my neck, resting on the curve of my cheek. "But it's *me* that owes you an apology, Julia. I shouldn't have pushed you like that. My feelings for you are really intense, and I just wanted *so* badly to break down this wall of yours. To really *see* you. You're this incredibly beautiful challenge to me. But I shouldn't have asked something of you that you weren't ready to give. I had no right to do that." He pressed his forehead to mine, his breath falling warm and soft across my skin. "But at the same time, I need you to know that it's all or nothing with me. If you want to explore what we could be together, I need you to be willing to show me what's inside."

His words cut into me, exposing the layers I had spent so much of my life erecting. Something cracked beneath, and my grip loosened its hold as all of my ache rushed out. Tears fell like a cleansing release against my skin, full of all the loneliness, anger, and fear that had woven itself so tightly to me like a suffocating cloak. It was an affliction too heavy for me to carry anymore.

My voice shook as I took his hand and placed it over my heart, curling my fingers tightly around his. "Then break my walls down. I don't want them anymore, Quinn. *I don't want them.*"

Chapter Fourteen

Quinn took my hand and led me into the darkness of his bedroom, closing the door softly behind us. The light from the streetlamps outside scattered across our skin, enclosing us in pale shadows as I stepped forward and sank into his arms.

"I'm dying," I choked out, "I'm dying, and I realize I haven't even lived yet." Anguish tore at the remnants of all the wasted years of my own self-imposed isolation, the wounds I tried to conceal, and the fear I allowed to imprison me. My entire body shook from the unforgiving reality of it all, and I wondered if I really could start over. Or was it too late?

Quinn's eyes blazed with intensity as he slid his hands into my hair and pulled me close, resting his forehead to mine. "But you're here *now*." His lips brushed across my cheek, stealing away the tears that streaked down my face. "This moment is the only thing that's real." Another kiss swept over my skin, his voice a fervent whisper in my ear. "And this moment is all that matters."

A shaky breath escaped me, and I gripped his arms, the heaviness inside fading away as his lips continued to follow the trail of my tears, running across my chin and down to the slope of my neck. Taking my hand, he led me to the bed, blankets yielding beneath me as he drew me down and pulled me close against his chest. His arms encircled me in silence, becoming my gravity as the last remnants of my grief spilled out across the sheets, leaving only a stillness behind.

Time fell away as he held me, my body curled into his. I had never truly laid beside a man like this, asking nothing of our bodies, only sharing the quiet rhythm of our heartbeats, fluid and soothing. The closeness enveloped me, softening all the sharp edges I had grown so accustomed to.

"I needed this," I whispered, the words falling from me like a confession as I looked into his eyes, my reflection swimming in the pool of his own emotion.

Quinn ran his hand up my neck and threaded his fingers in my hair, his thumb drawing a slow circle against my temple. "This is how I've always wanted to be with you, Julia. Real and raw, and open."

I tilted my head and found his lips, losing myself in the slow dance of his kiss, his mouth like fire and honey. Everything threatened to burst open, and I clung to him, gasping as I searched for my air, his hands holding me together.

He traced the plane of my face, fingers delicately traveling across my cheeks and brushing over my lips. "I want you to know you can fall with me, Julia. I'll catch you."

"Then catch me," I breathed as my words trembled against him, lost in the feel of his touch, tender and consuming. "I need you to catch me."

A sigh rose in his throat, his lips seeking the salt of my skin in an aching caress as his mouth crept to the pulse of my neck. "I promise I'll catch you." His words took hold of me as he traced out a language across my body, a language I had never spoken before, born not out of desire, but a longing to connect.

Grasping at his shirt, I pulled it over his head as he unbuttoned my own. Slowly unveiling me, he slid my pants down past my legs and discarded his, the last of the barriers between us now tangled and forgotten on the floor.

I watched him as he hovered above me. Beyond the grappling of clothes and furtive touches, I had never really looked at a man in full honesty. I had always been focused on the outcome, on the escape. Even that night with him in my kitchen, I had looked away.

Sitting up, I took him by the shoulders and gently pressed him onto his back, my hands running over his chest, tracing the ink on his skin, the definition of muscle that traveled down to his hips. My fingers feathered across his thighs, and he sucked in a breath, reaching out to clasp my arms as I snaked my hand up the length of him, feeling the pulse of his heat against my palm.

With a groan, he pulled me into his arms, his mouth falling on mine once more as he threaded his fingers into my hair. The remnants of his kiss flooded me with warmth as he drew back, his eyes piercing into mine. I was caught and bound within his gaze, and for the first time in my life, this vulnerability felt liberating, like something expanding inside my chest. Something aching to be free.

He lowered me onto the sheets, and I arched myself into him as the press of his arousal rested against my sex, like a gentle question waiting for an answer, waiting to go deeper. A broken gasp escaped the both of us as I reached down and slid him inside me, our eyes locking together as he began to move within, tender and unhurried. Never had I felt so exposed, pinned beneath him, all the pieces of myself magnified. This naked vulnerability tore away at me, revealing the marrow inside, but I didn't shrink away. I let go and stared into his eyes. I wanted him to see me. I wanted him to see all of me.

A fire burned in the space between us, solidifying something unspoken, something that took me apart, and then put me back together again. Tears gathered once more and ran a trail down my cheeks. My heart stretched and swollen beneath the weight of his gaze.

"There you are." His voice shook as he continued his slow thrusts inside me. "My God, you're so beautiful."

A fractured cry I could not hold back tumbled from my lips, foreign and filling the room with a wildness. I had become untamed earth, a purging storm, and my body only a vessel. I buried the intensity of the sound against his skin as another one rose to the surface, born of ache and abandon, our eyes seeking each other out in the darkness of the room. And then I was gone, exploding beneath him in a consuming rush of pleasure as he called my name out like a plea and joined me, the bright flash of release claiming us both.

My heart thrummed out a rhythm that matched his own as he buried his mouth against my neck and rolled me onto my side, his lips brushing across my ear. "I could stay inside you like this forever."

My body lay blissfully languid as I pushed my hips against him, the last bit of his seed trickling into me. "Then stay." I gripped his hair and pulled his face toward mine. "Stay with me."

Everything within me felt raw and uncovered. And hidden beneath the layers I had just unpeeled with him, something awoke, and a strength uncoiled inside.

In silence, we laid together, skin around skin and limbs entwined as the sleepy hum of the city slowed down outside the window. The room lay awash in fragmented light as we watched shadows play upon the walls like slivers of dreams which had slipped through cracked doorways.

We eventually untangled from our embrace, and he slid out of me, shifting me in his arms so that I now lay on top, head cradled on his shoulder, my hand resting over the phoenix on his chest. I outlined the curve of its wings with my fingers, the fire that licked around the feathers as it rose beyond the flames.

"When did you get this? It's beautiful."

"When I lived in Spain."

I looked up at him, his eyes soft and sleepy in the dim light. "When did you live in Spain?"

"I went on a two-year spiritual pilgrimage of sorts when I was in my early twenties. I traveled all around Europe. I guess I was trying to find myself."

"And did you?"

"I did in a lot of ways." He brushed back a strand of hair from my cheek, his hand sliding across the curve of my neck, sending goosebumps traveling across my skin. "I challenged myself. I spent a lot of time reflecting on the things that had been holding me back." He glanced down at his tattoo. "I got this to represent growth, and a new chapter in my life."

I stared at the ink, into the piercing gaze of the bird, as if it held my own secrets in the fire. "I guess it never loses its meaning, does it?"

"No. It doesn't. Life is just a series of re-births."

A lightness took hold of me. A whisper of restoration cradled in possibility. And suddenly everything felt so deeply significant.

"Thank you."

"For what?" A smile washed over his face as he watched me from across the pillow, his fingers trailing patterns along my skin.

"For finding me." I dropped my head to his chest, listening to the gentle rise and fall of his breath, the warmth of him a safe harbor. "I just wish we had met each other sooner."

He tilted my head to meet his eyes. "*This* is when we were supposed to meet, Julia."

With a sigh, I wrapped myself around him, wishing I could crawl into his skin and stay cradled forever in this delicate moment of whispered words and fervent hope. But I knew our time was borrowed, and there were things that sat beside us like restless phantoms seeking absolution.

I shifted myself and looked at him, my fingers sweeping down his arm. "Quinn."

"Yes." His voice fell soft against my cheek.

"You need to tell Jasper."

Tension flickered in his eyes, and he rolled away from me, staring up at the ceiling. "I don't know if I can."

"You have to." I sat up and placed my open palm on his chest, feeling the heavy rhythm of his heartbeat, his anguish trapped within. Just like mine. "Did you know that I was his age when I lost my mom?"

His eyes skittered back to me, his pain obscured within the shadows of the room, pulling at the threads of my own.

"My mom, she killed herself." The words rushed from my mouth, sharp and resolute, slicing into the tender space between us. I realized I had never talked about this with anyone before. I had kept this truth locked so tightly away, hidden beneath the veneer, so afraid that if I released my story, it would shatter whatever was left of me.

Quinn took my hand, his fingers threading through mine. "I had no idea."

"I was the one who found her."

Memories rushed at me, clawing into the space I had suddenly allowed to open inside. I took a deep breath, allowing them to settle into the corners, giving room to their demands. I no longer wanted to carry this story alone in the dark.

"I came home from school one day, and she was in her room in bed. That wasn't unusual. Sometimes she would lock herself in there for days. I used to sit beside the door and tell her stories, hoping she would stop crying. Hoping she would open the door and be my mom again." My throat constricted as my words tumbled out, full of all the terror that small child still clutched against her chest. "I was sitting on her bed, talking about this school project I was working on, and then I touched her hand." Tears welled up, choking the air from my lungs, and

I closed my eyes, trying to shroud that moment etched so brutally in my mind. A nightmare I could never erase. "And she was *so cold.*"

"Oh, Julia. *My god.*" Quinn sat up and enfolded me, soothing away the icy chill of my brutal recollections. "No child should ever experience that. I'm so sorry."

White pills and lifeless eyes. Those were the last memories I had of my mother. Images that stole away everything else. The sound of her laughter, the feel of her arms around me, I couldn't find those. They were buried beneath the crushing weight of losing her.

I looked up at him, my pain holding space in the depths of his eyes. "I would have given *anything* to have another moment with my mom. To know how much time I had left with her. But I didn't get that. And then she was just... gone." I shook my head. "Jasper deserves to know. You have to tell him now, Quinn. He's going to find out sooner or later."

He nodded somberly as a tear escaped and rolled down his cheek. "I know."

Finding his hand, I entangled my fingers through his and squeezed tight. "Take this time you still have, and give him some good memories, ones that will hopefully ease the sting of the bad ones. He needs the chance to say goodbye to his dad."

This time, it was Quinn who collapsed against me. His tears soaked my skin as he released whatever he had been holding in, the soft center of his sorrow merging with mine until it became something beautiful and sacred, forged in the fire of a shared vulnerability. My heart stirred like a song among the darkness, the broken pieces of myself coalescing with his to make something new, something whole. And a question rose inside, hesitant and pressing, daring me to answer.

Was this what love felt like?

Chapter Fifteen

y eyes drifted open, meeting the brightness of a morning that spilled into the corners of Quinn's room. I reached out for him, but the sheets beside me lay empty. From outside the door, I could hear the faint gurgle of a coffee machine and the thumping of feet down the hall. A smile spread across my lips, memories from the night before whispering across my skin. The delicate vulnerability. The intensity and euphoria. The feel of him inside me. The way he held me in his arms.

The sound of the bathroom door opening startled me, pulling me from my thoughts as I rolled over to see Quinn standing beside the bed, his phone clenched in his fist, eyes rimmed with red as if he'd been crying.

"What *happened*?" I rose from the tangle of blankets.

"I just got off the phone with Bethany, Jasper's mom." His voice came out choked as he sat on the bed beside me. "I told her."

"You did?" I scooted closer to him, slid my arms around his waist and rested my head on his back. Still reeling from the night before, I took this small act of intimacy as a gift. I wanted so badly to soothe away whatever was churning inside him. "How did she take it?"

Quinn grew rigid against me. "She freaked out. Just like I

knew she would." He raked his fingers through his hair and let out another long sigh. "I just need to give her time to process all this before I tell Jasper."

Drawing back, I looked at him as he turned and pulled me into his arms, placing a soft kiss against my temple. "I was up all night thinking about what you said. And you're right, it's time he knows the truth."

I threaded my fingers through his, noticing the way our hands contrasted but fit so perfectly together. His gentle strength engulfing my fragility. The shape of him interlocking with mine, forming the landscape of a puzzle I wanted to explore deeper. "I know this is going to be hard for both of you. And he may not understand all of it right now, but one day he will."

A forlorn smile crept across Quinn's face as he looked at me. "I hope so."

"Dad!" Jasper's voice in the other room broke us from our moment, and with a sigh, Quinn rose from the bed.

"I'm going to go make some breakfast. Why don't I bring you some?"

"No, it's okay, I'll get up," I said, reaching for my shirt on the floor.

Quinn's hand rested on my arm, his eyes shifting and growing heavy as they trailed along the length of my body. "Is it wrong of me to admit that I really love the idea of you, beautiful and naked, waiting for breakfast in my bed?"

I smiled and ran my fingers through his hair. "Are you trying to keep me a little secret?"

"No, Jasper knows you're here." He placed a soft kiss on my lips. "I just don't want you to put your clothes on yet."

"And he's okay with me being here?" A slight discomfort overcame me as I looked at him, not wanting to encroach upon the quiet world they orbited together.

"Yes, he actually wanted to knock on the door early this

morning and see if you wanted some cereal." A slow smile crept across the corners of his mouth. "But I told him you needed your rest."

I leaned back against the bed, watching as he closed the door behind him,, and then wrapped the blankets around myself, breathing in the comforting scent of him mingled within the fabric. The familiar clawing emptiness inside was now replaced with a soft murmur of possibility as I closed my eyes, cloaked in the richness of what was growing between us.

I must have fallen back to sleep, for I awoke to the smell of eggs and Quinn's hand sweeping down my back. "You hungry, pussycat?"

"Pussycat?" I rolled over and stretched, shooting him a sleepy look of amusement. "Is that your new name for me now?"

"Yes." He leaned close to me with a smile and slid the plate of eggs and toast across the bed to me. "I think it suits you."

Sitting against the pillows, Quinn watched me as I ate. His eyes drank me in like hands stroking my skin, stirring the embers of the night before, and a flush of arousal coursed through me.

"You're staring, Quinn."

"I can't help myself." His voice grew husky as he slid his hand beneath the covers, fingers tracing along the inside of my thigh. "I want to photograph every inch of you right now."

I raised my eyebrow playfully. "While I'm eating?"

His eyes grew heated, and he leaned in close to me as a knock sounded on the bedroom door.

"Dad, I'm ready to go."

Quinn dropped his forehead to mine. "I promised Jasper a trip to the arcade today. Do you want to tag along?"

"I'll let you guys have your time together." I pressed my mouth to his, tasting coffee. "Call me later, okay?"

With a nod, he rose from the bed and shot me a soft smile. "Make yourself at home."

"Maybe I will." I reclined on the sheets, shooting him an enticing look.

"Damn it." He hovered over me with a low growl and bent down to nip at my ear. "Stop teasing me right now." Reluctantly, he backed his way toward the door with a playful wink before closing it behind him.

The pattering of feet down the hall was followed by Quinn's motorcycle revving from the street, the sound filtering in through the window as I stood from the bed to retrieve my clothes.

My stomach housed a cacophony of butterflies inside, reminding me of my first kiss. Thirteen years old and standing beneath the oak tree by the middle school, his mouth tasting of soda pop, hands warm on my back. The elation that followed me as I walked home, the world suddenly full of color and possibility.

Sun peeked through the clouds, bathing the sidewalk in a burst of bright light which matched the buoyancy inside me as I stepped out of Quinn's apartment building and made my way to my car.

Everything looked rinsed in gold as I drove through the city, my eyes taking in details I had never noticed before. The way the water encompassed the horizon like a blanket of silk. The way the branches of the trees gracefully danced against the canvas of the sky. I was overcome with a sensation of perfection. Everything had its place in this wildly beautiful stage we called life, and for the first time, I felt connected to it all.

Lightness followed me into my apartment, my body humming with energy as my phone sounded in my purse, an unfamiliar number flashing across the screen.

"Julia, it's me, Amelia."

I sank down onto the couch, her voice a sweet song in my ear. "Amelia, I'm so glad you called."

"Oh, good. I was wondering if you wanted to meet up for coffee today?"

A smile rested on my lips as I ran my hands across the fabric of the pillows. "I would love to."

* * *

Standing in the charmingly cramped used bookstore downtown, my eyes scanned the shelves while I waited for Amelia. The rich, smokey aroma of coffee and the hiss of the espresso machine in the far corner of the room filled the space with comforting warmth as I found myself reaching for a worn travel book, its edges curled with faint creases.

"Tibet. Have you ever been there?"

I turned to find Amelia standing beside me, her cheeks flushed from the breeze, and her dark hair peeking out from beneath a brightly colored knit beanie. I stared down at the cover, the majestic rise of Everest towering above the lush green landscape of rolling plateaus, and a peculiar feeling stirred within, like a whisper of longing, causing goosebumps to rise along my arms. "No, I haven't."

"Me neither, but I've always wanted to go." She shrugged off her coat, draped it over her arm, and motioned to the espresso stand. "They have the best coffee at this place. That's why I wanted to meet you here."

With a nod, I followed Amelia to the counter, the book of Tibet clutched in my hand. Pulling out my debit card, I handed it to the woman behind the register. "We'll have two coffees and this book, please."

After our drinks arrived, we found a table nestled beside the window and slid into the seats across from one another, steam rising between us from our cups. "Thank you so much for calling and inviting me here." I traced my finger along the rim of my cup. "You are under no obligation to try and establish a relationship with me. So, it means a lot that you reached out like this."

Amelia nodded and took a sip of her coffee, her eyes glancing from me to the window. "Well, I actually brought you here because I had some more questions."

"Of course. Ask away." I wrapped my hands around my cup and met her open stare.

"You lied to me."

Her words fell harsh and clipped from her mouth, and I leaned against the stiff plastic chair, the edges digging uncomfortably into my back. *Did she somehow find out about my cancer?* Anxiety coiled within as I realized I had no idea how to navigate around this topic. I knew it sat beside me like a dark secret waiting to be revealed. But I wanted to nurture this fragile growth between us before I tarnished it with the truth of my diagnosis. It was all I had. A sliver of beauty my illness had yet to touch.

"What did I lie about, Amelia?"

"You said it was just you. That you had no other family. But who's Russell Marino?"

He's still alive.

My father's name hit me with a sickening weight that lodged itself in my chest, and I clenched my eyes closed for a moment. "How do you know about him?"

She shrugged, glancing down at her coffee. "I googled you the other day, and he came up."

I ran my fingers through my hair, a sigh lodged in the back of my throat. "That would be your grandfather, I suppose."

"You suppose?" She leaned forward, regarding me with a furrowed brow.

I shook my head, trying to push away the memories which still haunted me after all these years. Blood streaming down my face as I scrambled frantically out the bedroom window, while my father banged on the door I had barricaded with my dresser. The wood of the frame splintering violently against his onslaught.

"I haven't spoken to him since I ran away at sixteen." My hands clenched underneath the table, nails biting into the flesh. "He was not a good man, Amelia."

"Why? What did he do?"

I tore my gaze to the window. The slivers of sunlight which had followed the day were now swallowed up beneath a thick layer of clouds, and a grey pallor stretched across the room. "You don't need to hear about my ugly past."

"Hey." Amelia leaned across the table, her eyes wide and direct. "I really want to get to know you. But I understand if there are things you just can't talk about."

I placed my hand over hers, her warmth radiating through the chill of my skin. Though I did not want to stain her with my story, I wanted to be transparent, to show her I was willing to open my door and let her inside. I squeezed her hand, my voice dropping to a whisper as if the soft tone could diminish the blow. "Let's just say he did horrible things to my mother and me, and he was the reason she took her own life."

Amelia stared at me in shock, empathy welling up within her eyes. "Oh, my God. I'm so sorry." I imagined her heart as a wide-open meadow, and I could see the streaks of color I had just dulled within.

"No, *I'm* sorry, Amelia. I really didn't want this conversation to get so heavy like this. But this is me trying to be as open as possible with you. I had a childhood that was really traumatic, and it has shaped me into who I've become as an adult." Amelia wrapped her fingers tighter around mine while I spoke, as if she were afraid I was going to fall away. "There's so much I've done that I'm not proud of. So much of my life I've wasted." A tear formed in the corner of my eye, running a slow path down my cheek that I didn't move to brush away. "But meeting you has been like a bright light shining through all the darkness. In a way, you've given me a chance to start over. To make amends for my mistakes and to hopefully heal from them." I stared into the depths of her chestnut eyes, so similar to my own. "So, I want to thank you for that. Thank you for having the courage to find me."

Amelia nodded, a tender smile sweeping across her face. "I'm glad I did." She let go of my hand and pulled her phone from her purse, placing it on the table between us. The screen lit up in front of me, casting an image of a little girl beside a lake, her hands holding on to the string of a kite. "I thought you might like to see some pictures of when I was a kid."

"I would love that." Emotion broke through as she began to swipe through her memories, sharing images of sunlight and wide smiles, and my heart swelled with gratitude. It was the vibrant color of a childhood bathed in the kind of joy I had desperately prayed she would find all those years ago. A childhood full of love.

Chapter Sixteen

Late night bathed my living room in the reflection of city lights as I sat on the couch staring at the computer, my eyes running through the long list of holistic alternatives for cancer patients. Everything from naturopaths and acupuncturists to energy healers and guided peyote sessions. A plethora of options crowded the screen before me, leaving me overwhelmed and exhausted. While the book on Tibet I had bought the other day stared at me from the coffee table, the contents within its pages still unread, but beckoning to me.

Every so often, I found myself glancing at my phone, hoping to see Quinn's name flash across the screen. I had not heard from him since the day before when he'd told me he was going to take Jasper up to their favorite hiking spot, and an unease gnawed at me. I was pretty sure he had told Jasper about his cancer on their hike together, and his silence felt like a warning bell.

With a sigh, I closed my laptop and pulled myself off the couch. Padding into the bathroom, I sat on the wide rim of the jetted tub and turned on the tap, watching as the water eddied against the porcelain, my thoughts hovering in the delicate space between joy and sorrow.

Something was opening within me, a flower quietly

revealing its petals to the sunlight. Quinn was like a fire, consuming my armor, while Amelia was earth, her gentle presence giving form beneath my feet. And beside me stood sorrow, with grey eyes watching, reminding me what little time I had left.

Removing my clothes, I added some bath salts and sank into the warmth, releasing a long exhale as it wound its way through my muscles, enfolding me in a delicious buoyancy. My hands traced patterns across the water, spirals and swirls that reminded me of the impermanence of form. All water led back to the source, to the churning depths of the ocean, and I wondered what source my soul would return to when it no longer held space in my body. Would I become a part of the stars? Was the sky above our own cosmic ocean, a state of dreams, cradled by an infinite sleep?

A knock on the door startled me from my musings, and I sat up abruptly, scrambling for a towel. Dripping a trail of water across the tile, an image of Quinn rose in my mind, and I threw my robe on and hurried into the living room, opening the door to find him standing there, his eyes bleak and desolate.

"I'm so sorry I didn't call."

"It's okay." I took his hand and guided him through the doorway.

He stood rigid for a moment, then relaxed as I pulled him against me. The cold from outside clung to his clothes, and his hair held the faint scent of wind and ocean. "I've been driving around all night, and I had to see you." His words were a whisper in my ear as he gripped my back, bunching up the silk of my robe. "You smell so good. Were you in the bath?" He nuzzled my neck, his breath growing labored as his hand slid underneath my robe. "You're still wet."

"Yes." My voice came out in a tremble as the chill of his fingers ran across my back, his lips teasing my skin.

"Julia." He tangled his hands into my hair, my name on his

lips a harsh and broken rasp as he rested his forehead to mine and pulled me in for a kiss.

A rush of heat burst inside me as his mouth fell hungry against mine, hands fervent and engulfing, his desire a demanding force, consuming me. Untying the sash, he slipped my robe down, the silk fabric pooling at my feet as he drew his mouth to my breasts, biting gently as he backed me into the living room and pressed me down onto the couch. A low growl escaped him while his fingers crept to my center, causing a gasp to tumble out as he dipped into my sex, slowly coaxing out my arousal.

Reaching for his belt buckle, he locked eyes with me, and I saw the pain there. The kind that took hold of me, like a shared breath. I knew he didn't want to talk, and so I let our bodies take over, offering him a safe place to fall, knowing that in this release, we would find each other.

He plunged into me, hot and fierce, his eyes piercing mine as he gripped my hips and angled me up, thrusting deeper while my hands clawed at his back, wanting more. This was not the soft lovemaking from the other night. This was raw and primal, as if we could rip away reality by the sheer force of our will, to tear at the threads that bound us to gravity. And for one brilliant moment, it almost felt like we could.

My body shuddered and broke open as my unrestrained cries filled the room, sending Quinn over the edge. He fell against me with a loud groan, meeting me in the middle of my frantic climax as he spilled himself inside. Then his lips were on mine, soft, languid kisses that drew out all my longing once more as we clasped our bodies tightly together, still moving to a rhythm now grown gentle, his clothes askew and tangled around his limbs.

I looked up at him, aglow in the hushed light of the room. "Hey there."

He swept the hair out of my face, a tender smile lighting up his eyes, pushing back the heavy debris of emotion he had carried into the apartment with him. "Hi, beautiful."

We lay there entwined for a moment, allowing the silence to speak for us, caught within the tide of a moment that had no words.

Shifting himself against the couch, I nestled my back to his chest as he pulled me into his arms, his breath resting in my ear like a warm caress. "I don't know why, but when I'm with you, I don't feel so lost."

"Me, too." I threaded my fingers through his and let out a sigh, my body humming with pleasure and a closeness that stripped me bare as I closed my eyes and pressed myself tighter against him, allowing the warmth of his skin to slip over me.

* * *

I awoke in my bed, momentarily confused, then realized Quinn must have carried me from the couch. I turned to see the shadowed outline of him lying beside me with his eyes open.

"When did I fall asleep?"

"About an hour ago." His hand ran across the length of my back. "The way the moonlight is hitting you right now, with the contrast of the shadows. I wish I had my camera with me."

A smile twitched at the corner of my mouth. "Have you been watching me this whole time?"

"Maybe."

I slid closer to him, reaching up to run my fingers through the strands of his hair. "Do you want to talk about what happened with Jasper?"

His jaw tensed, and he stiffened next to me, that vacant sorrow pooling once more in the depths of his eyes.

"It was soul-crushing, Julia. It was everything I was afraid it was going to be." He sighed and pulled away from me, running his hand down his face. "He's *so* angry." Quinn looked over at me, his gaze trembling with tears. "He told me he hates me and that he never wants to see me again."

I shook my head, placing my hand on his chest, I felt the strident thrum of his heart battling with the vastitude of his emotion. I knew I couldn't take it away, but I wanted so badly to try. "You know he doesn't mean that. It's not *you* he's angry at, it's the cancer. He's angry at the cancer."

"I am too, Julia." His eyes blazed with intensity. "You know what I realized? This whole fucking time I have been lying to myself, just going through the motions. But I haven't fully accepted this. And when I told Jasper today, it all suddenly became very real. I can't hide from this anymore."

Pulling him close, I wrapped myself around him, as if my limbs could anchor the weight of his sorrow. He clung to me while his hands ran through my hair and gripped tightly, his voice spilling out in a fragmented cry as his grief pounded against me. "God damn it, Julia. *God dammit.*"

There were no words for the place the mind goes when it is forced to face an inevitability so harsh it cuts away at your very foundation. But here I was, standing in it beside Quinn, and even though that swirling darkness was terrifying, there was a power and comfort in knowing we didn't have to face it alone. We had found one another at a time when we needed each other the most, and the beauty of that gift was staggering.

* * *

My fingers traced Quinn's brow, watching his eyes flutter beneath his lids, delivering himself to some dream as the night deepened and danced across the sheets. I had held him until his grief wrung itself out, molding a space for a tenderness I'd never felt the depths of before, and my heart was bursting with an emotion that longed for release.

Slipping from the bed, I grabbed my robe Quinn had left

draped across the chair and walked over to my cello, moving it into the living and closing the bedroom door quietly behind me. Settling into the chair by the window, I plucked a few strings, adjusting the pegs at the bottom before I rested the cool wood against my chest, closed my eyes and drew the bow softly across the strings. I didn't need light this time. I didn't need my eyes to find the chords. There was a song within me, and I let it swell upwards, to claim my body, to translate what lay hidden beneath the silence.

Time snuck away from me as the slow, deep notes took hold. The vibration of bow across string reached deep inside, wrapping me within a story much larger than my own. It was the encumbrance of pain colliding with the vibrancy of love. And I realized the two could not exist without each other. That life could not exist without death. We were the dancers, locked within this endless embrace of duality.

The sound of footsteps extracted me from the music, and I opened my eyes to find Quinn standing in the living room watching me.

"I'm sorry. I didn't mean to intrude. I know your music is private. But that piece..." He walked over and crouched beside me, his eyes swimming with tears as he brushed his hand through my hair. "It got into my dreams."

I set the bow on the floor beside us, noticing my hands were shaking, my body spent from whatever I had just channeled through the strings. "You're not intruding." I moved to stand, but my legs had grown heavy, and I faltered, gravity yanking me back down.

Leaning the cello against the wall, I sank into Quinn as he gently pulled me from the chair and to the floor beside him, his arms encircling me, breath warm in my ear as I curled myself onto his lap. "That song was beautiful. It reminded me of the feeling when you stand at the top of a high peak, and you suddenly see all the things you never knew were there before. The way the light hits the top of the trees. The endless sky." His lips rested on my neck, sending threads of warmth unraveling inside. "That's what it feels like being with you. You're a vista to me, Julia."

I turned to him and threaded my fingers in his hair. Between the darkness, the pale sliver of the moon played across his eyes, and I saw a reverence there that made me ache inside, made me feel sanctified.

My mouth found his in a kiss that stripped me of words. Our lips and tongues became whispered declarations only our bodies could understand. His hands slipped in between the fabric of my robe, his touch like a pulse of electricity pulling me closer, filling me up, tethering us together.

With our limbs interlocked, we held each other, rocking slowly to the remnants of the song I had left in the corners of the room. A song that spoke of fire.

A fire that dared me to rise above the ashes.

* * *

I stood by the bedroom window as soft light played across my skin and collided with the steam that rose from my cup of coffee. I wondered where Quinn was as I looked down at the city below. The space beside my bed had been empty when I awoke this morning with my dream from the night before still clinging to me. Images of sunlight, and the sound of the wind rustling through tall grass.

The sound of the front door closing pulled my gaze away from the window, and I turned to see Quinn leaning in the doorway of the bedroom holding a paper bag in his hand.

"Hey there, pussycat."

My heart fluttered at the sight of him. He looked rugged and gorgeous with his tousled hair and warm smile, and the clarity in his eyes was concentrated, as if last night had ripped him open, had ripped us both open.

"Where did you run off to?"

He held up the bag. "I remembered you talking about that breakfast place down the street from here. Thought I'd surprise you. But there was a really long line."

"Wow, thanks for doing that." Moved by his sweet gesture, I set my coffee on the table beside the bed and sank back onto the sheets, patting the space beside me. "You look like you're feeling better."

"I am feeling *much* better." He joined me on the bed, sweeping his hand up my arm. "And once we finally made it back to the bedroom, I had some of the best sleep I've had in months. You have an incredible effect on me. Last night was..."

"I know." I nodded slowly as he ran his fingers across my cheek and leaned in for a kiss. His lips lingered against mine before pulling away, his gaze full of a sentiment neither of us needed words for.

The aroma of smoked salmon and egg croissants beckoned to me, my appetite suddenly ravenous, plucking at my attention. "Oh my God. How did you know this is my favorite thing to get at that place?" My eyes widened as I looked down at the bag in his hand.

He shrugged and threw me a playful smile. "Lucky guess?"

"I love you. You know that?"

With a chuckle, he pulled out the sandwich and handed it to me. "Wow, I didn't know you were so easy to please."

"No, I'm *serious*, Quinn." My voice came out soft and hesitant, and my pulse jumped in my throat as I realized how good it felt to say those words out loud. Words that had been hovering within my chest, yearning for a voice to give it language. Time had grown delicate, and I did not want to dance around a truth that longed to claim itself, to squander another moment holding myself back.

Overcome with a freedom that burst within me like wings, I set the food down on the bed beside us and climbed onto his lap. Bending to kiss his mouth, the sentiment tumbled out once more against his lips. "*I love you.*" I ran my fingers along the stubble of his jaw as he looked back at me with tears dancing in his eyes. I allowed the vulnerability of this confession to settle between us, not wanting anything in return. This was my offering to him.

"You don't need to say it back. I just want you to know how I feel."

He shook his head, clasping my hands as his voice grew choked. "*Julia.* Ever since the moment we met, you have captivated me. And when you finally let me in the day you came to my apartment... my God, it was so beautiful." He cupped my face in his hands, the light wavering in his eyes as he drew me closer, resting his forehead to mine. "How could I not love *everything* about you."

With the food momentarily forgotten, he lay me down onto the sheets. His mouth was tender and soft against mine, filling me with a lightness that brought tears to my eyes as I gently fell back from the last pinnacle of my lonely height and let him catch me in his arms.

Chapter Seventeen

The last remnants of autumn receded into a memory, and the assurance of winter crept in with stark grey eyes and chilly fingers. The hazy light of midafternoon bathed the trees in shadows as Quinn pulled the car to a stop at the trailhead and turned to look at Jasper, who sat hunched in the back seat. "We're here."

Jasper flung himself against the door, hurling it open and slamming it shut behind him. Quinn flinched. "He didn't even want to come with me this morning." His voice came out choked as he stared out the window to where Jasper stood beside the trailhead, swinging a stick at a tree. "He said he would only go if you came too."

Reaching for his hand, I squeezed it tightly. "He just doesn't know what to do with all this hurt inside him."

"I know, and I've been trying to talk to him about it all, but he just completely shuts down. Slams the door in my face. Tells me to go away. It's killing me, Julia. I don't know what to do." He sighed and ran his hands vigorously through his hair. "I've been wanting to ask Bethany if I could have him for a few extra days during the week, but I don't want to force him to spend time with me if he doesn't want to."

"You know he does. You're his dad. You're his whole world.

This is just how he's processing things right now." I leaned across the seat and smoothed his hair back, revealing eyes clouded with anguish. "Just give him time."

He looked at me morosely. "I don't have much time left, Julia."

The tide of my breath caught in my throat as I stared into the depths of his sorrow. It was a howling storm that battered into me, clawing at both of us. "It's going to work itself out." My words came out pressing and hopeful, trying to soften the sting.

Removing the keys from the ignition, he shot me a wan smile as he grabbed the backpack from the seat behind us and opened the car door. "I hope so."

The wind tugged at my jacket as I got out of the car, watching as he made his way over to Jasper. "You ready to go on a hike, bud?"

With a shrug, Jasper moved away from him and walked in step beside me. Our footsteps crunched lightly on the gravel as we walked through the trees, dappled sunlight piercing through the canopy of green as a heavy silence settled between us.

Jasper eventually broke the quiet and began to chatter to me about birds and plants, his young mind bursting with information, all the while ignoring his father's attempts to engage with him. I knew I was here as a buffer, a way to quiet the scream of all the emotions that raged inside them both, like an endless void with no tether to cling to.

We stopped at a bend in the trail where an outcropping of rocks huddled in a wide circle beyond the path. "Do you want to go check out that spot again, Jasper?" Quinn asked with a small smile, nodding toward the rocks. "You remember, we found some great treasures last time we were here."

Jasper furrowed his brow and stared at his feet. "No."

With a sigh, Quinn stepped closer to him, placing his hand on his shoulder. "Hey, bud-"

"Don't touch me!" Jasper's voice was a sharp cry slicing through the forest as he yanked himself away from Quinn and bolted down the path.

Quinn stood there, arms dangling limp, his face a mask of defeat. My heart clenched in my chest as I came up to him and rested my hand on his back, feeling his muscles contract against my touch. "Let me see if I can talk to him, okay?"

He only nodded, his jaw tense while he stared into the trees as if their whispers held the answers to the questions we were all too reluctant to speak aloud.

The path wound upwards, a dense thicket hugging the landscape of pine as I walked, a chill in the air hinting of snow. From the corner of my eye, I could make out a flash of Jasper's blue jacket off to the side of the trail. Pushing my way through branches, I saw him standing on the edge of a steep slope that cradled the stretch of valley below. Taking a deep breath, I cautiously approached him. "Do you feel like talking? It's okay if you don't. But I'm a pretty good listener. So, I'm here if you feel like sharing."

"He lied to me!" he spat out as he kicked a rock, sending it tumbling down the ravine. His face scrunched up in the kind of pain no child should ever have to grapple with. I thought of Amelia and all the truths stumbling around in my mind that I had yet to find the strength to share with her.

Bending down beside Jasper, I placed my hand on his shoulder and looked into dark eyes full of tears. "You know, sometimes parents have to lie, because it's their job to keep their children safe. Your dad was only trying to protect you from all this hurt you're feeling inside right now."

He sniffed, and with clenched fists, ran the sleeve of his coat across his face, staring out into the endless expanse of sky stretching above us. "It's not fair. Why does he have to be sick?" His lip trembled as he spoke, and I resisted the urge to take him into my arms.

In that moment, I saw myself in him, that small child so lost and confused, wondering why her mom was suddenly yanked from her. And I knew there was nothing I could say to make that pain go away. It would be a wound he would always carry with him, but one that, hopefully in time, would give him strength.

"Life doesn't always have the answer to these things." I sighed and followed his gaze to the peaks of the mountains in the distance. "I was your age when I lost my mom."

He turned to me with wide eyes. "You lost your mom?"

"I did, and I never had the chance to say goodbye to her. I was never given the opportunity to do that. Your dad is really strong, Jasper, and this monster inside him, well, he's going to fight it for as long as he can. He's going to fight it for you. Because *you're* his whole life, you know that? And he's going to do everything he can to be with you for as long as possible." I choked back the swell of my own emotion as it crept to the surface. "And your dad will always be by your side, even when the day comes that you won't be able to see him anymore."

Jasper let out a shaky breath and nodded as the weight against him seemed to loosen its hold for a moment. "That's what my mom said."

"Your mom sounds pretty smart." With a trembling smile, I quickly brushed away the tear that had escaped down my cheek.

Jasper narrowed his eyes at me. "So, are you my dad's girlfriend?"

"I guess you could say I am. Are you okay with me being his girlfriend?"

Jasper shrugged and kicked at a few more loose stones. "I guess so." He looked at me, his gaze full of the same stark intensity as his father. "Are you sad about my dad, too?"

A lump rose in my throat, and I struggled with what to say,

not wanting to introduce another element of loss to his world just yet. "Yes, I am sad about your dad being sick, but I am going to try to enjoy all the time we still have together."

Jasper sat on the ground and began sifting through the dirt, picking up certain stones and placing them into a pile. I watched him in silence as he arranged the rocks into a precarious stack, every teetering addition bringing it closer to its eventual fall, and when it did, he calmly started over. If only we could navigate our lives with such grace, to serenely rebuild among the rubble, knowing collapse was inevitable and necessary for growth.

The wind rippled through the trees, green limbs dancing like waves in an ocean as I glanced down the path. "Do you think we should go check on your dad? He might be getting kinda lonely back there all by himself."

Jasper nodded and quickly jumped to his feet, shaking dirt from his pants, his fist tightly clenched around a rock. "Yeah, I'm gonna go show him what I just found."

I followed him through the trees and stopped when I saw him wrap his arms around his father. I stood there, giving them their moment, watching as Quinn's face relaxed into a warm smile and he bent down to say something, his hands clasping over the rock Jasper handed him.

A tenderness overcame me, born of hope. I may not have had the chance to tell my mom all the things I wanted to say to her, but Jasper did, and that was a gift I knew he would cherish one day. It was a gift I knew I needed to give Amelia as well.

The last of the afternoon light rested above the tops of the trees as we made our way back to the parking lot. Jasper scrambled into the back seat as Quinn turned to me beside the car and drew me close against him.

"I don't know what you said to him back there, but thank you."

I shook my head, reaching up to fiddle with the buttons on his coat. "I think he just needed to get some things off his chest."

He cupped my face in his hands and placed a soft kiss on my lips. "Thank you."

"Eww, gross, Dad," Jasper called through the window.

Quinn laughed and released me, opening the door with a flourish before striding over to the driver's side. Settling into the front seat, he looked back at Jasper with a conspiratorial grin. "So, what do you think, bud? Should we drop Julia off at her place, or kidnap her for the rest of the day?"

"Kidnap her!" Jasper shouted with a wide smile as Quinn raised his eyebrow playfully at me.

"And what should we do with our hostage?"

"Go get hot chocolate!" Jasper bounced in the backseat.

Spinning around, my eyes went wide with mock horror as I gaped back at Jasper. "Oh, no, anything but that."

Jasper let out a giggle as Quinn fished through his pockets and retrieved the rock Jasper had given him. Placing it on the dash, he started the car and backed out of the parking lot, his eyes glancing up at Jasper through the rearview mirror. "Hot chocolate it is, then."

Reaching out for the rock, I held it in the palm of my hand. A rough grey stone with edges broken into the shape of a heart.

I looked at Quinn. "This is beautiful." My voice cracked as my fingers traced along the jagged edges.

"I know." His words came out in a whisper, his angled profile capturing the lines of emotion hovering at the surface, and I wondered if he saw the same thing I did? The deeper layer of meaning hidden beneath.

Perhaps we have to break apart first, before we can truly find the love inside us.

Quinn's hand rested on my thigh as we drove, his fingers running slow circles against the fabric of my pants, causing a warmth to rise within me. With Jasper humming happily along to the radio in the back, and Quinn's sturdy presence beside me, everything felt perfect, a moment encapsulated and weightless, and I held on tight to this bud of happiness which whispered inside. With a smile, I rested my head on the seat, watching the trees rush by and drinking in this moment so seamlessly captured beneath the moody Seattle sky.

The holidays were quickly approaching. I could see it in the stride of people pushing along the sidewalks, the storefronts now displaying pumpkins and painted turkeys on the glass. And I watched it all through a new lens, soaking in every detail as life rushed by, impervious and unaware of my own fleeting narrative.

Quinn unlocked the door to his apartment and ushered me inside, throwing his keys on the counter.

"So, it looks like we have a little over four hours until I need to be back in town to pick up Jasper from school. Let me just grab my camera, and we can head out."

"Still being illusive about where we're going, huh?" I glanced at him playfully from across the kitchen as I ran my fingers along the tile of the counter, eyeing the plate of bread crusts and sticky jelly, remnants from a sandwich Jasper must have eaten.

"Yep." He shot me a crooked smile and came up behind me,

placing a kiss against my neck as he ran his hands slowly down my arms. "I like leaving you in a state of anticipation."

"Oh, really?" A throaty chuckled spilled from me as I leaned into him.

"Oh, yes." His lips teased my ear before he pulled away. "I'll be right back."

With a nod, I walked to the window, folding my arms around myself while I stared out into the grey sky. Sun streamed momentarily through a thin break in a cloud, rinsing my skin in tentative light.

"Wow."

I turned to see Quinn standing in the doorway to his room, clutching his camera and watching me with a look of wonder in his eyes.

"You look so incredible right now with the way the light is hitting you. Don't move." He stepped closer and adjusted the lens on his camera, holding it up to me, and letting out a series of rapid clicks.

I turned my head from him, suddenly feeling shy under the scrutiny of his lens. "Okay, I think you got enough there."

He lowered the camera and leaned in to brush away a strand of hair from my face. "I can never get enough of you."

Heat rose to my cheeks as his fingers rested along the curve of my neck. "This place right here, I've been wanting to capture from the moment I first saw you." He leaned in and placed a kiss against the pulse of my neck. "And here..." His lips trailed up toward my ear, gliding along the lobe and causing a stuttered exhale to escape me, my limbs growing heavy as his breath danced across my skin. "I want to photograph all of you. Will you let me?"

"Right now?"

"Yes."

Caught beneath the weight of his alluring request, I relaxed and allowed whatever was left of my insecurity to dissipate under the tender burn of his gaze.

"Okay." My answer came out in a whisper as Quinn positioned me closer to the window, angling my body into the light. The intensity in his eyes devoured me as he began to shoot, and the space between us quivered with an intimacy that reached right through me as I stood there, offering myself up to his silent reverence.

He sat me gently on the wide ledge of the windowsill, his hands molding me, fingers adjusting the strands of my hair. "Your eyes..." He lowered the camera for a moment, staring into the depths of them. "I don't think I've ever seen a color like this before, the way they change in the light. It's haunting."

He leaned in closer, taking a round of close-ups as my hands fell to my shirt, undoing the buttons and allowing the fabric to slip down my arms. Quinn stopped shooting and watched me with a languid heat as I removed my bra and shimmied my pants down my legs. Lowering himself to his knees, he adjusted his lens again. "Lean back on the glass." His voice was soft as his camera began to click again, every shutter of the lens like a kiss against my skin, stirring the embers of my longing.

I ached for his hands on me as he continued to caress my body with the camera, making love to every dip and plane of my skin. I felt beautiful in a way I never had before, as if he was reaching beneath the physical definitions and into something vast and unexplored, the true essence of who I was captured through his eyes.

The sound of the camera being placed on the coffee table jolted me from my languid state, and Quinn's lips swept up my thighs, trailing a rush of warmth through every inch of me. "God, you're so beautiful."

I let out a soft moan as his hands ran along my body, his mouth exploring my skin with kisses that bloomed across my hips and belly and then slipped down to my sex. On instinct, I tensed, and drew my legs closed. He looked up at me in momentary confusion.

"I'm sorry," I said, reaching for him. "I've just never had anyone down there before."

"Really?"

"Yeah." I ran my hands through his hair, fiddling with the strands. "It's always felt... too intimate."

"Oh, Julia. You're missing out." A fervor grew in his eyes as his fingers stroked the inside of my thigh.

"Am I?"

"Yes." His reply was low and throaty as his lips fell against me once more, tracing patterns of desire along my skin.

"Just let me clean up a little down there first," I said, moving to stand.

Quinn took my arm and guided me back down to the ledge of the windowsill. "Please don't." He leaned close to me, his voice warm and smokey in my ear. "I want to taste you."

His words were like an electric shock to my senses, causing my core to tighten with arousal. I let out a sharp breath and opened my legs for him.

With a groan, he dipped down to my center, his lips teasing me with featherlight kisses that ignited my whole body. "Do you like that?"

His breath was a tantalizing sensation of heat, and my voice came out shaky as I arched my hips toward him. "Yes."

"Do you want more?"

"Uh, huh." I closed my eyes and gasped as his tongue ran slow circles along my sex, hitting every nerve ending and causing me to jerk. "Oh, my god, Quinn." I clutched at him, my fingers deep in his hair as he grabbed my waist and slid me closer, his arms reaching up to wrap my legs around his shoulders.

His mouth consumed me, and my hand flew to the window

frame and gripped hard, my fingernails digging into the paint as a torrent of sensation cascaded over me. I felt my eyes roll back, and I let out a strangled cry, completely lost in the feeling of his lips and tongue, drawing out a pleasure that stripped me of all other senses, leaving me weightless and exposed. "Don't stop," I panted as I writhed against him, so close to the edge that every muscle trembled in anticipation.

Another piercing cry spilled from me as I let go. Rocking and moaning with the last wave of my climax, Quinn slowed his pace to a light flicker and then drew himself up with a groan, his eyes flashing with desire as his thumb traced along my bottom lip. I parted my mouth and pressed the tip of his thumb along my teeth, biting down softly as my words came out breathless. "How do I taste?"

"Absolutely amazing."

My limbs buzzed with a delicious weakness, and I pulled him to me, feeling sensual and alive as I tasted the remnants of my release on his lips. "What you just did to me was *absolutely amazing.*"

"And I could do it all day. I love watching you. And the sounds that you make... my *God*," he murmured as his mouth drifted to my neck.

I leaned against the window with a sleepy smile and glanced out into the city below us. "Do you think we gave anybody a show?"

"I don't care," he growled, lifting me into his arms. "Do you?"

"No." Clinging to him, I let him carry me into the bedroom full of dim light and soft sheets, the press of his arousal like a tantalizing promise of more.

* * *

Entangled in each other's arms, we lay together, listening to the sound of life moving around us. The hissing of brakes on a bus, the muffled sound of closing doors within the building. Cocooned in the safety of our little world, I felt untouchable. Even the cancer growing inside, persistent, and unrelenting, seemed to fade from my mind until it was nothing more than an idea, a story that was only one of many. All that mattered was my steady breath beside his, and my heart, still courageously beating within my chest, giving me another moment, another day.

Quinn brushed his hand down my back. "I'm sorry. I was supposed to take you on that little date today."

My fingers skirted across the planes of his chest, tracing the black ink embedded below his skin, the Phoenix staring up at me with wild eyes. "And where *were* you planning on taking me, anyway?"

"Jetty Island."

"It's okay." With a playful smile, I rolled on top of him and pinned his arms to the bed, feeling the remnants of his release trickle out of me. "We ended up having a very nice photo shoot instead."

"We did, didn't we?" With a groan, he broke away from my grasp and pulled me in for a long kiss, stilling my breath and making me ache for him once more.

"I could do this all day, you know," I whispered as I ran my lips slowly across his chest, my tongue teasing circles along his skin as I traveled down to the soft coils of hair below.

"Me, too." His words became a tangled exhale as he gripped my arms and stirred against me.

A harsh knock on the door caused my pulse to jump, startling me from my explorations. I looked up to see Quinn swivel his head toward the living room with a look of mild annoyance and concern. Rising from the bed, he grabbed his pants and yanked them on as another frantic knock rang through the apartment.

"Jesus Christ, hold on." He let out a frustrated exhale and turned to me. "I'll be right back."

I nodded and pulled the covers up as he walked out. From the bedroom, I heard Quinn's sharp tone as the front door opened. "Bethany, what are you doing here?"

The door abruptly slammed closed as a woman's angry voice flooded inside. "We need to talk. Right now."

Chapter Eighteen

y heart lurched, and I found myself slipping deeper into the blankets as Bethany's voice in the other room grew louder.

"So why am I just hearing about this now from Jasper? I thought we were going to discuss these things before we introduced someone else into his life."

"What's there to discuss, Bethany? I don't need your permission." Quinn's words were a low hiss. "This is not the time to come barging in here. You need to leave. Now."

"Oh, I'm sorry. Am I interrupting something?" There was a long pause as footsteps walked closer. Through the crack in the bedroom door, I could see a pair of heels, and my eyes fell to my clothes laying in a pile on the living room floor. "Oh, is Julia in there?"

"Get out *now*, Bethany."

"But I'd really like to meet her. Come on out here, *hon*." Her voice was taunting, and a sharp twinge of anger coiled around me. I was trapped like a fly in a web, and I had no option but to face her. Yanking the sheet from the bed, I wrapped it against myself and flung open the bedroom door.

Steely grey eyes and wild red hair greeted me as Quinn crossed the room and took her by the arm. "Time to go."

She pulled away from him, teetering on her heels and

shooting me a smirk. "So, you're the woman that my husband's been fucking?"

My gut tumbled in confusion, and my mouth grew dry as I looked at Quinn, who shook his head at me, his eyes pleading.

"Oh, did you not tell her?" She turned to me with a cat-like smile. "We're still married, you know."

Quinn stood there with his jaw tightly clenched. "Okay. The Jerry Springer show is over, Bethany. You can go now."

"You know what?" I brushed past her as I bent down to grab my clothes. "I'm going to go. It sounds like you two have some things to figure out."

"Julia." Quinn's voice called out as I shut the bedroom door behind me. Dressing quickly with shaky hands, I tried to still the racing of my heart. I had opened myself up to him, and he never bothered to tell me he was still married. The sting of that hit me like a sudden blow.

I opened the door and peered out to find her standing in the kitchen with Quinn. Grabbing my purse from the couch, I tried to make my way past them, but Quinn reached out and clutched my hand, stopping me. "Please, don't go."

"Yes, please stay, Julia," Bethany goaded, her painted lips slurring over the words.

"Jesus Christ, are you drunk right now?" Quinn whipped his head around, eyes hard.

"What the fuck do you care?"

I twisted out of his hold and raised my hands in the air. "I'm not going to be in the middle of this."

"There's nothing to be in the middle of." Quinn raked his fingers through his hair, frustration etched across his face. "Do you want to know why we're still married?" He swept his hand out toward Bethany. "Because *she* refuses to sign the papers."

A tangled lock of red hair had fallen into Bethany's eyes, and I saw tears there. A wave of empathy overcame me. It was suddenly so clear. She was hurting too, and I knew all too well that anger was only a buffer from grief.

I placed my palm on Quinn's chest, feeling his heart tumbling around inside. "We'll talk later, okay?"

Slipping out the door, I left them to their broken discourse, the threads of their story unraveling behind me.

* * *

Fatigue pressed against my body as I walked into my apartment, but this time the silence I found inside did not claw at my skin, nor did it demand something of me. Instead, it stood beside me like a comforting friend, and I realized it had always been there, this soothing quiet. I just needed to open myself to it.

I made my way to the couch and sank into the cushions, watching the clouds drift past the living room window. Despite the events that had unfolded at Quinn's apartment, my mind was blissfully light. I waited for the rush of the usual churning thoughts to engulf me, but they were nowhere to be found. Only a peace rested between the stillness as I allowed the gentle hand of sleep to steal me away.

A knock on the door stirred me from dreams, vivid images of snowcapped mountains and valleys that tugged at a place inside me I couldn't quite define. The sky lay dark beyond the windows, and a full moon rested above the tops of the buildings as I rolled over and untangled myself from the couch.

I opened the door to find Quinn standing there, his face tense and washed in remorse as he gripped the doorframe. "I'm so sorry about all that."

The sight of him enfolded me like a warm blanket I longed to curl into, and the discomfort in his eyes was a tight band pressed against my own skin. I motioned for him to come inside, closing the door behind him. "It's okay."

He shook his head, a faint flash of anger brooding in his gaze. "No, it isn't. This is what Bethany loves to do. She stirs up drama whenever she can. It's exhausting."

I sighed and ran my hands down his arms. "She's hurting right now. You *do* know that, right?"

He stared at me in silence as I took his hand and led him to the couch. "Why didn't you share all this with me before?" I curled my legs to my chest. "That's what initially upset me. It's not the fact that you're still married. It's the fact that I had to find out about it through her."

"I know." He leaned forward and buried his face in his hands. "I fucked this all up, didn't I?"

"You didn't fuck anything up." I rested my hand on his back, my fingers brushing across the knots of tension hidden beneath. "I just want to know why you didn't tell me."

He stared at the floor, a long sigh tumbling from his lips. "I've been battling with her for years. This constant anger between us was just sucking all the life out of me." He turned to me, his eyes rimmed in red. "And then I met you. And I didn't want her to be a part of this. Of what we have together. It's beautiful and sacred to me, and I wanted to keep it separate somehow."

Reaching out, I entwined my fingers through his. I understood the need to preserve, to hold secret what was good for fear that hands would tarnish it. "I know relationships are complicated, one of the many reasons why I think I avoided them for so much of my life. But I think it's important that you find a way to heal with Bethany." My fingers traced the calloused ridges of his palm, noticing the branched lifeline in the middle that veered off in two directions like a fork in a road. The blueprint of choices that define us. "You can't keep compartmentalizing it. I don't know what you two have been through, but whatever it is, it's a part of your life you just can't push away anymore."

"I know. You're right, I've been stuffing it all down for way too long." Quinn leaned against the couch, his eyes heavy with confliction. "There's just so much baggage there."

"Talk to me, then. Tell me what happened between you guys."

Squeezing my hand, he ran his thumb vigorously up and down the length of my wrist, as if trying to wipe away the remnants of a past he didn't want to sit with. "Jasper was four when she left us. Took up with some guy she met at her gym and just disappeared. We didn't hear from her for almost a year. When she finally came back, saying what a terrible mistake she had made, begging to make things right, for me to take her back, for us to be a family again, it was too late." His voice was low and tense, and I could see all the years of pent-up resentment suspended in his gaze as he spoke. "She has spent the last six years trying to convince me she's no longer that person, but I guess a part of me has never forgiven her. It wasn't the fact that she cheated on me. It was that she left her own child to do it. Jasper was absolutely devastated." He ran his hands across his face. "What kind of mother just abandons her child?"

The sharp pang of guilt, like an old familiar foe, suddenly reared up, and I sucked in a sharp breath. As if reading my mind, Quinn turned to me, his eyes growing soft as he reached over and cupped my cheek. "Julia, I didn't mean it like that. You gave up Amelia because you felt you had no other choice at the time. Bethany *did* have a choice, and she *chose* to leave Jasper because she wanted to be wild and free again. It was selfish and careless, and I lost so much respect for her."

I leaned my head on his shoulder, my voice tumbling through the heaviness. "I'm sorry you had to go through all that. I can't imagine what that must have felt like, and what it must have been like for Jasper."

Glancing out the window, I wondered how many people out

there were locked within the tight confinements of mistakes they could not rectify? We were all imperfect creatures, trying to make amends for the choices we made in the desperation of our own discontent. I looked back at him, catching his eyes. "But don't you think it's time you found a way to forgive her?"

"You're right. I need to let go of all this anger." Quinn's voice was a slow sigh as he drew me into his arms and placed a soft kiss on my forehead. "What you saw back there at my apartment..." He trailed off for a moment, his eyes clouded in thought. "She doesn't usually drink like that. The thing is, she *is* a good mom *now*, and there's comfort in knowing that. Knowing she'll be able to take care of Jasper when I'm no longer around."

I clasped his hand in mine as a silence settled in between the spaces of a life that would eventually go on without us. I wondered if I would ever find that place inside that held forgiveness for all the things my father did to me. All we had were tiny precious moments left, and carrying resentment was only a bitter pill that slowly poisoned you. Every breath was a chance to live as honestly as possible. I knew that now, with every fiber of my being. Life was precious and fleeting, and our job was to live compassionately within the pages of our stories.

I looked at him, caught in the weight of his gaze, which burned both fierce and gentle. So much of myself I had found within the warmth of his fire, a second skin I could slip over my own scars, and my heart swelled with gratitude. Not only had he helped me find love, but he had given me courage. My story was not over. I realized it had only just begun.

Threading my fingers through his, I allowed the words to tumble out of me, unrehearsed and full of a deep significance I could barely grasp. "I've been thinking about going to Tibet for a while."

Quinn pulled back, a look of surprise flickering across his face. "When?"

"Soon." I ran my hand along his cheek. "There's this Tibetan healer I stumbled across a few weeks ago online. But it's more than that. I feel like something is pulling me there. And I think it's time for me to go and figure out what that is."

"I get it." He smiled at me, the corners of his eyes creasing. "Everyone has a journey they need to go on. This is yours."

"That's what it feels like. A journey I need to take." My fingers swept across his bottom lip. "I really want you to come with me. But I know you can't."

His brow furrowed, and confliction danced in his eyes. "Yeah, I can't leave Jasper right now."

"I know, and I wouldn't want you to."

Chapter Nineteen

"*W*ow. You're going to Tibet."

Amelia's eyes grew wide as we sat together on the shore of Puget Sound, a fine layer of mist clinging to our clothes as the waves slapped lazily against the sand.

"I am." I smiled at her as the press of anticipation hovered within me.

In one week, I would be on an airplane flying to East Asia. What was waiting for me there, I had no idea. All I knew was that I wanted to stand beside something much larger than myself, to push beyond the world I had fashioned, to answer that persistent call which had been growing inside me for weeks now. Every moment had become desperately precious.

With a sigh, she looked out toward the water, and I followed her gaze, watching the surface glisten with streaks of sunlight that made a tentative debut between the blanket of clouds. "I miss traveling."

I ran my fingers through the cool sand as a timid thought pulled at me once more. Since the moment I had decided to go on this journey, I kept seeing her with me, but the definitions of our relationship were still so tentative. How could I navigate a question like that?

"But it's time to start adulting, right?" she said with a chuckle, jolting me from my thoughts.

I shook my head playfully at her. "You do know that adulting is highly overrated."

She turned to me with a soft smile. "I'm beginning to realize that." Standing, she squinted down the beach to where her dog, Ziggy, was rolling around in the sand, kicking up his legs in exuberant animation. "So, when are you leaving?"

"The day after Thanksgiving."

"Oh, wow. That's really soon."

"I know." I stood and placed my hand on her arm. "Speaking of which, I'm sure you have plans with your family for Thanksgiving, but I wanted to invite you over to my place. I'm having a small gathering with a friend of mine and his son, and I would really love for you to be there."

She turned to me as the wind attempted to gather up her short hair, creating a halo above her. "I would really like that. My parents usually do an early dinner, so I could easily make room for a second one." A wide grin played across her face, filling my heart with buoyancy as the cautious steps of our growing relationship moved a little closer to each other.

Ziggy loped toward us and jumped onto my chest, his eager tongue colliding with my face.

"Ziggy!" Amelia yanked him down. "He really likes you," she said with a laugh.

I bent over and threaded my fingers through his dense, curly coat, scratching behind his ears. "I've always wanted to get a dog."

"Then why haven't you?"

I shrugged as I picked up a stick that lay beside me in the sand and threw it out toward the water, watching as Ziggy bound after it. "I used to work really long hours." I paused for a moment, realizing how untethered I had become from the life that had defined so much of me. I could barely recognize the woman I used to be. "It just felt cruel to leave an animal alone all day."

"That's too bad, but I caught the *used to,* there." She tilted her head at me. "Do you not work at your job anymore?"

"I quit recently."

"Really? Why did you quit?"

My thoughts tangled with her question like a relentless whisper. How long was I going to dance around the truth with her? "I needed to make some changes in my life."

Ziggy ran back to us, and Amelia flinched as he shook his coat vigorously and splattered her with sea water, causing laughter to tumble out. "Well, this has always been my favorite place to go with this crazy beast, so I was really happy you suggested we meet here."

I gazed out toward the lighthouse in the distance. "This used to be my place. I would come out here all the time when I was a kid and spend hours drawing." Memories of riding my bike down here when I was younger washed over me. Sitting perched on the large outcropping of rocks that jutted out to the water. Nothing but my notebook, pencil, and the sound of the ocean. Capturing the way the waves lapped beneath me, as if they could swallow up all my pain.

"Seriously?" Amelia's eyes lit up. "I used to draw all the time when I was a kid, too. My mom said I was always scribbling away in a notepad."

"I think you might have gotten that from me," I said with a small smile as we began to walk along the shoreline together, the placid waves teasing our feet. "And I'm so glad to see that you're still making art." I gazed into the sky as a flicker of sunlight burst through before it was enclosed once more in clouds. "It's really important to have something in life that defines us, something that no one can take away."

"It is." Amelia looked at me, her eyes full of a playful curiosity. "I wonder what else we have in common?"

"I want to be an open book with you, Amelia. Ask away."

"Okay, let's start with the basics. Favorite food." She pointed her finger at me with a grin.

"Um, I think I would have to say sushi."

"I freaking *love* sushi."

"Well, that's an easy one. I mean, who doesn't love sushi, right?" I said with a laugh. "Though I know some may argue with us on that one."

"True. What about favorite color?"

I looked down at my muted attire. "Black, I guess?"

"Well, that's obviously not mine." She motioned to her colorful skirt and brightly patterned jacket.

A warm smile bloomed across my lips as I looked at her. "No, you're a rainbow."

"Okay, what about your favorite way to unwind?"

"Very hot baths."

"Me, too!"

Her voice grew more animated as we continued our back-and-forth banter, seeming to revel in the tiny similarities between us, the intricate threads that bound us together.

"There is something I've been meaning to ask you." Amelia stopped walking and wrapped her arms around herself as a gust of chilly wind blew against us. "It's about my family history. All those boxes I can never fill out on my medical forms." She turned to me, looking abruptly pensive. "I've always wondered about it. I mean, do I have any genetic predisposition to anything?"

I sighed and ran my fingers through my hair. "Well, there is definitely alcoholism, anxiety, and depression that run on my side of things, but I don't know how much of that is circumstantial."

She tilted her head and regarded me with an open gaze full of questions, and my heart stilled. There it was. The cracked door I couldn't shut. I stared into her bright amber eyes, and I knew I had to tell her. She deserved the truth. If I wanted to continue this relationship with her, I couldn't hide this from her anymore. "Amelia." My voice came out dry and brittle as I struggled with my breath, struggled with the words that tore into me. That day I stood with Jasper beside the cliff, came rushing back, the parallel drawing goosebumps across my skin. "There *is* something I need to tell you."

"What?" Her face paled, and she blinked at me with wide eyes.

"I don't know if this is hereditary or not, but I have what is called Primary Cardiac Sarcoma."

She looked at me, her brow furrowing. "What is that?"

"It's a rare type of heart cancer."

The space between us became ominous and heavy as I watched Amelia grapple with what I had just revealed. Her face scrunched into a frown, and she let out a long burst of air between her lips. "What does that mean?"

I stepped closer to her, placing my hands lightly on her shoulders. "It means there is no cure, and that I only have a few more months left."

"You're dying?" Her words came out dissonant.

"Yes. I'm dying." There was a strength in that statement. A power I had never felt before. For the first time, I was owning this reality, bravely facing the monster before me, and it no longer seemed so vicious and cruel, only sorrowful and resolute.

I only wished I could transmute this feeling to her as her face crumbled before me, and she violently yanked herself away. Anger mixed with the trembling rise of tears swam in her eyes. "Did you only reach out to me because of this... because you're dying?"

I opened my mouth to speak, but all that came out was a strangled breath. My hands grasped at the air as if I could claw her back to me as she stood there shaking her head.

"I can't believe this... I can't." She blinked back her tears, her face awash in a torment that seemed to crush the oxygen from my lungs.

"Amelia. I'm so sorry."

"No." She threw the word at me like a buffer. "I can't do this... I have to go." Whipping around, she called out to Ziggy, her voice harsh and choked, the wind carrying her muffled pain across the water.

My heart lurched against my chest, and tears tumbled to the surface as I watched the outline of my daughter quickly recede into the distance, all the colors of her leaving me like a flash of light swallowed by the grey landscape of sand and sky.

And then she was gone.

Chapter Twenty

I sat in my living room, staring out into the dark of the sky, twining my hair around my finger as I replayed over and over what had happened on the beach. My heart sat heavy in my chest, and the bright spark that had been steadily burning inside was now faded to an ember choked out by the weight of Amelia's pain. I wanted so desperately to call her, but I knew she needed time to process the bomb I had just dropped.

Reaching for my phone, I dialed Quinn instead, knowing he would understand what I was going through. Once again, our worlds assembled like a mirror, reflecting the same struggles within.

"Hey, beautiful." The gentle sound of his voice was a lifeline, quelling the ache inside, and I let out a long breath as I released the events of the day to him, the splintered words and broken communication that now stood between Amelia and me.

"I'm so sorry." Quinn's words were low and filled with sympathy. "I guess it's my turn to say that all you can do is wait until she's ready to talk."

"I know." I sighed and ran my fingers absentmindedly across the couch, picking at the woven fibers. "I miss you."

"I miss you, too. I seem to be having a hard time going a day without you. Especially now that I know you'll be leaving soon." He spoke in a throaty whisper that made me long for the feel of his arms holding me, soothing away all the noise inside my mind. "I have Jasper until tomorrow morning, but why don't you come over?"

"Are you sure?"

"Julia." His voice grew firm, as if calling out my hesitancy, reminding me that we were way beyond the dancing around of formalities. "*Of course* I'm sure."

A tired smile slipped from the corners of my mouth. "Okay then."

"Good. I'll see you soon."

Hanging up the phone, I pulled myself off the couch and went into the bedroom to grab my toothbrush and a change of clothes. Stuffing everything into a bag, I turned to flick off the lights when a knock startled me. I moved to the door, my breath catching in my throat as I opened it to find Amelia standing there.

"I'm sorry for just barging over like this, but I need to talk to you, and I didn't want to do it over the phone." She ran her hand through her hair, a faint tremble visible in her fingers. "So, I googled your address. I hope that's okay." Her eyes were bloodshot and weary as they trailed down to the bag in my hands. "Oh, were you leaving?"

"No." I set the bag down in the corner and opened the door for her. "Please, come in." My voice wavered as relief flooded through me. "I'm really glad you're here."

She stepped into my apartment, taking in the view of the city that sprawled across the horizon. "Your place is really nice."

"Thanks," I said with a small smile as I closed the door behind me. She stood in the middle of the living room, her head tilted like a nervous bird, hands clenched tightly together as if afraid she was going to break something. I walked over to her, resisting the urge to reach out and place my hand on her shoulder, to pull her into my arms and feel her heartbeat against mine. For the first time, I finally understood what it felt like to be a mother, that longing to protect someone from the wounds that life inflicts, and the crushing pain when you realize you can't. That there are some things you can only watch unfold while you stand helpless and pleading.

Clearing my throat, I swept my arm out toward the couch. "Go ahead and make yourself comfortable. I can make us some tea if you'd like?"

"No thanks." She sat on the edge of the couch and looked up at me, her eyes wavering with tears. "I'm sorry I ran off like that today."

I shook my head, taking a seat beside her. "Don't be sorry. You had every right to react the way you did. I should have been honest with you from the very beginning."

"It wasn't just that." She twisted her fingers together and took a shaky breath. "I mean, I *was* angry. Really angry. But then I realized that it's not *you*." She wiped at a tear that had escaped down her cheek. "I had all these ideas in my head. Stories of us getting to know each other, things we would do together. I finally met you after all these years, and now you're being taken away from me. That's what I'm *really* angry about."

I reached my hand out to her, and she took it, the warmth of her skin cradled in mine. "I've spent a long time being angry myself. But you know what? A part of me is beginning to feel that this cancer, in some ways, has actually been a gift." Tears welled up as the enormity of it all hit me, and my voice wavered. "It made me stop and reevaluate my life. It made me realize how much I needed to change. I'm not the same person I was before my diagnosis. I wasn't ready to face my past. And honestly, I don't think you would've liked me very much."

"What do you mean?"

"Well," I said bluntly, "I was kind of a closed-off bitch."

Her face contorted into a hesitant smile, and she let out a

snort, causing a tangled laugh to spill from her lips. "I'm sorry," she choked. "It's not funny... I think I'm just feeling a little hysterical right now."

"No, it's okay. Maybe it *is* a little funny. The thing is, this cancer opened me up in a way I never thought was possible, and it brought me some wonderful things I never had before. One of them being *you*."

Amelia wiped away a tear and squeezed my hand, the reflection of light dancing in her eyes, the softness returning.

* * *

Night spilled across our laps as we sat side by side on the couch, sharing pieces of ourselves, stories of our lives, and all the years we had missed together. Amelia spoke of her childhood and of her travels after high school. She seemed to have embraced her life whole heartedly. Guided by an optimism of spirit and an intrinsic connection between herself and the world around her, possessing a wisdom seldom seen in someone her age. There was an unbroken ease and a quiet elation between us as we talked, and I cradled it close to me, reveling in the sweetness of our exchange.

Amelia stared at her phone, her eyes growing wide. "Oh, my God. I had no idea how late it was getting. I'm sorry. You probably want to get some sleep."

I waved my hand at her. "No, it's okay. I've been having such a good time talking with you."

"So have I," she said with a sigh. "I kinda don't want to leave."

I leaned forward, placing my cup of tea on the table beside the couch. "Why don't you stay then? This couch folds out into a bed." I motioned over to the cushions. "I've never used it before, but I'm sure it's pretty comfy."

Her eyes lit up. "I would love that."

"What about Ziggy, though?" I stood and stretched out my limbs, which had become numb from sitting in one place for so long, a sensation that had been growing more common lately. A tingle ran through them, the circulation struggling to regain itself.

"Oh, he has a doggy door, and I fed him before I left. He'll be fine." She stood with a wave of her hand and grabbed a cushion off the couch, placing it on the floor beside her.

"Okay, let me just go get some bedding for you then."

As I walked past the kitchen to grab some extra blankets from the bedroom, I noticed the blue glow of my phone in my purse, and I scrambled to answer it, realizing Quinn had probably been trying to call me for the past hour, wondering where I was.

"I'm so sorry, Quinn." I spoke into the phone as I made my way into the bedroom, my words breathless. "I didn't realize my ringer was turned off. Amelia stopped by as I was leaving, and we've been talking this whole time."

"*Jesus Christ,* Julia." His voice trembled with relief. "I was just about to pull Jasper out of bed and go over there. You scared the crap out of me."

"I'm sorry. I should have called. We just got caught up in conversation. I didn't mean to worry you." I sank onto the bed, realizing how fragile we had become to one another. One missed call, one late arrival, and we suddenly feared the worst.

"It's okay... I'm just so glad to hear your voice right now." He let out a long sigh. "How are things between you and Amelia?"

"Good, really good. In fact, she's going to be staying here tonight, so I won't be able to come over after all."

"You girls having a little slumber party?" he asked with a light chuckle.

"Yeah, something like that. I can come over tomorrow morning, though. I'll even bring breakfast if you'd like?"

"Mmmm... I'd like that *very* much." His voice took on a

raspy growl that hinted at more than breakfast, and my core tightened with the blush of arousal.

"Okay, then," I whispered back seductively, "I'll see you in the morning."

"I love you, Julia."

Warmth bloomed within, those three words a refuge that enfolded me. "I love you, too."

"I heard that." Amelia stood beside the couch with a playful grin as I returned with the blankets. "Who was that? Oh wait!" She wiggled her eyebrows at me. "He's that friend of yours you wanted me to meet, isn't he?"

I nodded, still feeling flushed from our brief correspondence over the phone. "Yes, he is."

"You guys sound pretty serious."

"We are." I placed the blankets on the couch and ran my hands through my hair with a soft smile.

She bit her lip, a sorrow sweeping across her face as she looked at me. "Does he *know*?"

"He does." I sat down for a moment, threading my fingers together. "He has cancer, too."

"Wait. What?" Amelia slowly lowered herself on the couch beside me, her eyes wide.

"That's how we met, at a support group."

"*Oh, my God...*" She gazed out the window, her brow furrowing as she took it all in. "You know, it's kinda beautiful in a way, though, don't you think?" She turned toward me, her eyes trembling with a wistful emotion. "Like star-crossed lovers."

I placed my hand on hers, the bittersweet reality of it reaching deep into me. "Yeah, maybe it is."

Turning down the lights in the living room, I watched a soft glow dance across the walls as I helped Amelia tuck the sheets and blankets into the fold-out couch. "You're right," she said as she nestled herself into the covers and let out a big yawn. "This bed is surprisingly comfortable."

"Oh, do you want me to go get you something to sleep in?"

"I'm okay. I have on my comfy pants that double as pajamas." Her head nestled into the pillow as she spoke, her eyes drowsy.

I sat beside her on the edge of the couch and leaned in, resting my hand on her shoulder. "Goodnight, Amelia." She smelled of shampoo, a floral scent reminding me of summer, and the prick of tears gathered in my eyes. I had missed so many of these moments with her. So many nighttime tuck-ins and bedtime stories, so many tears, scraped knees, and kisses that made it all better. How I wished I could go back and do it differently, to be the kind of mother she needed, but all I had left were stolen moments with a child someone else had loved in my place.

The familiar and bitter sting of regret rose within, threatening to pull me back down to its place of darkness, but then Amelia looked at me and murmured goodnight with a sleepy smile like a promise of absolution, and that was enough.

This moment was enough.

* * *

Morning woke me from a deep sleep full of bright color. The sensation of lightness rose within me as I got out of bed and peeked into the living room. Amelia was still awash in her own dreams. Her arm thrown back against the mattress, sheets tangled and spilling off the bed, as if she slept the same way she lived, unabashedly claiming the space around her, filling it with vibrancy. I stood there for a moment watching her, my heart dancing in my chest.

Quietly, I moved into the kitchen and put coffee into the machine to brew, the gurgle and hiss softly filling the room.

"Morning."

I turned to see Amelia sliding onto the barstool chair across the counter from me, her hair tousled from sleep.

"Oh, did I wake you? I was trying to be quiet."

"No." She shook her head and propped her elbows on the counter, resting her chin in her hands.

"Do you want some coffee?"

"Yes, please." Her sweet smile lit up the kitchen as I reached into the cupboard for the mugs and slid one over to her.

Wrapping her hands around the coffee, she stared into the murky depths before lifting her eyes to mine. "I want to spend as much time with you as I possibly can."

I leaned across the counter, my fingers brushing over hers. "Me too." The words spilled from me, no longer hesitant, but filled with resolve. "Amelia. I've been wanting to ask you this, but I didn't know how to at first." I took her hand and squeezed tightly, my warmth enfolding hers. "It would mean so much if you would consider coming with me to Tibet."

Light flickered in the depths of her gaze and a faint smile spread across her face. "I was hoping you would ask me."

Chapter Twenty-One

The rich aroma of spices from the turkey cooking in the oven drifted through my apartment as I stood beside the kitchen sink, peeling potatoes. A misty rain fell outside, obscuring the view from the window in a familiar palette of grey.

A knock on the door stirred me from my quiet thoughts, and I grabbed a dish towel, wiping my hands as I went to answer.

"Happy Thanksgiving!" Quinn's and Jasper's jubilant voices rang out in unison as they stood together in the hallway. Quinn held a bottle of cabernet, and behind him were two tall dark-haired women with matching smiles.

"Julia, these are my sisters I was telling you about, Trina and Tabitha." He swept his hand out toward them with a sheepish smile. "They kinda showed up and surprised me as we were heading out. I hope them coming over is okay? I know it's last minute."

"Of course. It's fine" A smile spread across my face as I opened the door for them to step inside. "I was actually worried that I had made too much food. So, this is perfect."

"It's such a pleasure to meet you, Julia. I'm Trina." Her hand enveloped mine in a firm shake. Wearing a sleek pantsuit, she radiated authority, her short bob peppered with strands of grey accentuating the plane of an angled jaw.

Her sister stood beside her, wearing a flowing dress of green indigo silk, her hair pulled into a messy bun, eyes soft and inviting. "And I'm Tabitha." She shot me a friendly wave as she looked around my apartment. "Thanks so much for letting us crash your dinner like this."

"It's not a problem at all," I said with a brush of my hand. "I'm glad I finally get to meet you two."

"You know, Quinn has been gushing about you for weeks now," Trina said, leaning in with a wink. Quinn gave me a slow smile as he helped Jasper out of his coat, watching while he bounded past us and into the living room.

"Wow, cool view!" I looked over to see Jasper pressing his face to the glass, his eyes wide with awe as he looked down at the city below.

From behind, Quinn slid his arms around me. "Hey there, beautiful." His voice was a whisper against my ear as he planted a quick kiss on my neck, and I leaned into him, my limbs growing languid as his breath teased my skin.

"I'm afraid I'm running a little behind on the food preparation," I said, motioning to the uncut potatoes still lying on the kitchen counter.

"And that's why we're here." Trina beamed. "Just show us the ropes, and we'll take over."

"Oh, no... you don't have to do that."

"Nonsense." Trina waved her hand at me. "You two sit back and relax."

"I think you should listen to Trina." Quinn shot me a playful smile. "She can be a little scary in the kitchen."

"I am *very* scary in the kitchen," Trina laughed as she grabbed an apron hanging on a peg by the fridge.

As I dictated the rest of the meal prep to Trina and Tabitha, Quinn opened the wine and poured us all a glass. "Here's to a beautiful life," he said, raising his glass to ours. The gentle clink of crystal filled the kitchen, preceded by a mournful silence that washed over all of us. The look in his sister's eyes were mirrors of unspoken sorrow, and I wondered if they knew about my own dance with time.

"Okay, let's get this show on the road, then." Trina clapped her hands and grabbed a pot by the sink, her bustling movements cutting through the sudden heaviness in the air.

Quinn took my hand and led me to the living room, settling onto the couch beside me. "When is Amelia supposed to show up?" He pulled me close and draped his arm across my shoulders, his fingers lightly running down my arm.

"She just called and said she was on her way."

Quinn nodded and looked over to where Jasper was holding a blown glass vase in his hands. "Hey, bud. Be careful with that."

"It's okay." I leaned into him, breathing in the rich spicy scent hovering on his skin. How I yearned to curl into his arms and lose myself in his eyes. Tomorrow, I would be leaving for Tibet with Amelia, and I wanted to savor every last moment together. "I don't care if he breaks it. It's just a vase," I whispered into his ear.

Quinn chuckled and ran his hands through my hair. "Well, it looks pretty expensive."

"It doesn't matter."

These days, all my possessions and money had begun to feel like nothing but objects that held me down, and I longed to release the burden of them all. I made a mental note to research charity organizations and to draw up a will when I got back. I had already decided the bulk of my finances would go to Amelia.

"Oh, wow. You have a smart oven!" Trina called out to me from the kitchen, jarring me from my thoughts. "I don't think I've ever seen one of these before."

"Yeah," I replied, taking a sip of my wine. "It came with the place. Do you want me to show you how it works?" I moved to pull myself from the couch, but Quinn placed his hand on my arm, shaking his head with a playful look in his eye.

"Oh, no. I got it figured out," Trina said with assurance as the sound of closing cupboards and sizzling vegetables in a pan filtered in from the kitchen.

"I have some news." Quinn took my hand in his as he spoke. His voice dropped to a whisper as he glanced over at Jasper, who had found my television and was now flipping through the channels, looking up at the big screen in a state of rapt attention. "My sisters just told me about this new clinical trial for pancreatic cancer patients."

"Really?" I shifted on the couch so I could face him better, resting the stem of my wine glass in my lap. "What is it?"

"Some new experimental drug that's supposed to bind around the pancreas and slow the growth of the cancer cells." He motioned toward Trina and Tabitha. "Those two, who apparently are just *full* of surprises, already got me approved for it. I start in a few days."

My heart fluttered with elation, and I threaded my fingers through his, squeezing tightly. "This is such great news. It could give you more time."

"I hope so. We'll see. It's still in phase one of trials." He brushed a strand of hair out of my face, his eyes full of his own gentle questions. "And what about you? Did you end up contacting that healer you found in Tibet?"

"I did. Yes." I looked down at my glass, my finger absentmindedly trailing across the condensation. "It's worth a shot, right?"

"It's worth *everything*." Quinn tipped my head up to meet his gaze, his eyes misty as he stroked my cheek with the pad of his thumb. "Every minute with you is precious to me, and I would move mountains to have as many of those with you as possible."

"I know."

My last bargaining chip was laid out between us, a thin sliver of hope dangling on a line of chance. Modern medicine had failed me. All I had left was a spiritual reprieve.

A knock on the door drew us from our moment of hushed words, and I rose from the couch. "That must be Amelia."

Trina took charge, opening the door in a flurry. The sound of cheery voices filtered through the apartment as Trina and Tabitha introduced themselves and ushered Amelia into the living room. Her cheeks were rosy from the cold, and rain dotted her eyelashes as I pulled her against me. "Thanks for coming."

"Thanks for inviting me." She looked around the room full of strangers, her eyes bright and open, taking in this assortment of family I had suddenly found myself a part of. How swiftly my life had stretched beyond the confinements I had erected, like a delicate gift I still wasn't sure was my own.

Quinn stood from the couch and extended his hand. "Amelia, it's so good to finally meet you."

A wide smile burst across her face as she took his hand in hers. "You, too."

Jasper had managed to wrench himself away from the television and was staring up at Amelia with a puzzled look on his face. "Are you Julia's sister?"

I let out a laugh and moved to ruffle his hair playfully. "Thanks for the compliment. But no, this is my daughter."

"Cool. I'm Jasper." He looked down at the bag in her hands. "What's in there?"

"Well, I happen to have a little thing for collecting games," Amelia said with a grin as she crouched down to open the bag, pulling out boxes of board games. "And I thought it might be fun to play some of these with everyone." Jasper knelt beside her as she handed him Clue. "I think you might like this one."

"Yes!" Jasper enthusiastically opened the box and began arranging the pieces along the board. "Can we play right now?"

"Sure." Amelia looked up at us with an encouraging wink. "You guys want to play?"

* * *

"So, you two are heading off to Tibet tomorrow?" Trina pointed her wineglass at us as we sat around the table together. Warmth and chatter filled the room as we finished up the last bit of food on our plates, while Tabitha brought in the pumpkin pie and ice cream.

"Yes, and I'm so excited," Amelia began. "I've never been to that part of the world before, but I've always wanted to go."

Quinn's hand found mine underneath the table and gave it a squeeze. A buoyant feeling of gratitude took flight beneath my chest as I entwined my fingers through his. My holidays had always been spent in silence, the weight of my loneliness a presence I constantly found myself running from. As if I could convince myself it was only an illusion, when in fact it was the very fiber of my soul crying out to be seen.

I looked at Quinn, caught in the anchoring depths of his gaze. Here I was, surrounded by people who were all connected by this delicately beautiful and impermanent thread of existence, and love was at the center of it all, the breath that kept our hearts beating, the music to our dance. A song I was only beginning to discover.

"Shall we bust out some Scrabble?" Tabitha asked with a wide smile as we finished our dessert.

A bustle of activity followed while dishes were cleared, and chairs scooted back from the table. I grabbed the empty bottles of wine and headed toward the kitchen while Quinn, Jasper, and Amelia set up the board in the living room. "Let's do teams, Dad." I heard Jasper call out.

"Oh, I kinda like that idea." Amelia looked back at me with a grin. "You want to be on my Scrabble team?"

"Of course, I would love to," I said as a warm smile bloomed across my face.

"You know, Julia," Trina said, sidling up next to me in the kitchen while Tabitha ran hot water over the dishes in the sink, "I have to say, you seem to have quite an effect on our little brother." A soft smile stretched across her face. "Despite the current circumstances." She paused for a moment, a sadness flickering in her eyes as she glanced at Quinn, who was hunched over his tiles with Jasper, debating what word to spell first. "I can't remember the last time I've seen him this happy."

"I can't either." Tabitha turned off the water and leaned against the counter, regarding me with a steady gaze. "What happened with Bethany really messed him up. I think he's been reluctant to let anyone in since then."

My mind flashed back to that moment in his living room, the night I released myself to him. *It's all or nothing with me,* he had said with such burning conviction, tearing down my fragile walls. That statement was a force which had propelled me to him, but I hadn't known at the time how powerful it really was. We had both let our walls down and chosen each other. Tears pricked at my eyes, and I hastily moved to brush them away.

"Oh, honey, let those tears come." Tabitha moved closer to me and placed her hand on my shoulder, her face full of tenderness. "Do you know what an incredible gift you two are to each other?"

I met her open gaze with trembling lips. "Do you know about me?"

She nodded, needing no further explanation. Her eyes spoke for both of us. "I do." Pulling me close, her words fell against my ear. "And I believe the two of you have been waiting for each other."

"It feels like that." Unbidden, my tears leaked onto the shoulder of Tabitha's silk dress, staining the green to black. "I just wish I knew how much time we have."

Tabitha pulled back and gave me a sad smile, the corners of her eyes dancing with tears of her own. "Do any of us ever really know how much time we have?"

* * *

The evening had grown late. Remnants from dinner had been put away hours ago, the board games tucked neatly back into their boxes, and the air infused with a drowsy hum that settled around us. The soft murmur of conversation drifted in from the living room as I stood in the bedroom, surveying my suitcases neatly packed and resting along the far wall.

Quinn came up from behind and slid his arms around me, placing a lingering kiss on my neck. "My sisters are going to stay with Jasper tonight." His voice was throaty against my ear, causing an ache to wash over me, weakening my limbs.

"Oh, really?" I breathed, leaning against him. "Does that mean you're staying over?"

His lips lazily ran down my neck, his breath teasing my skin. "Only if you want me to."

"Hey, you guys." Trina's voice startled us from our stolen moment, and I pulled away from Quinn as she stepped into the room. "We're going to call it a night and get Jasper into bed. That little guy is all tuckered out." She shot me a wink. "Thanks for the great dinner."

"Thanks for helping cook it," I replied with a smile as Quinn and I followed her back into the living room.

There was a flurry of coats being put on and animated but hesitant goodbyes. Trina and Tabitha pulled me into long, crushing hugs, smelling faintly of flowers and wine. "Thank you for finding our brother." Trina grasped my hands tightly as we stood in the doorway together, the last bits of the evening hovering between us. "I feel good knowing he has you in his life. And please, don't ever hesitate to reach out to either of us if you guys need anything."

"Of course." I squeezed her hand before she let go and sprinted after Jasper and Tabitha, who held the elevator door open for her, their voices disappearing behind the closing doors.

Amelia stood beside me, her eyes bright with enthusiasm as she leaned in for a hug. "I'll see you at the airport tomorrow morning."

I enfolded my arms around her, feeling the healthy pulse of her beating heart close to mine. "I can't wait."

I shut the door behind us, enclosing the apartment in a sudden stillness, with only the sound of the rain pattering steadily upon the roof. Quinn's eyes burned with heat as he gently backed me up against the door and drew me into a lengthy kiss that stole my breath and spoke of all the promises we made together in the dark.

"God, you make me so love-drunk," he growled in my ear, sending a tantalizing shiver across my skin.

I chuckled and sucked in a hiss of air as his hands ran a slow trail underneath my dress to the soft flesh of my inner thigh. "Are you sure that isn't the wine talking?"

"No. It's *definitely* you," he murmured as his mouth slid down to my neck. "I didn't even finish my glass from earlier."

Inching my leg up, I wrapped it around his waist, urgently pressing into him as I grasped at his shirt.

With a groan, he pulled back. "Okay, as much as I want to take you up against this door right now, I have plans to savor every inch of you tonight." Taking my hand, he led me into the bedroom and turned on the lamp beside us, flooding the room with a soft amber light. "And I want to see all of you."

With a sigh, I lowered myself onto the bed. I had always preferred being with him in the dark. The grip of cancer muted and set aside when touch replaced sight. Hesitation hovered within me as I slowly slid down the straps of my dress and unhooked my bra, revealing what was left of a body receding. A body that reminded me of all the things his hands made me forget.

As if reading my mind, he bent in front of me, drinking me in with the intensity of his eyes while his hands traced the slope of my breasts, cupping loose skin which once held form. "Every time I look at you, all I see is beauty." He leaned in and brushed his lips across my nipples, the warmth of his mouth replacing the fabric that had clung to my skin as his hands slid the rest of the cloth down my hips. "You are such an endless landscape to me, Julia."

Vanquished by the blaze of his sentiment, I gripped his hair, drawing him close to me as my words brushed across his cheek. "And you are the one who brought it to life."

* * *

Night deepened around us, pulling strands of moonlight through the curtains of the bedroom. Propped up on his elbow, Quinn gazed at me, coiling my hair through his fingers. "Is it selfish of me to admit there's a part of me that doesn't want you to go? I'm going to miss you like crazy."

"I am, too." Pulling him close to me, I ran my hand across the plane of his back, suspended in a state of elation as I came down from our tangled high, my body humming with energy. "I wish you could come with me."

"If only I could." His lips rested against my neck, his voice smokey. "Two weeks is such a long time."

I tilted his face to mine, my fingers running over the stubble along his jaw. "I'll be back before you know it. In the meantime, you have some cancer to fight."

"I guess I do, don't I?" He nodded, his tone growing somber. "And maybe you do as well?"

"We'll see."

A sad smile rested on my lips. I knew the healer in Tibet wouldn't be able to cure my cancer. There was no cure. All he could promise me was a lessening of my symptoms, a brief alleviation from the fatigue and shortness of breath. A gentle push against the quickening of time.

"I'm really glad Amelia is going to be there with you. The thought of something happening, and you being alone..." He trailed off, a look of apprehension sweeping across his face.

Rolling him onto his back, I slid on top, pressing my body into his warmth. "Don't worry. Everything's going to be okay."

"We don't know that, Julia."

I placed a soft kiss on his lips, stilling his words. "True, but I'm going to be bold and believe that it will be."

Chapter Twenty-Two

The bustle of people around us was a steady hum as Quinn and I stood together at the entrance of the airport.

"I already miss you," he whispered as his arms enfolded me.

"Me, too." A tight band of reluctance clung to me, and I found it hard to extract myself from his arms. Cupping his cheek, I swept my thumb across his lips as early morning crept through the windows of the airport, bathing his face in soft light. "You have the number of the place we'll be at in Lhasa, and I'll call you when we get there."

Quinn nodded and released me, turning to Amelia with a playful grin. "You take care of her for me, okay?"

"Of course." She smiled up at him as she grabbed her duffle bag and swung it over her shoulder.

I love you, Quinn mouthed to me as he stood with his hands in his pockets, watching while we made our way toward the security line. I turned back to catch one last glance at him, his eyes never leaving mine until the crush of people swallowed him from view.

"The way he looks at you." Amelia shook her head, a wistfulness gathering in her eyes. "One day, I hope I find someone who looks at me that way."

"Oh, you will," I said with tenderness. "You're only twenty-one. You are going to have a lifetime of guys lining up to love you."

She shrugged and adjusted the shoulder strap on her bag. "I don't know... I just don't get guys sometimes. One day they're admiring you with their puppy dog eyes, and then the next minute, they tuck tail and run."

I laughed, running my hands through my hair. "Yeah, guys can be weird like that. But *some* of them do grow up eventually."

She smirked and then drew in a breath, her brows knitting together. "But sometimes I wonder if I only *think* that's what I want because society has convinced me." A tiny spark lit within her eyes. "There's actually this girl at my work who I think I might have a little crush on."

A smile stretched across my face, touched by the fact she felt comfortable enough to share that with me. "Well, I think that might be something worth exploring, don't you think?"

A mottled blush spread across her cheeks as she glanced at me. "Maybe."

"Amelia..." I stopped walking and placed my hand on her shoulder. "If there's one thing I've learned recently, it's that life is too short to hide away from the things that could bring us happiness."

She took a deep breath, that hopeful spark of youth dancing in her gaze. "You're right. It's just so hard to put yourself out there sometimes."

"Believe me, I know how hard it is. But it's *always* worth the risk. When you find the courage to be vulnerable, that's when you truly find yourself."

"Have you found yourself?"

Her question hit me like a wave. *Had I found myself?* Releasing my hand from her shoulder, I gave her a smile. "I think I've found enough parts of myself to have the strength to find the rest."

The jostle of people around us stirred us from our moment,

THE LIFE WE DREAM OF

and we continued walking, allowing the rush of bodies to propel us forward as Amelia reached out and slipped her hand through mine.

* * *

I slept through most of the trip, fatigue gripping me like a vice as the next thirty-two hours became a blur of airports, drink carts, and layovers. Amelia took charge, navigating us through the terminals and flight changes, gently nudging me awake every so often to make sure I had something to eat and drink.

I sat next to the window, watching the clouds drift below us, suspended in a dream-like state, the seat beneath, my only anchor between earth and sky. Our last flight out had been from Beijing, a large, pulsing airport filled with flashing neon signs and a cacophony of electronic voices spilling from speakers in a foreign tongue. It was chaotic and dissonant, and I looked forward to the quiet reprieve of the mountains that awaited us in Tibet.

"Oh, I almost forgot," Amelia said as she dug through her bag and handed me a bottle. "It's Ginko Biloba. It's supposed to help you with the altitude when we get there."

"Thanks." I took the bottle from her. "You know, you don't have to stay at Lhasa with me the whole time. You can do some traveling on your own if you want."

She followed my gaze out the window, a flicker of hesitancy flashing across her face. "I might. I just want to make sure you acclimate first."

Amelia had apparently done extensive research on the altitude of the region before we left, expressing concern over the condition of my heart and how it might affect me. And so we had decided I would venture no higher than Lhasa. I knew it was still a risk, but one I was willing to take. I did not want to spend my last moments making choices based on fear. I had spent my whole life doing that.

Amelia tapped on the computer screen attached to the seat in front of her. "We're almost to Lhasa," she said with growing enthusiasm. "Just one more hour to go."

Leaning against the seat, I turned to her. "I've been meaning to ask you, Amelia. Do your parents know you're traveling with me?"

She nodded and shifted her position, folding her knees onto the seat as she faced me. "Yeah, I've told them everything."

"And they're okay with it all?" I tried to imagine what it would feel like to have a child whom you loved and raised as your own, suddenly establish a relationship with their birth mother. Would there be some lingering concern?

"Of course. They've been really supportive. In fact, they were the ones who convinced me to reach out to you in the first place."

"Really?" I leaned forward in my seat.

She shrugged, her fingers fiddling with the fabric of her pants. "Yeah. I guess they thought it would help me discover more about myself, to find all those missing pieces I always wondered about."

I rested my hand on hers. "And have you?"

She looked at me, her brow furrowing in thought. "I think I have."

"I think I found some of those missing pieces, too." With a smile, I squeezed her hand and closed my eyes, resting my head against the seat as the lure of dreams beckoned me back into their encompassing fold.

I awoke to Amelia's soft voice in my ear. "We're about to land."

The plane jolted as it made its slow descent into Lhasa's Gonggar airport. Pulling myself from the haze of sleep, I gazed down at the snow-covered mountains that loomed below, their peaks rising above the clouds in a majestic display, leaving me dizzy.

The plane hit the tarmac and slowed to a shuddering stop, the whine of the motor dying to a soft hum. The sudden shifting of bodies filled the cabin with sound while I stared out the window, a tug of excitement growing within.

I was here. I was in Tibet with my daughter.

* * *

I stood on the balcony of our hotel room, the steep rise of the Himalayan Mountain range surrounding us like an enfolding embrace. My eyes followed the last rays of the sun as it dipped behind the peaks, washing the sky in a vibrant shade of pink and gold.

The air was thin, and the short walk to the room had winded me considerably, but there was a crisp tang to the evening that lifted my spirits. A mixture of wind, snow and the faint hint of incense wafted from the marketplace below. The melodic tinkling of bells and the murmuring of voices rose from the street and curled around me in a comforting song, filling me with a mixture of elation and sorrow. There was so much beauty in the world, and I wanted more time with it.

"Oh my God. This place is so amazing," Amelia said with a sigh as she joined me on the balcony. Zipping up her jacket, she leaned against the railing, soaking in the expansive view stretched out before us. Hugging the slopes of the plateau, the snow-capped mountains jutted upward, piercing the sky, the magnitude of them beckoning forth a persuasive sensation of awe.

I nodded and reached out to give her shoulder a gentle squeeze. "I'm so glad you're here to share this with me."

"So am I." She turned to me with a soft smile. "Are you going to see that healer tomorrow?"

"I am." The chill of the wind settled into my skin, and I pulled my sweater tight around me. "We'll see if he has something that will help."

Amelia's eyes lit up with the press of hope, a tiny bud unfurling within the landscape of uncertainty, and I tried to extract that same feeling for myself. But I knew I did not have enough currency to bargain with time. Nothing was guaranteed. All I had left was the courage to keep trying.

"How are you feeling?"

"Tired. But I'm always tired these days."

"Why don't you go lie down, and I can grab some food for us?" Her voice was tinged with concern as she bent to retrieve a bottle of water that had been sitting on the table beside us. "And don't forget to hydrate." She handed the bottle to me with a playful wink.

Her fussing filled me with warmth. The tender feeling of being cared for was a soothing balm stretched over skin which had been exposed to the elements for far too long. I clasped the bottle in my hand as a heaviness settled into my limbs. "I will. I'm just going to give Quinn a quick call first."

Amelia slipped out of the hotel room, and I sank onto the bed, the silk brocade blanket shifting beneath me as I took out my phone and dialed Quinn's number. I knew it was late where he was, but he had told me he would be waiting for my call.

"Hello, beautiful. You made it."

Quinn's voice was soft with sleep. The deep and gentle resonance of his words were a delicate cord connecting across the thousands of miles now stretched between us.

"I did."

"How is it over there?"

"It's breathtaking." I leaned back against the pillows, watching the last bit of vivid color wash across the darkening sky. "Everything is so quiet here, even though we're staying in the city."

"Mmm... I wish I was there with you." The sound of rustling blankets drifted through the receiver as Quinn shifted in bed. "I'd be holding you right now."

A smile bloomed on my lips, and I could almost feel his arms around me, his touch rinsing away all the fatigue that clung to my skin and burrowed beneath my bones. "I wish you were here, too. You should see the sunset. It's so beautiful."

Afternoon spilled through the thin clouds, casting prisms of shadowed light across brick buildings as we navigated our way through the cobbled streets of Lhasa. The storefronts wore cheerful displays of colors set against an array of gilded Buddha statues and handheld prayer wheels.

The rich burgundy fabric of robes trailed past us as monks made their way into the large ornate building of the Jokhang temple. I stopped walking and took in the striking sweep of the roof that looked as if it had been dipped in gold. Decorative engravings lined the building, its walls splashed in vivid colors of orange and yellow, accentuated by tones of deep blue. The pictures I had seen in my travel book did not do justice to the vibrance now in front of me.

I took a deep breath, the air thick with the overwhelming scent of burning incense. Notes of juniper wafted from the entrance, which was crowded with people prostrating, their arms and legs spread out upon the ground, creating a fluid wave of movement, lost to the rhythm of their own silent prayers.

I had a sudden urge to join them. To kneel on the ground and offer myself up to an unseen force greater than my own mind. What kind of peace would I have found in my life if only I had believed in something? Learned how to relinquish my control to a faith that cradled me in the whisperings of absolution.

"Is it okay if you meet me back here after your appointment?" Amelia pointed to the temple. "I would really like to spend some time inside."

"Of course." I retrieved the piece of paper from my pocket that I had scrawled the physician's address on and glanced down the street. "I shouldn't be no more than an hour."

With a wave, Amelia strolled toward the temple doors, pulled on the frayed multi-colored rope that hung against the deep scarlet paint, and disappeared into the fold of the corridor.

Following the worn brick beneath my feet, I navigated through the crowd of people, glancing over at doorways in search of the doctor's office. In the distance, the whitewashed stone and infinite windows of the Potala Palace loomed above me like its own sacred mountain, terraces of long stairs rising upward.

I spotted the address of the office, and placed my hand on the brass knob, a melody of bells tinkling softly above as I opened the door. The scent of sweet resin hit me as I stepped inside. Pale gauzy curtains blocked out the bustle of the street, and my eyes fell to the walls, adorned with tapestries depicting various Buddhist deities, the serenity on their faces instantly calming my nerves.

"You must be Julia?" A man appeared from the hallway. His dark, smiling eyes crinkled around the edges as he spoke, hair peppered with faint strands of grey. "It is pleasure to meet you."

His soft voice held notes of a thick accent as he walked forward and extended his hand, his grip warm and firm. "I'm Doctor Kunchen."

I nodded. "Thank you for seeing me on such short notice."

Our correspondence had consisted of only a handful of brief emails after I had stumbled across him on the internet a few weeks before. A shot in the dark that he had assured me held a promise of light.

"No problem at all." He motioned down the hall for me to follow. "So glad you could come."

Settling myself in a chair next to him, I watched him briefly look at the notes on his desk before reaching over and taking my wrist. His face was furrowed in concentration as his fingers rested lightly against my vein. "You have deep pulse." He released my hand and motioned for me to open my mouth, peering at my tongue. "Deep pulse and too much Loong."

"What does that mean?"

His eyes filled with sorrow. "The cancer inside you is moving too fast. Stealing your Qi. Your life energy."

The words pressed against me, crushing whatever vague hope I had nurtured before coming here. "How fast?"

"Faster than would like to see." He rose from his seat and walked to a cabinet by the far wall, opening drawers and pulling out various bags of dried herbs. "I make mixture for you to take every day with hot water. It will help body with symptoms. To slow down disbalance." He began deftly measuring out the bags into a glass jar as he continued to speak. "I would also like you to come back in few days for stylostixis and moxibustion treatment."

"And what is that, exactly?" I folded my arms across my chest as I tensely leaned forward in my chair, unfamiliar with the terminology.

"Acupuncture and heat therapy." Closing the lid on the jar, he regarded me with a somber look. "What I practice is called

Sowa Rigpa. The science of healing. It is relationship between mind, body, and environment." He returned to his chair beside me, placing the jar of herbs on his desk. "Your mind has been in suffering for long time. Disease be traced back to Karma. The inherent nature of self is battling with body. You need to find balance."

My throat felt dry as I struggled with my words. "And will this help me find balance?"

"It will help." He shifted in his seat, folding his hands in his lap. "But to purify and minimize your karmic influences, you must seek Semde. The clear and natural mind. Meditation is way to achieve this."

I nodded and bit my lip, staring up at a painting of Buddha which hung behind him on the wall. His calm, knowing gaze penetrating through the layers of paint and canvas.

Doctor Kunchen leaned forward, resting his hand on my arm, his eyes open and warm. "Death is only another journey. It is not death we run from. It is fear. When you learn to embrace fear, to face karma from this life, there will be no more suffering. You will find release of fear. You will find Semde."

I stared at him, trying to grasp the complexities of what he was trying to say. "And meditation can help with the fear?"

He nodded slowly. "The mind is like child, always running. You need to be like mother. Have gentle spirit. Sit with child." He placed his hand over his heart, his wizened smile enveloping me in a feeling of love, like a father's comfort I never knew.

Tears gathered in the corners of my eyes, and I let them fall, knowing I was safe with this man who spoke soft wisdom in a quiet room surrounded by mountains and sky. We sat in silence for a moment, his eyes calm pools of compassion, patiently holding space for me as I allowed the swell of acceptance to release and trickle down my skin.

* * *

I stood at the entrance to the Jokhong Temple, my hand pressed against the worn grooves of the painted wood. A hushed stillness settled over me as I stepped inside the dimly lit building. Removing my shoes, I placed them beside the assortment of others that lay neatly arranged by the door like well-behaved children awaiting the return of their parents.

My bare feet padded silently upon the tile floor of the corridor as I passed people in various states of prayer, strings of beads entangled between their fingers.

Transfixed, I stared at the dazzling array of color. Walking past cushions nestled beside columns draped in cloth, I came to a large Buddha which sat as the centerpiece of an open room. Surrounding the base of the statue, lay flickering votive candles, and offerings of flowers, jewelry, and fruit.

A hand rested on my shoulder, and I turned to see Amelia standing beside me. "It's pretty incredible in here, isn't it?" She spoke in a whisper as she pointed to the golden Buddha in front of us, adorned with a headdress of jewels. "I was just talking to one of the monks here in the temple. This statue is one of the most sacred to the Tibetan Buddists. It's called Jowo Rinpoche. The Precious One." She knelt and settled herself on a cushion, patting the space next to her.

I joined her on the floor, drawing my knees to my chest as thoughts tumbled around in my mind, a relentless pull of questions with no answer. As if sensing my distraction, Amelia leaned in close to me. "How did it go with the doctor?"

"He gave me some herbs and wants me to come back for some further treatment." I smiled wanly at her, my voice matching her hushed tone. "He says I need to meditate."

"Really?" She swept her hand out towards the room. "Well, I guess you're in the right place for that."

"I guess I am. He also spoke of karma in our lives and how it affects our health." I bit my lip, recalling his words to me as we sat together in his office, laying bare the truth that my body was only giving up the fight my mind had started so many years before.

Amelia regarded me in silence for a moment. "Do you believe that's true?"

I looked up into the tranquil features of the Buddha which seemed to gaze down at me as if he held the silent answers hidden within the folds of his offerings. "A part of me thinks there's some truth to that. I have lived so much of my life running from the pain of my past. Cut off from myself."

"And is there something still holding you back from releasing that pain?"

Her frankness stilled my breath, extracting a truth I was still reluctant to face. My vision wavered as my words stumbled out in a long shuddering sigh. "My father. I still hold a lot of anger for what he did to my mother. For what he did to me."

Amelia entwined her fingers through mine. "Maybe this is the place where you're meant to let all that go."

Chapter Twenty-Three

Sitting cross-legged on the bed of the hotel room, I flirted with the idea of stillness. I had never sat within the space of my mind and allowed it to cease its constant chatter. To no longer give weight to its demands. The endless barrage of thoughts had always been my companion, a buffer from the loneliness of my life.

But the loneliness wasn't there anymore. I searched around for it, but it had quietly slipped away, leaving only a soft tenderness behind. Within the gentle eyes of my daughter and the encompassing support of Quinn, I was buoyed by something greater than I could ever have envisioned. I had found love within myself.

Amelia breezed in, pulling me from my silence and trailing the scent of onions, garlic, and ginger in her wake. Her cheeks were flushed from the bite of the wind, which blustered outside, sending the colorful prayer flags across the street into a frenzied dance outside the window. She set the paper bag on the bed beside me, pulling out what looked like dumplings, aromatic steam rising from within the thick dough.

"I got us some momos," she said with a wide smile. "You have to try these. They're *so* good." She flopped down on the bed beside me and began to root through the bag. "Did you ever get ahold of Quinn today?"

I shook my head, trying to push back the nagging concern which had taken root. "No, his phone's been turned off. I'm sure he's with Jasper or something." I reached over and took one of the dumplings from her hand. "I know he just finished up his fourth day of that experimental therapy."

"Oh, yeah?" She looked over at me as she bit into her Momo. "And how's that been going?"

"It seems to be good so far. He did complain of a headache the other day when I talked to him on the phone, but other than that, he said he's been feeling fine."

With a sigh, I glanced out the window as the last bit of daylight was swallowed up by the darkness. A part of me wished I was there with him. The distance between us left me stretched in two directions. But I knew that we were both on our own private journey of healing, and our roads would eventually lead us back to each other.

"You miss him, don't you?" Amelia roused me from my thoughts.

Turning toward her, I leaned back against the pillows. "I do."

She smiled and scooted closer to me on the bed. "So, how exactly did you guys become close, if you don't mind me asking? I mean, who made the first move?" She wiggled her eyebrows playfully at me.

I let out a small chuckle. "Well, it was me, actually. But it didn't go too well the first time... or the second time, for that matter." I inwardly cringed as I recalled that tense moment between us in the kitchen, and the catalyst which made me finally break down my walls. "I needed to find the strength to open myself up."

"I'm so glad you have someone like that in your life. Someone who challenges you." Amelia ran her fingers across the bedspread, tracing the patterns embroidered into the cloth. "I remember when you showed up at my house the day we first met. And you just looked so sad." She glanced up at me, her eyes piercing into mine. "But you don't look that way anymore."

I stared at her for a moment, awash in the truth of her statement. "Do you know how beautiful you are, Amelia?"

She shot me a sheepish look and raked her fingers through her hair. "Uh, thanks. I guess I have you to thank for that," she said with a shrug.

"I'm not talking about the way you look, though you *are* gorgeous." I smiled at her and took a bite of the Momo, the savory juices filling my palate. "I'm talking about who you are. And for that, you have your parents to thank."

Her gaze flickered with emotion. "Do you ever think about what would have happened if you hadn't given me up for adoption?"

I grabbed a napkin from the bag and wiped my fingers. "All the time. But you were meant to have the family that you do. For years, I've carried so much regret about giving you up, but I don't anymore. In a way, even though I was never able to be your mom, I was able to give you the chance to have the best life possible." I reached out and touched her arm. "And *that* I would never take back."

She leaned into me, resting her head on my shoulder. "You're my mom, too, you know."

Her words were sunlight, filtering through the depths and exposing all the shadowed places inside me, and I choked back the tears that threatened their way to the surface. "You don't know how much that means to me, but I don't think I deserve the title."

She sat up and took my hand in hers. "But it's true. I *have* a mom, an amazing, wonderful mom who raised me and loved me with everything she had in her." She squeezed my hands, her eyes full of conviction. "But I also have a mom who gave birth to me, who gave me the chance at life. I wouldn't exist if it weren't for you."

I allowed the tears to slip down my cheeks. Her words were a beautiful offering, an invitation for me to step fully into her life. For the first time, I was given the chance to explore what it would feel like to be a mother. The impact of this was overwhelming and profound.

My voice came out in a choked whisper as I pulled her close and wrapped my arms tightly around her. "Thank you, Amelia."

A brisk wind blew against us as Amelia and I walked through the market. The aroma of incense mixed with spices from the vendor stalls lining the streets filled me with an intoxicating lightness. There was a humming energy within this city that seemed to infuse the air. Color and life teemed around every corner, and beneath it all lay the pulse of reverence as hundreds of spiritual seekers crowded the streets and spilled from the temples. Time took on a new meaning here; it was slow and humble, giving room for something new to take root.

We ducked inside a small store selling trinkets. Amelia walked beside me, scanning the tables, her fingers running over painted statues and prayer flags. She picked up a small, carved wooden flower with intricate petals unfolding. Holding it in the palm of her hand, her eyes grew wide as she looked at me. "This reminds me of a dream I had last night. We were here in Tibet, standing in the marketplace." She stretched out her arm, gesturing to the street outside. "And you were holding something in your hand." She furrowed her brow as if lost in thought for a moment. "I asked you what it was, and you said it was your heart, that you wanted me to have it." She set the carving down on the table, tracing the petals. "But when you gave it to me, it wasn't your heart at all. It was a rose, a huge red rose with its petals wide open."

Amelia wandered past the table to a rack of scarves, and I scrambled for my purse, retrieving a few bills and handing them to the woman who sat beside the cash register. My breath hitched in my throat and goosebumps trailed along my arms as I picked up the carved flower and discreetly slipped it into my coat pocket.

I drew her close to me as we stepped out of the store. "You know, I used to think our dreams were just repressed emotion, things we were too afraid to face. But I'm beginning to realize they are much more than that."

"I think so, too." She gazed up into the opaque sky with a faint smile, her eyes dancing across the expanse above us. "I think so many of our dreams are, in fact, messages. We just have to be willing to listen to them."

Arm in arm, we continued down the street, the old stone beneath us bearing the weight of all the many steps taken. The ones that came before us and the ones yet to be made. I didn't know how many I had left, but in this moment, walking beside Amelia, surrounded by sacred temples and breathtaking mountains, everything felt limitless.

The next morning, we stood outside the hotel room together. Dawn had stretched across the sky, showering the buildings in a rosy glow.

"I wish I could come with you."

"I wish you could, too. But the elevation is just too high up there." Amelia adjusted the straps on her backpack and slid it over her shoulders. "It's only a two-and-a-half-hour drive by bus to Yamdrok Lake. I'll be back this evening."

"You don't need to come back so soon, you know. You can stay overnight if you want."

She placed her hand on my arm. "I only plan to be gone for the day." She nodded up at the hotel room with a smile. "The beds here are just too comfortable to miss out on."

I could see that twinge of concern in her eyes as she spoke. She didn't want to admit it to me, but I knew she was scared. My cancer had become a lurking monster to her, waiting to snatch me up in the dark unaware. I had caught her the other night while she thought I was asleep, her hand hovering over my chest, watching the slow rise and fall of my breath.

"So, what are *you* going to do today?"

Amelia's question tugged me from my thoughts, and I glanced into the sky as the rays of the sun flirted with the deep blue, staining it a pale pink like watercolor spilled across a damp page. "Well, I have that acupuncture appointment with the doctor. And then I think I'll maybe go visit one of the temples and do some meditation." I gave her a smile. "You know, try to find my inner Zen."

"Well, I hope you find it." She pulled me in for a quick hug. "I'll see you soon, okay?"

With a nod, I watched as she made her way down the long stretch of empty street before shooting me a wave and disappearing around a corner.

I wrapped my sweater around myself, looking forward to a day full of quiet introspection. This place cradled me, washing out all the debris and leaving a stillness behind. It was a sensation unfamiliar but deeply comforting, and for a moment, my sickness did not feel so pressing and ominous.

* * *

Afternoon light glinted off the mountains as I meandered through the streets of Lhasa toward the physician's office. Approaching the Jokong Temple, I ran my hand along the inscriptions of the large gold-and-bronze prayer wheels outside the entrance. Amelia had explained to me that these represented *the turning wheel of dharma*, sending your blessings and prayers out into the universe.

I closed my eyes for a moment, evoking a prayer as I slowly turned the wheel. It wasn't a prayer born of words but more a yearning fashioned from a sensation of peace. A growing strength inside that plucked at the shadowed pieces of my past, unraveling them gently into the endlessness of the sky. It was a prayer for acceptance.

I continued walking, feeling buoyed as I slipped past the market stalls with their beckoning scents of spices and herbs. The bustle of people created a hum that surrounded me, enfolded me, the streets alive with color and movement. And I was a part of it all. A tiny spark of life briefly dancing among so many others.

The bell sang above me as I opened the door to the doctor's office.

"Welcome back, Julia." The soft cadence of his voice filtered from the hall, and he appeared from a room, his eyes warm as he nodded for me to follow him to his office.

A raised table now stood in the center of the room with a white cloth draped over the cushions.

"Please." He swept his hand toward the table. "Remove shirt and shoes and make yourself comfortable. I will be back soon." He glided from the room, closing the door softly behind him.

Removing my shirt and shoes, I positioned myself on the table and leaned back, drawing the thin sheet to my shoulders. I looked around the room, noticing the cracks and chips in the paint, the worn desk in the corner. There was no sleek furniture, pretty flowers, or potted plants. No music drifting through speakers or magazines to distract you. Other than the few tapestries that adorned his walls, there was a stark simplicity to his office, a disrepair that spoke of honesty. Wood becomes worn, cracks appear in paint, the blemishes of life were not meant to be disguised.

The door opened, pulling me from my thoughts, and I looked over to see various thin needles and herbs arranged neatly on the tray he carried in his hands.

"Ready?"

I nodded and adjusted the sheet around my shoulders. "I've never done acupuncture before. Will it hurt?"

Setting the tray on the counter beside us, he retrieved a small tube from a drawer and began to fill it with the herbs from the tray. "You may feel small poke at beginning. But pain is very mild. Should be no discomfort when needles are fully inserted." His fingers fell to my wrist, searching for the pulse beneath. "If I could have you move to stomach, we will begin."

"Of course." Shifting on the table, I rolled over and rested my head on the cushion. "And what are the herbs for?"

"Moxibustion." Pulling the sheet to my waist, his hands lightly pressed along my back. "This treatment I give you today, help in removing blockage of energy. Blockage of qi. Try to relax. Close eyes." I watched him as he moved from the table and struck a match against the tube, sending a large plume of smoke to drift upward, the scent strong and reminiscent of marijuana. "Mugwort." The crinkles around his eyes deepened as he smiled down at me. "Will help draw out imbalance inside you."

Taking a deep breath, I closed my eyes, allowing my body to relax into the table as heat from the burning herbs hovered above my skin, instantly soothing the tense muscles along my back.

I don't know how long I drifted, the warmth coiling through me, sending a rush of lightness to wash through my limbs, but eventually the sensation faded and was replaced by the coolness of his hands.

"I insert needles now." His voice floated above me as I lay there. The prick against my skin claimed my attention for only a moment and then receded, leaving a pulse of energy vibrating beneath the surface. The room dimmed, and the soft cadence of his words sounded from somewhere far away. "You rest now."

The door closed, and silence slipped into the room. The kind of silence I had never heard before. It was internal. As if the noise within had been turned down to a faint hum, and I could feel the separation between myself and my body. Breath filled my lungs, my heart pumped blood, but for a moment, I was weightless, untethered from the dependance.

Behind the curtain of my eyes, images swam in my mind. Amelia's eyes, Quinn's voice soft in my ear. Rain on my skin and the breath of the ocean. The blush of a morning sky.

Then I fell deeper. Into the chill of the dark spaces locked tight within me.

The sound of my mother crying, her body slumped against the cabinet. The taste of blood in my mouth. Broken glass on the kitchen floor. My father's fists meeting my face once more. *"I didn't do anything, Daddy. Please. Stop. I didn't do anything."*

A hand rested on my arm, jolting me back. I opened my eyes. Cheeks wet.

I hadn't realized I'd been crying.

"It is okay." His voice was soothing, hands deftly removing the needles. "You are releasing blockages. Memories stored in body. This is process of healing."

* * *

Dazed, I clutched my purse and stepped out into the pale afternoon light, closing the office door behind me. My feet made purchase on the cobbled stones as a wave of vitality and euphoria coursed through my limbs. Something had loosened inside, and I walked with no destination in mind, following the stream of people around me.

Eventually the streets widened, and the tightly clustered buildings grew further apart, opening up to the surrounding vista. My shoes met uneven ground as I skirted away from the road and took what looked like a worn path through a maze of rocks and long tufted grass, their golden fronds waving in the wind.

I debated going further as the trail wound its way steadily upward, but my legs propelled me forward, eyes trained to the view ahead. My breath grew labored as my lungs grasped for air, and my head began to swim, trees and rocks wavering like an image on rippling water.

My hands scrambled at the air as I fell, my feet losing traction on the loose gravel as a sudden rush of dizziness overcame me. I grabbed onto a large rock as I went down, allowing it to buffer me from the impact of my fall. With my heart pounding violently in my ears and my knees throbbing, I sat there couched on the ground, praying for the swirling to stop.

Eventually, my vision slowed to stillness, my head clearing enough to move, and I looked up to see the white peaks of the mountains in the distance, with a small ledge to my right. On shaky legs, I pulled myself off the ground and slowly made my way to the rock outcropping.

Beyond me lay an unbroken stretch of cloud and mist curling around a vast fortress of stone. The view stilled the frantic thrashing of my heart, and I lowered myself back to solid ground. Closing my eyes, I took slow, deep breaths and waited for my mind to settle.

I lost track of how long I sat there while the cold bite of the wind blew against me, suspended in a state of calm detachment, as if I were observing myself from above. My mind skittered through thoughts like tiny stones dropping into water. And then the angry eyes and tired lines etched into the grooves of my father's face rose before me.

The ghost I could never outpace.

I sucked in a deep breath, knowing I could no longer push him away. I allowed him to stand there quietly before me, and within that space something softened, and the layers peeled back. I saw for the first time the terrified man he really was. Bound and broken from decades of fighting a battle with himself, a war he was powerless to stop, for it was all he'd ever known. And beneath the rubble of his life lay a sorrow so vast it brought tears to my eyes, for I could finally see all the anguish and fear hidden behind the rusted armor of his anger.

And I knew he couldn't hurt me anymore.

Raising my head to the sky, I opened my eyes, allowing the pain to release itself into the wind as the rush of fresh tears streamed down my face. I knew what I needed to do.

It was time for me to face him.

* * *

Evening had fallen, and I sat out on the balcony of the hotel, sipping the bitter herbal mixture the doctor had given me, watching as the moon rose into the ink of the night.

A lightness bloomed within. Between my treatment at the doctor's office and my moment on the hill, I had purged something. As if I had opened the last door which had been so tightly locked, and that small child inside me was no longer trapped within the confines of the protective cage I had built around her.

She was unbound.

The sound of the door opening stirred me from my thoughts, and I turned to see Amelia walking in. She threw her backpack on the bed and stepped out onto the balcony.

"Oh, my God. That lake was *so* gorgeous." She wore a wide smile as she sank into the chair beside me. "I had such a good time, and I took a bunch of pictures for you."

"I'm so glad to hear that." I rested the back of my head against the chair, closing my eyes for a moment as the sudden pull of fatigue which had been looming, finally took hold of me.

The exhaustion had been more frequent these past five days. I wasn't sure if it was due to the travel, elevation, or the comment the doctor had made the first day I saw him, the one that still sounded in my head like a haunting reminder that claimed my breath. *The cancer inside you is moving very fast.*

"Are you okay?" Amelia's voice came out hesitant, worry etching her words as her hand fell to my leg.

"Yes." I opened my eyes and leaned forward, giving her hand a reassuring squeeze as the faint tendrils of apprehension loosened their grip for a moment. "I just had a bit of a long day."

She shot me a small smile. "Did you find your Zen?"

I chuckled and took another sip of my tea, the warmth settling in my belly. "I found *something*."

"Really?" Her eyes met mine, the light from the room illuminating her face in a soft halo. "What did you find?"

"Strength." I let out a long sigh as my finger traced along the rim of my cup. "I think it's time I confronted my father."

"Wow. When was the last time you saw him?"

"Over twenty years ago." I shook my head, staring into the contents of my cup as memories flooded me. Eye swollen shut, blood trickling from my nose. My heart screaming inside my chest as I scrambled from my window for the very last time and ran blindly into the darkness, away from all the fear and hurt, away from the house that had never been a home.

"I need to face this part of my past so that I can finally let it go."

Amelia leaned back in her chair, her eyes wide and fixed on me. "That's really brave."

My fingers clenched the cup as I looked at her. "Time has become way too precious not to be brave."

"I guess you're right." A sadness washed across her face, and she wrapped her arms around herself, looking up into the glittering milk of the sky. "I wish we knew where we went when we died."

I found her hand in the darkness and gave it a squeeze as I followed her gaze toward the sky, the multitude of space spinning violently above us. "Maybe we go back up there. We are stars, too, you know." I looked at her as a wave of emotion hit me, bringing fresh tears to my eyes. "Some of us burn brightly and light up the night. Others are only a glowing ember keeping company in the dark. But we're all beautiful, and in the end, we're all the same. Just dust and matter dancing together." My voice came out in a whisper, a hopeful wish I was afraid to startle. "I like to think that we don't disappear. We just reappear somewhere else."

Amelia continued staring up at the sky, a faint smile playing across her lips. "I like that idea."

A silence rested between us as we sat together watching the stars, our private thoughts dancing beneath the limitless fold of the night sky. From beyond the open door, I could hear the faint ring of my phone, and I scrambled out of the chair to answer it.

"That's probably Quinn," I said, quickly setting my cup of tea on the table next to me. "I've been trying to reach him for the past two days."

Seeing his name flash across the screen, I eagerly grabbed the phone from the nightstand and pressed it against my ear, a smile playing across my lips. "Hey you."

"Is this Julia?" A woman's voice wavered with static through the receiver.

"Yes, this is." Confusion slammed into me, causing heat to prickle my skin. "Who's this?"

"It's Bethany."

My heart lurched in my throat. *Why was Bethany calling me from Quinn's phone?*

"Julia, Quinn is in the hospital." Her voice sounded choked and so far away as the colors in the room began to lose focus. "He's in a coma."

Chapter Twenty-Four

I gripped the armrests of the car as Amelia sped through the dark toward the airport. *Quinn was in a coma.* I covered my mouth with my trembling hand, trying to stifle the loud sob that wanted to rush out.

Amelia reached over and rested her hand on my arm in an attempt to comfort me, her face etched with concern as she steered the rental car through the narrow, winding road. "Something tells me he's going to be okay. We *have* to believe that."

I nodded blankly, choking on the words trapped in my mouth. The world beyond my window rushed past in a blur as the sickening grip of anxiety clawed at me. Bethany had said she found him unconscious on his apartment floor when she went to drop off Jasper the night before. *Hypertensive encephalopathy,* the doctors had told her. Apparently, a complication from his experimental treatment. I squeezed my eyes closed, trying to block out the thoughts of him lying lifeless in a hospital bed.

Through my haze, I noticed we had arrived at the airport. Amelia parked the car by the rental shop and ushered me quickly inside the lobby with our bags. The airport was eerily quiet, as if the pulse of life had been extinguished. I sat stiffly on a chair, biting my lip as Amelia stood at the counter, navigating arrangements for our flight back home.

"We got lucky," she said as she sat down next to me, holding out my ticket. "They had available seats for the next flight out. It leaves in an hour."

I stared out the window of the airport as the faint light of morning rose above the mountains. This was not how I envisioned leaving Tibet, shaking and full of apprehension. "I'm sorry, Amelia."

She looked at me, her brow furrowing. "What do you mean?"

I sighed and twisted my fingers together in my lap. "I'm sorry that we have to leave like this. I know you wanted to stay longer."

She shook her head and took my hand, squeezing it tightly. "Don't be sorry. I didn't really come here to see Tibet. I came here to be with you."

Tears clouded my vision, making her face waver and dance before me. "And I'm so glad you did."

She scooted closer to me and rested her head on my shoulder as we sat together in heavy silence, waiting for our flight. Her presence was a gentle solace that quieted the shrieking inside as I stared out the window of the airport, saying my goodbye to this place and sending out a fervent prayer to the mountains which cradled this land so rich in secrets and reverence.

Please let him be okay. Please have him wake up.

* * *

The trip back home was a flurry of plane changes interspersed with frantic attempts to contact Bethany, hoping for good news. But there was none. Quinn remained the same, trapped in a state of paralysis while we glided over an endless ocean. The only comfort was held in the last breath of each agonizing hour, knowing it was bringing me closer to him.

We touched down onto the Seattle tarmac, early morning spreading its winter cloak across the sky as I shuffled from the plane, bleary eyed and exhausted from lack of sleep and the sickening jaws of worry which had gnawed at me relentlessly for all the hours that had stretched between Tibet and home. Amelia took me by the arm, and I stumbled through the hush of the terminal, my legs weak and uncooperative as I followed the silent march of the other passengers.

I sat slumped in the passenger seat of my car while Amelia drove through the blush of the approaching day and toward the hospital. I turned on my phone, the glow of the screen lighting up momentarily before going blank. "Shit!" I fumbled around in my bag for the charger chord. "I forgot to charge my phone on the last flight. It's dead now." My search came up futile, and frustration coiled inside as I realized I must have left the cable behind at the last airport layover. "My charging cable is gone. How am I going to call Bethany?" My voice rose in distress as I raked my shaky fingers through my hair.

"It'll be okay." Amelia glanced over at me as she merged the car onto the freeway. "She knows when our flight came in. She said she'd be waiting for us in the lobby." The warmth of her hand fell on mine. "We're almost there."

My heart pounded erratically, and a rush of dizziness overcame me for a moment. I clasped her hand and tried to slow my breathing, grateful for her calming presence, which had infused our entire trip back, the steady anchor holding port from the hurricane of my apprehensions.

A light mist curled around us, the cold sinking into my bones as we made our way across the parking lot and slipped through the doors of Bonner General Health hospital. My eyes scanned the rows of chairs and seated people inside the waiting room, desperately searching for a flash of bright red hair.

"Julia?"

I turned to find Bethany standing behind me, the look on her face causing the faint press of hope to whither inside. My hands clenched together. "My phone died on the trip back, so I've been unable to check in. How is he?"

"The same." She brushed away a lock of tangled hair that obscured tired eyes. "Do you want to see him?"

"Yes. Of course, I do." My voice came out frantic as Amelia reached for my bag, nodding to one of the chairs in the lobby.

"I'll be right here."

My body was leaden, wanting so desperately to collapse, but the thought of seeing him sent adrenaline rushing to the surface as I quickly followed Bethany down the long white hallway, the echo of our footsteps piercing the stillness of the early morning.

She stopped at one of the doors of the ICU and turned to me, her fingers resting against the silver handle. "If anyone asks, just say you're his sister."

"Do they know?"

"Yes. They do. They tried to get a flight out last night, but planes are grounded right now because of a storm. I've been keeping them updated." A long sigh tumbled from her lips as her eyes skirted down the hall. "I'll let you have some time alone with him. I'm going to go check on Jasper. He's in the cafeteria having breakfast."

My hand fell on her shoulder, the contact causing her to momentarily stiffen. "How is Jasper handling all this?"

Bethany shook her head, her voice low. "He's trying to be brave, but he's *so* scared."

My heart lurched, and I felt the same stab of pain that Bethany had hidden behind her eyes. The pain of a mother trying to shield her child from a reality that held no answers, only a desperate plea silently screaming into the void of the unknown. I watched as she turned from me and disappeared down the hallway, her pace brisk and frantic, as if trying to outrun her own thoughts.

I opened the door and was met with bright lights and the steady beep of a monitor. My breath knotted in my throat as I stepped closer. Quinn's face was like a painting enclosed in glass. Lost in a place I could not reach. With trembling legs, I walked to him, crossing the space between the door and the bed, my hands reaching out, grasping at the familiar solidity of his skin that did not respond to my touch.

"Quinn." His name spilled out of me in a moan as I collapsed into the chair beside his bed, my fingers tightly curling around his. "I'm here." I rested my head on the sheets, allowing the tears I had been holding back to pour out of me, broken and untamed. "Please, wake up... You need to wake up. *Please*. I don't think I can do this without you."

I don't know how long I sat there with a sickening weight lodged in my gut, clutching his hand, willing him to come back to the world. I needed to hear the deep rumble of his voice, to lose myself in the gentle harbor of his eyes, to watch him enfold his son in a crushing hug, the kind that chased away the monsters in the dark.

But wherever he was, I couldn't reach him. None of us could. Only silence answered back. The kind of silence that shrieked through the sound of the monitors and scraped against your skin, a cold grip that wouldn't let go.

"The doctors aren't telling us why he hasn't woken up yet. All we can do is wait and stay hopeful."

The sound of Bethany's voice startled me, and I turned to see her standing in the doorway, her eyes flickering across Quinn's motionless form. "Why don't you go home and get some rest? I know you've had a long flight. I promise I'll call you if anything changes."

I shook my head, unable to extract my hand from his, not

wanting to leave him, but knowing that Amelia waited for me in a room with upholstered chairs and ticking clocks.

On shaky legs, I pulled myself from the bed and wiped away the remainder of my tears with my sleeve. Bending down, I touched my lips to Quinn's forehead, lingering against the warmth of his skin.

"I'll be back soon."

* * *

Hazy afternoon light peeked through the curtains of my apartment, and a cold I could not banish crept through the blankets as I attempted sleep. Restless, I scattered my body across the sheets, limbs weary as foreboding thoughts snuck through and taunted me with images that sent my heart racing, skin chilled with sweat.

What if this was the end? What if our time together was up? These questions tore at me, relentless and unforgiving, the answers unwanted. I couldn't sit with them. The very idea of losing him stole my breath.

I stared at the clock beside the bed, waiting for my mind to calm down, waiting for the phone to ring, for something to change. The memory of Amelia's face, lined with worry as she helped me into the apartment a few hours ago, stood beside the rush of my thoughts. The feel of her arms around me was like a promise I held on to. When had she become the caregiver of my grief? And how much longer did I have until her own grief filled the room, demanding promises I could not give?

Untangling myself from the bed, I grabbed my phone and headed into the kitchen. My hands shook as I placed the kettle on the stove and rooted through the cupboard for some tea, hoping something solid and warm would still the fluttering of my heart, the tremble in my out-breath.

I stood at the counter and waited for the water to boil, my

eyes falling to the cello which rested beside the living room window. The last time I had played was the night he had taken me into his arms on the floor. The night he held me against him like I was something beautiful and wild, and then made love to me so slow and deep it left us both in tears. Never could I have imagined the heights he brought me to, and my chest constricted with a choking sob that pushed its way toward the surface.

My phone lit up beside me, blue light flashing across the tiles on the counter, and I grabbed it, fingers frantically pressing at the screen.

"Bethany?"

"Yes, it's me. He's awake. He woke up about twenty minutes ago."

"*Oh, thank God.*" My voice wavered as a violent surge of relief coursed through me, releasing the grip of all the anguished emotions which had sat beside me for the last thirty-six hours.

"I'll be right there."

Chapter Twenty-Five

My heart soared as I propelled myself through the double doors of the hospital, the familiar outline of the waiting room a blur as I rushed past and headed down the long, white hallway toward Quinn's room.

Opening the door, I saw him propped up in bed, with Jasper and Bethany standing beside him. The sight of him awake was a burst of oxygen rushing into my lungs. He looked fragile and gaunt beneath the sheets, but then the brightness of his eyes met mine, bringing everything back into focus.

He reached his hand out to me and with a strangled gasp, I careened toward him, collapsing into the feel of his arms. "Oh my God, Quinn," I choked out as tears broke the surface, releasing a stream down my cheeks. "I was *so* scared."

Everything in the room momentarily fell away as his hands slid up to cup my face, pulling me close to him. "I'm okay, Julia. I'm okay."

"Don't you ever do that to me again, *dammit*." I whispered against his lips as they softly met mine.

"I'm sorry I scared you." Light stubble brushed across my skin as he kissed away my tears, his breath a gentle wave of relief washing along my shore.

From the corner of my eye, I saw Bethany quietly shuffle Jasper out of the room and close the door behind her, giving us a moment alone. I inhaled a sharp breath and threaded my fingers through his hair. "What happened?"

Quinn furrowed his brow. "I'm not quite sure. I was feeling a little out of it the other day and had a pretty bad headache. I remember I was standing in the kitchen when my vision started to waver, and the next minute everything went dark."

I rested my forehead against his, breathing in the scent of him, an earthy musk hidden beneath the layer of hospital disinfectant. Gratitude encompassed me, and fresh tears pooled in the corners of my eyes. "I don't know what I would have done if something had happened to you."

"Hey." Quinn pulled back to look at me. "I'm all right. The doctors have me on medication that is stabilizing my blood pressure. And I'm going to pull out of the clinical trial." His thumb trailed along my cheek and hovered gently above my lips as his tone grew somber. "But you know it's only a matter of time with the two of us. And I *need* to know you're going to be okay if I go before you."

His eyes flashed with intensity, the weight of his words pulling me down to the gravity of a future I didn't want to sit with.

"Stop, Quinn." I grasped his hands, my fingers trembling around his. "I don't want to think about that right now, okay?"

Pulling me closer, he placed my hand on his chest. "*Please.* Just promise me." His voice was ardent and pleading, asking for a strength I wasn't sure I had. But I would give him all of myself if I could. I would give him everything.

"I promise." My words came out shaky as I pressed my palm over the thrum of his heart. "I promise I'll be okay."

"Good." A slow smile crept across his face. "I missed you like crazy, you know." His hands encircled me and swept up my back, fingers lost in my hair as he drew me tight against him, creating a bloom of warmth that chased away my entangled emotions.

"I missed *you*." I closed my eyes, my fingers digging into his back as if the sheer force of pressure could obliterate the impermanence of everything.

The sound of the door opening jolted us from our embrace, and I looked up to see a doctor walk in, grey hair framing a wizened face.

"Why hello there, Quinn." He grabbed a chair beside us. "It's nice to see you back in business."

He shot us a playful wink and Quinn chuckled, threading his fingers through mine. "Yes. I think I'm ready to get out of here."

The doctor peered down at the tablet in his hands, swiping through Quinn's chart. "Well, all your tests came out good. But we do want to keep you one more night for observation." He closed the file and looked at us with a smile. "If everything checks out, you'll be a free man tomorrow morning."

"Thank you." Quinn nodded as the doctor stood from the chair.

"Can I stay with him?" I asked, as he made his way to the door.

He stopped and glanced at his watch. "Visiting hours are over at six. So, you have until then."

I turned back to Quinn as the doctor shut the door quietly behind himself. "I want to make a quick call to Amelia and let her know what's going on."

"Okay. And then you can tell me all about your adventures in Tibet." Quinn's voice grew soft as he brushed his finger across my cheek. "But you should probably go out into the lobby. The reception's pretty bad in here."

"Have you talked to your sisters? Are they flying out?"

"No." He leaned back onto the pillows with a sigh. "I told them not to bother. They were just here. I don't need them fussing over me."

A tentative smile slipped out as I danced my hand up his leg. "What if I had plans to do that?"

He clasped my wrist as a grin slowly bloomed across his lips. "Oh, *you* can fuss over me all you want."

"Good. I'll be right back, then."

Slipping out the door and down the hallway to the waiting area, I pulled my phone from my purse and dialed Amelia. She answered on the first ring, her voice rising in animation as I shared with her the news about Quinn.

As we talked, I looked across the room to see Bethany sitting in the corner of the lobby, eyes vacant as she stared at the floor.

"I'm going to stay here with Quinn for the day," I spoke quietly into the receiver.

"Okay. I'll check in with you later. Try to get some rest if you can."

"I will. Thanks, Amelia."

I hung up the phone and walked over to where Bethany sat stiffly in a chair, fiddling with the wrapper of a water bottle, her fingers peeling the plastic off in jagged strips. I took a seat beside her, my hand resting momentarily on her arm. "I've been meaning to thank you for calling me in Tibet."

Her eyes shot up. "Of course." She placed the water bottle on the table beside her and leaned against the chair with a sigh. "Quinn was holding his phone when I found him, and your number was on his screen. I guess he had been trying to call you at the hotel."

My throat grew tight as the image of him lying on the floor flashed through my mind. "That must have been really scary, finding him like that."

"It was." She glanced over at Jasper, who was coming toward us from the bathroom. "I'm just glad Jasper was still in the hallway when I walked in. I somehow managed to keep him from seeing his dad on the floor. But he watched him get wheeled out on the stretcher." Her eyes wavered with tears, and she quickly wiped them away as Jasper plopped himself down in the seat next to us, regarding me with his wide brown eyes.

"Did you get to climb Mt. Everest when you were in Tibet?" he asked, tapping his feet against the tile floor.

I smiled at him, reaching out to ruffle his hair. "No. I wish. That would have been really cool."

He pursed his lips, letting out a puff of air as he appeared to be lost in thought for a moment. "Yeah, that would have been cool."

"Hey, Jasper." Bethany took a few bills out of her purse and handed them to him. "Why don't you get yourself a little snack from the vending machine while I talk to Julia for a minute?"

"Okay." Grabbing the money, he sprang from his seat and weaved through the maze of chairs.

"He's been such a trooper these last few days," Bethany said, her voice dropping to a whisper. "This kinda felt like a practice run for us."

She looked at me, her gaze open and sincere, and I knew we shared the same fear. The woman sitting next to me was not the same woman who had barged into Quinn's apartment all those weeks ago, throwing her words like daggers. Grief had swallowed the anger, replacing it with a mournful acceptance.

"I've been meaning to apologize for the way I acted with you." Bethany clenched her hands together as she spoke, her brow furrowed. "It's just been so hard for me to come to terms with everything."

"I know." I leaned back in the chair as the bustle of people moved around us. "Dealing with something like this can feel so impossible."

"It's not just his cancer diagnosis. Seeing you two together like that in the hospital room..." she trailed off, her eyes growing misty again. "I've never stopped loving him. And a part of me hoped this would be our chance to start over." Bethany's tears fell freely now, her confession a delicate release that broke through whatever barrier had been between us. "Is that selfish of me? To want these last moments with him? *Every day* I regret the way I messed everything up between us."

"No. It's not selfish. It's human." I leaned over and gave her hand a gentle squeeze. "And I'm very familiar with regret. It has haunted me most of my life. But I realize now that everything happens for a reason, and regret is only a poison. You have to find a way to forgive yourself."

She nodded, grabbing a tissue from the box that sat on the table next to us. "I'm trying." Wiping the tears from her cheeks, she twisted the tissue in between her fingers. "And even though it's hard to see him look at you the way he does, I'm so happy he's found love. He deserves it. He's *such* a good man, Julia."

"I know." My lip quivered, and tears pricked at my eyes. "He's one of the best things that has ever happened to me."

Bethany locked her gaze with mine, her sorrow matching the current of my own. "I can't imagine how hard this must be for you, too. Knowing you only have so much time together. How do you do it?"

"Did Quinn not tell you?"

Confusion swam across her features. "Tell me what?"

I sighed and rested my head against the chair. "We're *both* dying, Bethany. That's how we met."

"What?" Her hand fell to her mouth as she stared at me in shock. "I had no idea."

I smiled at her. "But you know, I wouldn't change a thing if I could. My cancer brought me to him, and he's been one of the most profound catalysts in my life. He's helped me learn how to live again. There's nothing more valuable in the world than that."

She reached for my hand as a silence took hold of us. There were no more words. No declarations that could soften the blow. Life was a fragile dance, and we all knew the song would eventually end, leaving only our footprints behind.

Jasper appeared next to us with a bag of chips, stirring us from the soft stillness of our shared moment. "Can we go home, Mom?"

Bethany roused herself, slipping her hand from mine. "Yeah, why don't you go get your stuff and say goodnight to your Dad." As Jasper bounded down the hall, Bethany fumbled for her purse, pulling out an envelope and handing it to me. "Can you give this to Quinn?"

"Sure."

I took it from her and placed it on the seat beside me as she stood and glanced pensively out the window of the lobby.

"You're right, you know." She looked at me with a tired smile. "There is nothing more valuable than learning how to live. I've been stuck in the past for so long now. I think it's time I try to let it go."

"And you will." I found myself standing and pulling her in for a hug. "I've come to realize that we're always much stronger than we think we are."

She wrapped her arms around me, her body relaxing into mine, all her rigid edges becoming soft. "I hope you're right." Her voice was muffled against my hair as we stood together in the lobby like two souls seeking refuge in the tide waters.

* * *

Late afternoon shadows slanted across the walls in fragmented patterns as I opened the door to Quinn's room. "Bethany left this for you." I placed the envelope on the bed beside him.

Quinn picked it up, turning the envelope over in his hands. "Did she tell you what it was?"

"No." I sank into the chair beside him, my legs shaking as

the leaden strain of the past few days hit me. "She just asked me to give it to you."

Opening the envelope, his brow furrowed as he read the documents, fingers hovering over Bethany's signature on the bottom. "She finally signed the divorce papers." He looked at me, his eyes clouded with confusion. "I don't know why she would bother to do this now."

My thoughts drifted back to our conversation in the waiting room. The shared sorrow that for a moment, wove us together like a tapestry, the marrow of our truths exposed. "Maybe it's a peace offering," I said as I ran my hand along his, tracing the lines of all the stories etched into his skin. "Her way of making amends."

"You know, I always had the option of going around her signature. But it was just another fight I didn't have the energy for." He looked out the window, a deep sigh running through him before he turned back toward me, his gaze wavering with an emotion I couldn't quite place. "About ten years ago, I took out a life insurance policy when I bought my motorcycle. Bethany never knew about it, but I suppose it will all be going to Jasper now."

Once again, I was reminded of the looming inevitability of all the things still left to pack away. The memories and moments tucked inside my bones. The legacy of my life stretched like a canvas slowly filling with color. *What would I be leaving behind for Amelia?*

Quinn folded the paper and slid it back into the envelope, placing it on the table beside him. "I'm relieved to have this finally over between us. This *was* a gift, Julia. It's you and me now, and however long we have together."

My eyes grew moist as the realization hit me. He was finally free from his tangled marriage. They both were.

"Come here." He took my hand and drew me onto the bed, sweeping his fingers across my cheek. "You look so tired."

"I am. I haven't really slept since I left Tibet."

Quinn pulled me close, and I sank into him, resting my head on his chest. My eyelids grew heavy as the comforting warmth of his arms enveloped me, the steady thrum of his heart a lullaby, quickly beckoning me into the depths of sleep.

Chapter Twenty-Six

The slate grey of an early morning sky loomed above me as the nurse escorted Quinn through the sliding doors of the hospital. He stood from the wheelchair with a sheepish smile and took my outstretched hand, allowing me to help him into the front seat of my car.

"How are you feeling?" I asked as I slipped into the driver's side and turned the ignition, inching my way into the steady stream of cars leaving the parking lot.

"I'm feeling good." His hand ran lazily up my thigh, his fingers sweeping slow circles across the fabric of my pants. "And Jasper's not coming over until six tonight. We have the whole day together."

I glanced at him, his eyes heavy with thoughts he didn't need to say aloud, eliciting a charge of electricity to travel through my core. "Did the doctor say it was okay to resume normal activities?"

Quinn chuckled as he slid his hand further up my thigh. "Define normal activities."

A flush overcame me, peppering my skin. "You know what I mean."

"Yes, Julia." His voice was husky as his fingers swept across my hip and lingered above the waistband of my pants. "And I plan on doing all kinds of *normal* activities with you when we get into that apartment of yours."

I tried to focus on driving, but his words and the rush of his touch flooded me with arousal as he slowly ran his thumb along my sex, teasing me through the thin fabric of my yoga pants. I sucked in a sharp breath. "I can't drive when you're doing that. You really need to stop." But my words came out breathless and void of meaning as I arched myself against his hand, wanting more.

"My apologies." He shot me a rakish grin as he pulled away and sat back in the seat. "It won't happen again."

"It had better." I threw him a playful smile as I navigated the car onto the freeway, delicate sunlight cutting through the clouds above us.

Quinn's brush with mortality was a reminder of how precious our time together was. All the days we had been apart now seemed to hover between us like an intoxicating band of energy demanding release. I ached for the feel of him inside me, to draw the bold colors of my longing across his skin. For him to take me to those wild places that stripped me bare and made me whole. To reach for every sublime moment we had left.

The drive back to my apartment took way too long, and we stumbled into the elevator together, our hands hungry and frantic. I fumbled for the buttons while Quinn pressed me to the wall with a groan. "The things I'm going to do to you." His words were a delicious promise that made me lightheaded as his lips trailed along the lobe of my ear.

"And what kind of things do you have in mind?"

"Well…" His fingers coiled into my hair as his teeth softly nipped at my neck, the stubble along his jaw grazing deliciously across my skin. "I have plans that might involve the kitchen counter."

"Oh, really?" A breathless chuckle escaped me as the doors

THE LIFE WE DREAM OF

to the elevator slid open, exposing us to the brightness of the hallway, the world outside separated by glass. With shaky limbs, I unlocked the door to my apartment and ushered him inside, my purse falling to the floor as he grabbed me from behind and drew me against him.

"I want you to take off your clothes. *Right now.*"

His command was tender but full of intensity, and I yielded to him, turning around and slipping off my jacket as he watched with eyes that burned into me. Unbuttoning my shirt, I dropped it onto the floor, along with my bra. Despite the chill in the apartment, my skin prickled with warmth as his gaze claimed me. Peeling away the rest of my clothes, I stood in front of him.

"Now lay back on the counter."

I hoisted myself onto the granite, the coolness of the tile deliciously contrasting the heat of my skin as I relinquished myself to his instructions. A fervent energy built between us as he stepped closer and spread my legs, running his hand along the length of my inner thigh, leaving a trail of desire across my skin.

"Quinn?" My voice trembled with anticipation as I grasped at him, wanting him closer, needing to feel all of him enfolding me.

"Shhh." Dropping his head, his lips drifted across my thighs, his breath brushing over my sex like an agonizing tease as he gently pinned my wrists to the counter. Bound beneath him, I allowed him to take control, knowing I was safe in his hold. I had always been safe.

I bucked against him as he dipped down and tasted me, his lips and tongue awaking all my senses. A wave of pleasure gripped me, fast and consuming, threatening to push me quickly over the edge.

I struggled in his grip, wanting to reach out and clutch at

him as the pressure built rapidly within. A moan spilled from my lips, pleading and breathless. "I'm going to come."

"Not yet." He pulled away from me with a groan and lifted me to his chest, his eyes full of fire as he ran his hand across my breasts and down past my stomach. Slipping two fingers inside me, he curled upward and hit a place so deep it made me gasp. "*Now* you can come for me."

Lost in the weight of his gaze, I clawed at his back, an untamed cry spilling from me and piercing the air as I shuddered and burst apart, my release breaking over me in waves.

"God, I love the way you let go." His voice was a low growl against my skin as his lips ran down my neck and grazed across my nipples, sending a renewed burst of desire to swell inside. "And I think we just made a much better memory on this counter."

"Yes, we did." My words floated lazily between us as I dropped my head to his chest, his arms encircling me as the frantic drumming of my heart slowed. "I never used to do that."

"Do what?" He titled my head to meet his eyes, thumb trailing across my cheek.

"Let go like that." I brushed a slow kiss across his fingers, the scent of my release lingering on his skin. "But you bring everything inside me to the surface."

"And you set me on fire, Julia." With a groan, his lips found mine, and I wrapped my legs around him as he lifted me up and carried me into the bedroom, laying me against the sheets.

Time moved gently as we entangled ourselves together, suspended in a place where our bodies spoke for us, a tender language that eliminated the last remnants of fear I had traveled home with.

He was here. *We were alive.* Spinning reckless and untethered, together in each other's arms.

* * *

Quinn lay beside me, his head resting on the pillow as he ran his hand through the strands of my tousled hair. "I love you..." tears gathered in his eyes as he traced my lips with his fingers, "so much it overwhelms me sometimes."

"*You* overwhelm me." I cupped his face in my hands, staring into the solace of his open gaze.

Life was a series of moments, some small and seemingly insignificant, others profound and life-altering. The day I had walked into the support group and sat hesitantly beside him was the moment everything changed, opening me up to possibilities I never thought I could have. Blown together by a course neither of us could predict, we had found a love that stripped us down, leaving behind a light that chased away the darkness.

Quinn drew me close, burying his face into my neck, his breath a warm assurance against my skin. "I'm so sorry I was the reason you had to leave Tibet early."

"Don't be sorry. Don't *ever* be sorry. I found what I went there for." I traced my fingers down his arm as memories of his silent body cloaked beneath hospital sheets flashed before me like a foreboding reminder. "What was it like being in a coma? Do you remember anything?"

He looked at me and shifted onto his side, propping himself up on his elbow. "I don't really know. It's like I wasn't there anymore, but at the same time, I was. My thoughts were not present, but this feeling of consciousness was." He furrowed his brow. "I can't really explain it. But it was peaceful."

My breath hitched in my throat as I tentatively sat beside the idea of existing beyond the self. "Do you think that's how death will be?"

"I hope so." He looked at me, his face bathed in the muted light that streamed in through the curtains. "When you were in Tibet, I had this dream that you were standing beside me on the edge of this cliff, and you turned to me and said, *don't be scared.* Then you jumped. I tried to grab you, but it was too late. I looked down, and you were gone." Traces of sorrow flashed within his eyes as he spoke; his voice choked. "But then this large white bird rose into the sky, and I knew it was you. I knew that wherever you were going, there was no more fear. There was only beauty. There was something that felt so profound about the dream that I actually woke up crying."

I rolled over and pressed my body against him, interlacing my fingers with his, as if I could fuse the tapestry of us together, weaving threads that could never unravel.

"I don't want to be scared of this, Julia."

"I don't either."

I sat at the kitchen counter, staring at the will I had printed out. I had been staring at it for so long the December sky now hung low beyond the window, scattering filtered light across the pages. My pen hovered over the assets and beneficiary section, the ink bleeding into the whiteness of the paper as I wrote in Amelia's name, solidifying my decision to leave her everything.

I looked around the apartment, taking stock of what I could donate and what she might want. Eventually, my external life would be whittled down to a handful of items neatly packed away into boxes. A lifetime of accumulation rendered obsolete, their worth void of meaning. Except for my cello.

Standing from the counter, I walked over to the window where it rested on its stand and ran my fingers over the polished wood. All the years of myself were stretched across the strings like an imprint of my soul, and I realized I had never shared my music with Amelia, and I suddenly wanted to. I wanted her to see the parts of me that had kept vigil against the pain of who I used to be. To see the whole story of who I was. The fractures and scars made beautiful by the fumbling journey toward healing.

The phone rang, jarring me from my thoughts, and I crossed the room to answer it. "You feel like going on an adventure?"

A playful smile slipped out as I leaned against the counter, Quinn's voice on the other end surrounding me like a soothing blanket. "Wait, haven't I heard this line before?"

He chuckled, his voice growing low. "Yes, and it worked the first time. I managed to get a beautiful, reluctant woman onto my motorcycle."

"Yes, you sure did."

"So, what do you say?"

"Okay. I think I could use an adventure right now. Where are we going?"

"It's a surprise. I'll be outside your apartment in twenty minutes."

I walked into the bedroom, my limbs prickling as the circulation struggled to catch up with my movements, my heart rapidly pounding within the cage of my chest. This sensation had been happening more frequently. And though the herbs and meditation seemed to push back the edges of the fatigue a little, I could feel my body growing weary of the battle inside. Raging silent and unseen, the pages within my story were growing thin, but I did not want to go in for a scan. I didn't want to know how close I truly was. Hope had taken on a new meaning for me now. It was no longer a frantic grappling with time, but an attempt to live courageously in the present. As Quinn had said to me all those nights ago when I stood in the darkness of his room unveiling the raw marrow of myself. *This moment is the only thing that's real, and this moment is all that matters.*

Standing beside the window, I gazed at the city below, watching the traffic as it silently rushed past, waiting for the familiar green of Quinn's hatchback to appear at the curb. When I finally saw him, I threw on my coat, grabbed my purse, and headed out the door, the grip of winter pulling at me as I stepped out onto the sidewalk.

Quinn left the engine idling as he leaned across the front seat to open the door for me, flashing me a warm smile as I slid in beside him. "You ready?"

With a nod, I entwined my fingers through his, the comforting scent of him enveloping me as we merged into the last remains of afternoon traffic.

We navigated through tree-lined streets and up a familiar slope of winding road, a smile tugging at the corners of my mouth as we pulled into the parking lot of Mount Baker Ridge.

Quinn cut the engine and slid the keys into his pocket before walking around to my side. The scent of pine hit me as he helped me out of the car and I took in the view surrounding us, the stillness punctuated only by the gentle whisper of the wind. "You brought me back here."

"Yep. This is where we began, Julia."

"It is, isn't it?" I sank into him as he guided me to the lookout point. Grasping the railing, I watched the fog as it snaked around the edges of the trees, shrouding the water in a gauzy cloak. How much of myself had I shed since I'd last touched these steel bars and gazed out into the abyss of mountains and water? It was a lifetime ago.

From behind, Quinn wrapped his arms around me. "I remember when I first took you up here. You were sitting on that bench, looking out toward the water, and the light was hitting you in a way that made my heart ache. You reminded me of this untamed and stunningly sorrowful creature, and I wanted nothing more than to take you into my arms. To take all your pain away."

"And you did." Tears brimmed in my eyes as I turned around and placed my hand on his cheek. "You helped me find so much of myself."

He smiled and leaned down, his lips falling on mine in a soft lingering kiss before pulling away and finding my eyes. "Do you know when I fell in love with you, Julia?"

"When?" My lips gently pressed against the question, leaving a whisper behind.

"It was the morning I stayed with you after you called me from the hospital. I had woken up to the feel of your hands running through my hair, and when I looked into your eyes, I saw so much love there, beneath the surface, just longing to be released. I knew in that moment I wanted to wake up to those eyes *over* and *over* again."

Quinn reached into his coat pocket and retrieved a small black box. "I've been thinking about marriage lately. The institution of it all. All the rules and paperwork. How even when I wanted to leave Bethany, she was able to use it as a leveraging device." He looked at me, his eyes wavering with emotion. "I don't want that with you. I want something different. I want something that transcends all that, something made just between the two of us."

"I do too." My heart fluttered within like exalted butterflies dancing upon something yet to be named.

"So, this isn't a ring. This is something you wear close to your heart." He placed the box in my palm, the wind whipping his hair wildly as his hands enfolded mine. "I want to honor

247

what *we* are together. I'm not asking for marriage. I'm giving you a promise that goes beyond that."

My hands shook as I opened the box. Nestled between tissue paper was a necklace in the shape of a star. Brilliant crystal shimmered on one side, while on the other was an inscription engraved into the silver.

Forever.

My throat constricted as I traced the words with my thumb. "This is beautiful."

Taking the necklace from the box, he unclasped the hook and slipped it around my neck. "You are my star, Julia. The light in my darkest nights." His fingers traced along the curve of my neck as he spoke, his eyes brimming with a reverence that stilled my breath. "We don't know where we'll go in the end, but I believe that love lives beyond death. And wherever we end up, I will find you again. I *will* always find you. That is my promise to you. That is my forever."

"Quinn." I gripped his face in my hands, pulling him close to me as a sob tumbled out, bitter and sweet, entangled in the threads of a story I knew would live beyond us. "You are all my forevers."

A wide smile lit up his face as he drew me in for a kiss, slow and tender as I trembled against his mouth, tasting my tears on his lips.

Under a somber sky, we held each other, creating our own quiet union birthed from the ashes and fire of who we once were, and who we had become.

Chapter Twenty-Seven

"Are you sure you don't want me to come with you?" Quinn stood beside my car, his eyes heavy with concern, the cold bite of the wind stinging our skin and tugging at our hair.

"I'm sure. I need to do this alone, okay?" I ran my hands down his chest and drew him against me, sinking into his warmth. "Don't be worried. He can't hurt me anymore. I know that now. I'm doing this so I can finally say goodbye."

"You could just write him a letter." Quinn gripped my arms, his reluctance to let me go evident in the pull of his brow.

"I need to face him."

"I know." His lips rested softly on mine. "Call me when you get there, okay?"

Nodding, I grabbed my keys from my purse and opened the car door, slipping into the driver's seat. I watched his form fade from the rear-view mirror as I pulled out of the parking garage and into the stream of afternoon traffic.

I drove north with my hands tightly gripping the wheel. The rush of green sped past my windows in a blur, tall trees shrouded in a landscape of fog as my thoughts trailed behind me, the road a compass steering me forward. The memory of my father was an ominous shape slowly taking tangible form as the ninety-minute drive closed in on me, every mile marker bringing me nearer to the small town of Rochester. The place where I grew up. The place I ran from all those years ago.

My heart pounded in my chest as I drove down familiar streets, the pavement of my childhood whispering beneath me. *Do you remember this?* The corner with the old oak tree I had fallen out of when I was eight, busting open my chin, and leaving behind a faint silver scar. The pink house with the tall hedge that still stood out front, in which my neighbor Billy and I had once carved a tunnel inside, dirty knees and stubbed toes, a safe place to trade stories and secrets only the branches could hear.

I parked the car alongside the curb and cut the engine. The rush of apprehension pressed in on me as I stared at the small, drab single-story house, the blue paint chipped and faded, the front porch sagging, as if it could no longer bear the weight of all the memories housed inside.

I had done my research. I knew he still had a job at the casino and never sold the house. I knew he wasn't working today, for I had called the casino ahead of time. I knew he was most likely sitting inside somewhere, oblivious to my upcoming and uninvited presence.

Taking a deep breath, I stepped out of the car and walked toward the house, my eyes following the lines of the cracked driveway up to the dented garage door my father had once plowed into during one of his drunken rages. A bent and rusted time capsule of a life I no longer wanted to define me.

I stood on the porch, my hand hovering over the doorbell, its once yellow glow now faded to a dim amber. I had no expectations, no hope he would greet me with anything other than a steely reserve. I was not here for a tearful reunion. I was here to let go of my ghost.

Pressing hard on the doorbell, my heart stilled and then picked up pace as the sound of footsteps grew close.

"Who's there?" Bloodshot eyes met mine as the door

THE LIFE WE DREAM OF

opened, and my father squinted down at me, gaunt and hardly recognizable.

"Hi, Dad." The name caught in my throat, a foreign word with a bitter aftertaste.

He gripped the doorframe, his face contorted in confusion. "Julia?"

"Yeah, it's me."

He looked at me, his eyes flickering back and forth like a caged animal seeking an escape. "What are you doing here?"

I held my hands out like an offering. "I came to talk."

"Talk, huh?" He snorted and flung the door open wide, motioning for me to come inside with a disinterested flick of his hand.

I stepped through the doorway, the house smelling of stale beer and unwashed linen. Everything looked the same. The couch, now threadbare and stained, slumped in the corner. The old bookshelf holding my mother's tattered romance novels were now covered in a thick layer of dust. Time had swept through, but nothing had altered. This was the house of all my wounded memories, now staring back at me like relics enclosed under glass.

He shuffled over to the couch, raking his fingers through thinning grey hair, and grabbed a beer that sat on the coffee table. His hand shook as he lifted the bottle to his mouth, taking a long pull from the neck. "So, what do you want? Money or something?"

"No. I don't want anything from you."

"Then why are you here?"

"I told you why."

"Oh, that's right. Because you *want to talk*." His mocking tone drew out the words like a petulant child. The same familiar bite that always made me recoil into myself. But it didn't touch me this time. He had become a caricature, his blows no longer powerful or precise. The looming man of angry words and heavy fists was now a frail body bent around a bottle, hiding from the world.

I leveled him with my gaze. "Are you capable of having a conversation with me? Or is this just going to be a waste of my time?"

"I don't give a shit what you do with your time. But I must say, it's pretty presumptuous of you to just show up like this after all these years." Spittle flew from his mouth as he spoke, and his eyes shifted from anger to a caged sorrow, the remnants of all our unspoken words now colliding in a room full of collateral damage. "You left." He pointed a gnarled finger in my direction. "You're no longer a daughter to me."

I shook my head, watching as he sank back onto the couch, his hands trembling, as if weakened from the strain of emotions locked inside. Twisted and choking the life from him. My father was nothing but a stranger to me. He had always been a stranger in my life. Full of shadows, rage, and loneliness. A broken soul screaming at the world. And I saw those pieces of myself in him. All those years I allowed my own body to splinter from the burden of my family's legacy.

But I no longer needed the armor of my own anger to protect me. All it had ever done was hold me down. He had been my suffering. He had given me his pain, and I diligently carried it for him.

And now it was time to let it go.

"You know, being your daughter was never something I wanted. It was always something I was trying to *escape* from. I've lived with this poison inside me for *so* long. But I don't want it anymore. I don't want you to be the monster in my story." I walked to the couch and crouched beside him, staring up into eyes that couldn't look back. "I'm here because I'm releasing our story. I *forgive you*, Dad."

"What the hell are you forgiving *me* for? What did I ever do to you? You're the one who left."

His words bristled and slurred around the murky waters of his own delusions. And I realized *he didn't know*. He didn't know what he had done to me, what he had done to my mother. All his memories had been stifled by alcohol, time, and the mind's powerful ability to warp your own story to fit the narrative you need to sleep at night.

To him, I was only the difficult daughter, the one that left.

"What did you *do*?" I leaned in closer to him, trying to pry at the bars of his cage, but his gaze was a barrier I couldn't budge. "You did *a lot* to me, Dad. You did *a lot* to Mom. And I have wasted *so much* of my life, angry and hurting from it all." Tears gathered in my eyes. The edges of my words blurred. "But you know what? I'm not hurting anymore. I've found *my* healing. And I only hope one day you'll be able to see clearly what happened. That *you* can find a way to make peace with yourself." Wiping my eyes, I stood and walked toward the door, knowing there was nothing more to say. He was lost, and I would never be able to reach him.

"Goodbye, Dad."

"Julia."

I turned to him, watching as he whipped his head around, grasping the arm of the couch. He cleared his throat, eyes glassy and darting from me to the door. "Are you happy?"

My hand rested on the knob, the metal worn and darkened from years of use. "I've found my happiness. Yes."

"That's good to hear. That you're happy." A hesitant smile pulled at the corners of his mouth, and for one brief moment, a glimmer of softness rested in his eyes, a vague outline of the father he could have been. Turning toward the window, he brushed his hand through the air as if trying to erase his words. "Goodbye, Julia."

With a nod, I closed the door behind me, trapping the remnants of my memories inside. I knew this would be the very last time I would ever see this house, this street with the rhododendron bushes lining the sidewalks, a summer's worth of crushed petals on the road like brown, withered relics.

I stood in the driveway for a moment, letting this truth claim me. No longer was I running from the shards of a broken past, from the scars that defined me.

I had finally faced them.

Chapter Twenty-Eight

*W*inter slipped by, and the world around us folded into itself. Christmas came and went, followed by the bold optimism of a new year as Amelia, Quinn, and I sat out on the roof of my apartment, watching fireworks explode in a cacophony against the cold night sky. Our hands curled around glasses of champagne, faces bathed in the fleeting light of color and fire. The vibrancy of life demanding to be seen, if only for the briefest of moments.

I clung to these days as time spun by me, and the grip of cold loosened, the warmth of spring teasing me with the fragrance of possibility. My mind was now spent in a form of constant prayer, every new morning a gift, every breath another chance to cherish the time I had left.

I *had* found happiness beneath the rubble of who I used to be, and I cradled this truth fervently.

I wasn't dying. I had found life.

"What are you thinking about?" Quinn's voice was soft as he lay beside me, trailing his fingers down my back.

Evening had fallen, and the last fragments of light bathed my bedroom in the muted glow of dusk as he swept his hand across my skin. These were the stolen hours we had together. The hours when Jasper was with his mom and Quinn would come over with whispered words among tangled sheets, kisses that made me languid.

"I'm thinking about what our life would look like if we had more time."

He sighed and pulled me into his arms, placing a kiss on my forehead. "What would you like it to be?"

I glanced around the room, the bare walls and empty corners a reminder of the person who used to inhabit this place, void of color and trapped in a state of inertia. "I would sell this apartment. Buy a house overlooking the water." I looked up at him with a soft smile. "One with an extra bedroom for Jasper."

"And a wide wrap-around porch." His eyes grew soft with sentiment as he ran his hand across my cheek. "So we can have dinners outside while we watch the sun go down over the water."

"We would get a dog."

He raised his eyebrow. "What kind of dog?"

"A dopey, happy lab." A warmth bloomed inside as I threaded my fingers in his hair.

"And what would we name it?"

"Lucky."

Quinn chuckled. "I like that."

My hands fell to my stomach, trailing along the concave slope of skin against bone. What was left of me had been given to Quinn, and he filled me, breathing beauty into all the empty spaces.

"Maybe we would have a child."

Tears swam in the depths of his gaze as he placed his hand atop mine. "I would love to have a child with you."

My cheeks stained with tears as I closed my eyes and saw our life stretched out before us. Endless days of laughter and light shining on water. A world full of possibilities we didn't have to borrow.

* * *

Mist coiled around my bare feet.

The ocean whispered beside the shore.

In the distance, I could make out a figure walking slowly toward me.

Long dark hair and amber eyes.

"Mom?"

She appeared beside me, and her hands clasped mine as the wind picked up, blowing her dress, a translucent silk the color of the fog, which threaded around her like a serpent.

"I've been waiting for you, Ju Ju."

Tears stung my eyes as the name rested on her lips. The name she would whisper in the dark while she rocked me to sleep as a child.

My words came out choked. "Where have you been?"

Her eyes shimmered like the water. "I've been between yesterday and tomorrow." She pulled me close, her arms encircling me. "But I've always been right here. And I have never stopped loving you."

The feel of her against me began to soften, her arms loosening into thin wisps of vapor.

"Wait, Mom. Don't go yet." My voice pleaded with her vanishing form as a broken sob spilled out.

"My sweet girl. Do not cry."

She was gone now. Only her voice remained, rising into the sky like a bird taking flight.

"I will see you soon."

* * *

Morning drifted through the curtains as I sat in bed beside Quinn, the gentle flutter of his eyelids indicating he was still lost in the depths of his own dreams. While mine lay beside me like a lucid memory.

My mom had always been the open wound that would not close, the part of my past I could never speak to, and now the soft cadence of her voice swam inside my mind like an evocation.

Pulling myself from the comfort of the blankets, I padded into the living room. Sunlight slanted across the tile, its light drawing my attention to the window. March had crept in, baring hesitant warmth against budding branches, and my heart fluttered with the thought of spring. It had always been my favorite season.

Would I have one last chance to watch it bloom?

Quinn emerged from the bedroom and slid his arms around me. "Morning, beautiful. How did you sleep? I noticed you were coughing a little last night."

"I'm okay." I leaned into him, placing my hand on his bare chest. My fingers traced along the grooves of muscle and skin, hoping to smooth away the look of concern that hovered in his eyes. "I dreamed about my mom last night." I looked up at him, all my unformed questions suspended within my chest. "I never dream about her. Which I realize now is so weird. But she finally came to me, and it felt so real." I furrowed my brow and glanced back out the window. "I had so many things to say to her, but she disappeared before I could."

Tilting my head to his, he placed a soft kiss on my lips. "Then say them to her now. I still talk to my dad. I know in some way that he hears me."

I nodded, pushing back the growing sense of unease which pressed into me, and slipped my fingers through his tangled hair. "Why don't I make us some breakfast before you go pick up Jasper?"

"Sounds good." He followed me into the kitchen and rested against the counter as I turned on the coffee maker and went to grab the eggs from the fridge. "What do you have planned for the day?"

Cracking the eggs into a bowl, I stared down at the swirling yolks as I blended them together. "Amelia invited me over for dinner tonight."

"Well, that sounds nice." He took the whisk from my hand, his lips sweeping across my forehead. "I changed my mind though. I'm going to make breakfast for you, okay?"

With a smile, I stepped away from the counter. "If you insist."

I watched him as he moved about the kitchen. His hair, which had begun to grow out, now brushed against his shoulders, tousled, and falling into his eyes. He looked full of vitality, as if the cancer inside had not touched him yet, and I fostered a sudden and buoyant hope that the clinical trial had helped. That somehow, the growth had slowed, giving him the kind of time that grew beyond measured days. I allowed the edges of reality to blur, our words from last night rising within me and painting a warm picture of Jasper standing taller beside him, a dog at their feet, laughter in a kitchen filled with life.

"Hey, there." Quinn rested his elbows on the counter, his

fingers reaching out to swipe a tear from my cheek. "What's tumbling around in that beautiful head of yours?"

"You are." I leaned my cheek into his hand. "If I could give you my time, I would."

"Don't say that." He shook his head, emotions like thunder rolling across the surface of his eyes. "Your time is just as important as mine."

"I know. That's not what I meant." I curled my fingers through his, tracing the grooves and ridges of his skin with my thumb. "I'm full, Quinn. I'm *full* of love. And isn't that all we really ask for in the end?"

He took me into his arms, his heart pounding out its own language within the cage of his chest. "I think it is. And I think it may be the only thing we can truly carry with us from this life." His hand ran slowly down my cheek as his eyes met mine. "I'm full, too, you know."

* * *

The chill of night pressed into me as I stepped from the car and walked across the stone pathway toward the front door, surprised to find myself already winded as I clutched the bottle of red wine in my hand. Amelia's window glowed with soft light that spilled between the curtains like a beacon, her door bursting open at the sound of my knock.

Ziggy loped around me in enthusiastic circles while Amelia ushered me inside, the house warm and rich with the aroma of spices. "I'm making Indian food." A wide smile spread across her face as she gestured toward the kitchen. "From scratch."

"Wow." I shrugged off my coat, hanging it on a hook beside the door. "It smells amazing."

"It's vindaloo and curry. You're going to love it." She took the wine from my hand and pulled me in for a long hug. "It's *so* good to see you."

Amelia's eyes shone with a sorrow I could see her trying to conceal as she took in my gaunt and pallid appearance. Our time together had begun to take on an undercurrent of fragile reverence. We both knew these moments together were fleeting.

Neither of us knew how many more we had.

Steam rose from the curry bubbling on the stove, fogging up the kitchen windows as I sat at the table, sipping from the small glass of wine I had poured.

"So, I finally gathered up the courage to ask my co-worker, Val, out on a date." Amelia said as she spooned the vindaloo and curry into bowls of white rice. Placing them on the table, she took a seat across from me. "And she said yes."

My heart swelled as I listened to her talk about their first date. Her cheeks flushed from the rush of a budding connection.

"And there was a *kiss*." Her eyes fell sheepishly to her glass of wine on the table, her fingers absentmindedly tracing the stem. "I think it may have been the best kiss I've ever had."

"I'm so happy for you. A kiss like that is always a good sign."

"I hope so." She ran her hands through her hair and raised her glass to mine with a playful grin. "Here's to great kisses."

"And many more to come." I clinked my glass against hers with a chuckle that quickly turned into a wet cough. Raising my napkin to my lips, I noticed splotches of red seeping into the fabric. My heart stilled as Amelia looked at me from across the table, her face etched in concern.

"Are you okay?"

"I'm fine," I said with a forced smile, placing the napkin discreetly in my lap, my hands shaking. "I think I may be coming down with a cold or something. I've just had a little cough the past few days."

"Oh, I can get you some echinacea if you'd like." She rose

from the table and walked over to a cupboard, rooting through the shelves. "It's really good for the immune system."

Another cough tumbled out, and I stood, gasping for breath as I clutched the table, a sudden wave of dizziness overcoming me. "I'm just going to use your bathroom for a sec. I'll be right back."

I managed to make my way down the hall, shutting the bathroom door quickly behind me. My breath came out in labored pants as I stared at my reflection in the mirror, a bubbling sensation of restriction rising in my chest.

Gripping the counter, another violent cough tore through me as I heard a tentative knock on the door.

"Are you sure you're okay in there?"

Amelia's voice sounded muffled and far away.

My vision blurred, and I dropped to my knees, hands grasping at cold tile.

And then everything went dark, silent and still.

Chapter Twenty-Nine

a voice stirred me from the darkness, a flash of bright light hitting my eyes as I fluttered them open. I lay on Amelia's bathroom floor, my head cradled in her lap.

"*Thank God,* you're awake." Amelia's words came out choked as she gripped my arms, her face pale and splintered by fear. "I called an ambulance. They're on their way."

I tried to sit up, but a debilitating weakness held me hostage, rendering my limbs useless. "What happened?" All that came out was a whisper as I struggled to take air into my lungs.

"You must have passed out." Her voice trembled. "I'm just so glad you didn't hit your head on anything."

"I'm so sorry." I reached out and found her hand, curling my fingers around hers. "I didn't mean to scare you like that."

She shook her head, tears wavering in her eyes. "Don't be sorry."

The sound of the door opening followed by Ziggy's frantic barking and footsteps rushing down the hall filled the house, as a sudden flurry of paramedics spilled into the bathroom.

Hands checked my vitals and placed an oxygen mask over my face, the cool rush of air instantly soothing my strangled breath.

Strapped to a board, I became airborne and weightless as I was carried out into the night, the sky alive with stars.

I knew what was happening.

My heart was failing.

Time had finally caught up with me, and I waited for the clawing hands of fear to take over. To fight against this truth. But the fear didn't come. What sat beside me instead was a quiet acceptance, as if I was ready to face what lay beyond me.

"I'll be right behind you, okay?" Amelia's voice was choked, her hand trembling as it slipped from mine and the doors to the ambulance closed with a muffled shudder.

* * *

I lay beneath the white hospital sheets, my body divided between wires and tubes monitoring breath and heart rate, filaments tethering me to a world that held death back with a detached precision. Amelia's face was pinched into a mask of apprehension as she sat on the edge of the chair beside me, her fingers tightly woven through mine.

"I finally got ahold of Quinn. He should be here soon."

Unable to speak, I nodded and squeezed back in reply.

"Oh, and the doctor I talked to in the hallway told me your scans will be ready in a few minutes." She bit her lip, glancing at the closed door as if fearful of it opening. She knew as well as I that the results were not going to be good.

Reaching up, I slid the oxygen mask off my face. "Amelia," I wheezed, my words a broken wound. "Thank you for being here. I know this isn't easy for you."

Tears gathered in her eyes, her mouth opening to speak, but no words came out.

The door opened, and Quinn rushed in. A tangle of fear, grief, and desperation swimming in his eyes. My name rushed from his lips in a strangled cry as he crossed the room and took my hand, gripping tightly. "I'm here," he whispered as he smoothed my hair back, tenderly running his thumb across my cheek. "I'm here."

A tired smile settled across my skin, a feeling of completion as everything that mattered was now beside me. Two hearts housed in bodies I desperately loved. Placing the oxygen mask back on, I looked over to see the doctor standing in the room.

"Julia. We have received the results of your scans." His face was grave as he took a seat beside the bed. "You have a large accumulation of fluid in your lungs. What we are going to do is perform a thoracentesis, which will drain the fluid and help you to breathe better." He sighed and swiped through my scans on the tablet. "But it is only a temporary solution, I'm afraid. The fluid will eventually return." He paused for a moment, regarding me with heavy eyes. "I am sorry to tell you this, but according to these scans, you are now in the end stages of heart failure."

Amelia stared at the doctor, her face ashen as a silence fell across the room, followed by the sharp intake of Quinn's breath.

"How long does she have?" Quinn's voice came out in a strangled whisper as he clenched my hand, leveling his gaze to mine. All the light inside his eyes extinguished.

We both knew this moment was coming, but it didn't make it any easier. I reached out, placing my palm on his cheek as if my touch could somehow soften the blow.

"A few weeks at the most." The doctor let the words settle around us for a moment before he continued, his tone resolute. "What we need to discuss at this stage is hospice care."

Quinn helped me through the door, holding me steady as the shadows of late afternoon traveled like hesitant whispers across my apartment.

The incision site where they had drained the fluid from my lungs the day before was tender and sore, but I was able to breathe again.

"I've set everything up with the hospice nurse," he said as he led me into the bedroom and helped me into bed, pulling the sheets back. "She'll be here first thing tomorrow morning, along with Amelia."

His words were soft and controlled, but I could see the silent scream trapped in his eyes. I knew he was trying to hold it together, to be the pillar against the wind. I rested my head on his chest, listening to the sound of his heart thrumming wildly within, battling with his breath.

He lay me back onto the pillows, removing my shoes and drawing the blankets around me. I winced as the incision site throbbed between the sheets and watched as he pulled the bottle of pain medication from his pocket, setting it on the table beside me. "I'll get you some water for these."

I nodded and closed my eyes for a moment, the rocking sensation of sleep beckoning like a seductive song. Quinn's touch stirred me, his hands delicately lifting my head and guiding the pill to my lips.

"You get some rest. I'll be right here."

"Quinn?"

"Yes?" His fingers threaded between mine as color washed across my eyelids in a kaleidoscope of patterns.

"Don't be scared."

"I'm trying."

* * *

Waves crashed upon the shore.

Salty spray tickled my skin.

And it was warm. Everything was so warm.

The outline of my mother appeared through mist. Her feet barely touched the ground as she glided toward me. The edges of her softened against dappled sunlight.

"Come sit with me for a while." She settled into the sand, patting the space next to her.

I sank down, folding my knees to my chest. "I know why you're here."

She smiled, her eyes bright and clear, reminiscent of the mother I knew before pills and depression took her away from me.

"Yes, Ju Ju. It is almost time to say goodbye."

Sorrow welled up in my chest. "Why did you leave me? I needed you."

She placed her hand over mine and leaned in close. "I was so lost, Julia. I couldn't find my way back to you. I didn't have the strength." Her eyes swirled in a palate of sudden grey. "There are no words to express how sorry I am for not trying harder. But I didn't know how."

She shook her head as her fingers swept through the air, leaving a trail of color behind.

"Life is a test of strength. One I didn't pass. But you did." Her smile pierced through, golden light shimmering between us.

"You rose above the wreckage."

* * *

My eyes shot open, yanking me from the depths of my dream. The faint light of the moon filtered in through the curtains, and from somewhere within the apartment came the sound of muffled sobs.

My body hummed from the pain medication, a euphoria that snaked its way through my blood as I got out of bed and made my way into the living room.

Quinn was slumped on the couch, his head crumpled in his hands, shoulders shaking. I sat beside him, reaching out to touch his arm. Pain lanced through me as he jerked his head up, revealing bloodshot eyes drowning in grief, a face marbled with tears.

"We were supposed to have *more* time."

"I know." My words whispered between us, a quiet acknowledgment of shared sorrow as I slipped my arms around him.

"It wasn't supposed to be like this." His voice became a broken moan as he buried his face in my neck, hands clutching at my back.

I grasped his shoulders, forcing him to look at me as I caught his tears with my fingers, my chest growing tight. The thought of leaving him with all this loss was a weight too crushing to sustain, and it stole away my breath. "Do you remember what you made me promise when you were in the hospital? Now it's your turn to make that promise." He stared back at me, eyes lost behind the curtain of his anguish. "Promise me, Quinn."

"I don't know if I can."

"*Promise me.*" I rested my forehead against his as he pulled me tightly to him, running his hands up the plane of my back, fingers sweeping across my shoulders, as if he was trying to trace the outline of me.

"I promise."

His words spilled out in a tangled sigh as I leaned into him, his warmth an anchor I could still cling to even as the storm inside me raged. Its last battle cry a mournful song of finality. "Come lie with me. I need to feel you."

Effortlessly, he lifted me into his arms, holding me against him, delicate and tender, as if I could break. He carried me into the bedroom and lay me down on the sheets, soft cotton brushing across my skin.

I unbuttoned my shirt, my eyes never leaving his as I placed his hand on my chest. "I'm not scared, you know. Everything I need, everything I have *ever* needed, is right here."

Fresh tears hovered in Quinn's eyes, his hands slowly running across what was left of me. Flesh and bone holding together all the memories we had made, his love woven into the fibers of my body.

"Make love to me."

"*Julia.*" He drew in a shaky breath as my fingers trailed down his chest, inching up the fabric of his shirt.

I knew this would be our last moment together like this, and I wanted to burn with him one final time. To feel him deep inside me, filling me up and stripping away the confinements of myself like a beautiful goodbye.

He shuddered as his lips met mine. Slow kisses mixed with the salt of our tears as we shed our clothes together. Gathering me into his arms, he rolled onto his back and pressed me gently to him.

He let out a cry as he entered me, eyes wide and full of ache, his hands tracing the last chapter of our story against my skin.

Slow and cautious, we entwined ourselves like new lovers, discovering each other all over again, making room for a love that had grown too large for our bodies to hold any longer.

Chapter Thirty

*D*ays slipped by like water between cracks.

The ebb and flow of my breath pulled by an invisible current as I unraveled.

Legs swollen with fluid.

Limbs weak.

Lungs labored.

I could no longer walk on my own, but someone was always there. Gentle voices, soothing hands, warm arms cradling what was left to hold on to.

As I shifted within myself, peeling back the last of my layers, an awareness had grown and taken root. A truth I knew had always been there. Death was not a monster lurking in the dark with sharp claws and hungry eyes. It was life's companion. And it now sat beside me, patiently waiting for its turn to speak.

Quinn stood by the bed watching me, his face etched in thoughts like dark clouds gliding between the light. My hand found his as he sank down next to me with a shattered sigh, his fingers tracing my skin, resting lightly against my cheek. "You have given me so much. So many beautiful moments."

I took his hand and lowered it to the rapid rise and fall of my chest. "And you will have more when I'm gone."

Tears gathered in the corners of his eyes as he leaned down and pressed his lips to my forehead, his voice a tremble across my skin. "But it won't be the same without you. *Nothing* will be the same."

Cradling his face in my hands, I stared into his anguish, so heavy and encompassing it splintered the space between us. How bold we were to love with such abandon, knowing how fragile we were inside. I longed to shield him from this goodbye, but I knew I couldn't. We were here to be broken and then put back together again. Our scars sinews of strength that told the story of a life that was lived.

"Go on that road trip with Jasper," I whispered. "Go have one last great adventure with your son. He needs this. You *both* do."

Quinn nodded and gathered me into his arms. Weary of gravity and longing for flight, we merged our bodies together, sharing our heartbeat, our breath, as we cast aside the weight of what time we had left.

Sunlight stretched across the blankets of my bedroom, casting images that flitted like tiny ballerinas against the fabric. I reached for them as if I could catch one in the palm of my hand.

The space between my dreams and reality was growing thinner, the veil lifting, leaving a childlike wonder behind.

Amelia sat beside me, her hands woven together as if in prayer, eyes lost behind the curtain of her melancholy.

Why did we fear death? Was it really for ourselves? Or was it for the pain we knew we would leave behind?

"Come here." My words came out splintered and frail as I patted the covers. "There's something I've been meaning to give you." I pointed to the jewelry box that sat on my dresser. "Open it. There should be a necklace inside. A carving."

Amelia slowly stood and crossed the room, her edges flickering with light. Everything was filled with light. I could see it now. It had always been there. We were all fallen stars, matter and energy dancing for one brief moment in the space between the darkness.

"This is the rose I saw in Tibet." Amelia turned to me with the carving in her hand, which I had taken to a jeweler a few weeks ago to have a silver chain fashioned through the wood. It now dangled between her fingers like a delicate thread.

"Yes, I wanted to give you this. I want you to know you will *always* have my heart."

Pressing the necklace to her chest, she curled onto the bed beside me, disturbing the shadows which now fell like petals against our skin. The weight of all the years filtered down to this moment, the small details encapsulated in a room with walls that held stories half finished.

"It's beautiful."

My fingers found hers, death entwining life as the soft shell of my tenuous heart stretched around her. "You're my angel, you know that? The *very best* thing that ever came from me."

Amelia's lip quivered, her hand squeezing my own. "I love you, Mom."

The light spilled from her, shimmering streaks of brilliant color filling me with buoyancy.

"And I love *you.*"

A tiny river trailed down her cheek, uncloaked and fragile, and I reached out to catch it. There were no more words left.

The silence spoke for us.

"Julia."

The soft murmur of Quinn's voice stirred me from the depths.

I had been floating between dreams. Whispers beckoning me closer to a stillness I could feel, like a patient friend waiting beyond a doorway.

It's almost time.

Quinn's hands smoothed back my hair, his lips leaving a brush of heat against my forehead. I fluttered my eyes open.

"You want to go on an adventure?" Sorrow clung to the edges of his smile as he spoke, and I nodded, my fingers reaching out to trace the plane of his cheek, memories embedded like ink upon his skin, endless and embracing.

I will always go on an adventure with you.

He lifted me from the bed and placed me gently in the wheelchair. Amelia's face appeared, floating like an apparition of my own youth as she tucked a blanket around me, and then a small hand slipped over mine. Jasper's wide brown eyes smiled down at me.

Amelia wheeled me through the living room and out into the hallway, while Quinn and Jasper walked beside me, Jasper's hand never leaving mine.

A warm breeze ruffled my hair, the air sweet upon my lips like delicate longing, awakening my senses as we glided through the doors and out into the blinding blue of an afternoon sky. I hovered between the spaces of myself, a glimmering flame burning its last bright dance as my eyes swept over the delicate details.

The rush of traffic like the city's ardent breath.

The way the sun hit the tall buildings like an ember enclosed in glass.

Movement above me as a bird untethered its wings, colliding with the sky.

All these things belonged to a world much larger than any of us. We were only a blush of life. A sunrise painted across the horizon.

The wheelchair stopped, and Quinn crouched next to me, his eyes glimmering as he pressed his lips to my hand and pointed to a tree above us. "Look, Julia."

My vision abruptly filled with brilliant color, shades of pink trembling before my eyes, bathing me in a landscape of rebirth. The wind picked up, scattering sunlight through the branches, and shaking loose the blossoms which fell around us like rain.

Opening my hand, a petal drifted into my palm.

Velvet and silk whispering against my skin.

Ocean water lapped at my bare feet.
A gentle tug coaxing me deeper into the sea.

My mother stood beside me, the warmth of her hand clasped in mine, eyes vibrant and alive.

"Are you ready, Julia?"

"Yes, I'm ready."

I stepped forward unafraid, waves wrapping around me like a languid embrace, pulling me closer.

Then I was weightless, my limbs unraveling into the depths.

Leaving nothing behind but the solace of my exhale.

Amelia

$\mathcal{I}$ stared at the envelope. My name written on the front in flowing cursive script. The last of my mother's words tucked neatly inside.

Opening the seal, I gently pulled out the contents, my hands shaking as my fingers brushed across a folded piece of paper and a photograph. She was bathed in light, sitting against the wide ledge of a window, her amber eyes piercing through the lens. The look on her face was one of open vulnerability, as if the person behind the camera had released something inside her. She looked beautiful and free, and my eyes clouded with the sting of fresh tears.

Unfolding the letter, I took a trembling breath and leaned back onto the couch, my hand reaching up to clasp the wooden rose around my neck.

Amelia,

As I write this, the sun is rising. The colors are so vibrant and alive, and I wish I had more of these moments. Ones we could share together.

You are my sunrise. A breathtaking dance of color that came into my life and rinsed the darkness away. You helped me believe in second chances. You helped me find the person I had locked away so long ago. And because of this, I'm not afraid of death. I'm not afraid because I have finally learned what it means to be alive.

Even though I missed so many years of being your mother, these precious months I've had with you have been timeless and reverent. And so, I want to leave you with my slivers of wisdom. The truths I found in my life.

Never run from your pain. There is healing waiting beneath it. For in order to find peace, you have to be willing to walk through the fire.

Never doubt yourself, for you have an untapped well of strength inside, and the more you draw from it, the deeper it becomes.

And always, always love with the fierceness of abandon. Love is what holds us in place. It's what gives this journey of ours meaning.

Thank you for finding me. Thank you for opening me up to endless possibilities. I am so full inside. And my love for you will not end with me. It will unfurl beyond my body and cradle you for as long as you carry breath.

And then one day, I know we will meet again. Maybe somewhere up there in the stars.

Go live a bold life full of love,

Julia

CPSIA information can be obtained
at www.ICGtesting.com
Printed in the USA
BVHW070950230323
661006BV00006B/356

9 781088 045817